The Slow Moon

THE SLOW MOON

A Novel

Elizabeth Cox

RANDOM HOUSE 🏠 NEW YORK

Published in the United States by Random House, an imprint of
The Random House Publishing Group, a division of Random House,
Inc., New York.

RANDOM HOUSE and colophon are registered trademarks of Random
House, Inc.

Library of Congress Cataloging-in-Publication Data

Cox, Elizabeth.
    The slow moon: a novel / Elizabeth Cox.
        p.   cm.
    ISBN 0-679-46328-3
        1. Teenagers—Fiction.   2. Tennessee—Fiction.   I.   Title.

PS3553.O9183S58 2006
813'.54—dc22   2005044781

Printed in the United States of America on acid-free paper

www.atrandom.com

9 8 7 6 5 4 3 2 1

First Edition

Book design by Simon M. Sullivan

To Kittsu Greenwood, my dear friend

*The long day wanes: the slow moon climbs: the deep
Moans round with many voices. Come, my friends,
'Tis not too late to seek a newer world.*

—Alfred, Lord Tennyson, "Ulysses"

I

A Dream of Love

One

So on that April evening in South Pittsburg, Tennessee, with spring just beginning, a copper moon rose, balanced like a huge persimmon, and two young teenagers, Crow Davenport and his girl Sophie, left a party and walked into the woods toward the river to be alone. They were quiet as they walked.

"You okay?" Crow asked her. They had already talked about what they would do tonight.

"I keep thinking somebody's following us," said Sophie. Her voice sounded thrilled, expectant.

"Who would follow us?" said Crow.

"I don't know."

"Don't you want to do this?" Crow felt eager but would acquiesce if Sophie changed her mind.

"No. I do." She looked around. "I do want to."

"Then what's the matter?" said Crow. He carried a small blanket from the house under his arm.

"Don't you hear something?" Sophie asked.

"An owl, maybe." They kept walking. Crow put his arm around her waist and pushed tree limbs away from her head.

"Wish I could see it," said Sophie.

"Yeah." Crow began to rub her shoulders, touching her long dark hair.

"If I could see it, I'd draw it," she told him.

Sophie's school notebooks were filled with drawings, and even though those drawings were not the first thing Crow had noticed, her notebook was something he could ask her about. Their first conversation was about how well she could draw.

"Right now?" he asked. "You'd want to draw something now?" He leaned her body against a tree and kissed her. He had kissed her the first time in her house, the odor of honeysuckle coming in like mist. They had heard a dog barking across the street. Crow had shown Sophie a slick gray stone that he carried in his pocket and asked if she liked it. She said she did, so he gave it to her, then kissed her on the lips, barely—a wing of moth.

But his desire to kiss her now felt urgent. Wind chimes hung on porches, sounding like temple bells.

"Let's stay here," said Sophie, and she led him deeper into the trees. And for a short while the night seemed to stop. "Put the blanket down," she urged. "We can lie on these leaves."

Here, at the mouth of a creek leading to the Tennessee River, in early evening, near the home where the Fairchilds lived—both parents away—a party was going on, alive with teenage bodies and hard music. But these two had wandered away from the party. Their love for each other made them feel separate from the others, better.

The day had been warm, with a brief rain, and the air hung like blue milk.

"Nobody'll see us," Crow tried to reassure himself. "Most everybody's drunk by now anyway, or stoned."

"I feel a little drunk myself," Sophie confessed.

"You're not used to it," Crow said.

"Well, that part's true."

"Sophie," he said, and kissed her again. He had not kissed her like this before. The creek widened, and from where they sat they heard water lap against the banks of sand and river foam. With no adults around, their dreams of pale longing increased in size. They believed they were grown. Flashes of heat lightning flickered, made them dizzy.

Sophie stepped backward, laughing. Flushed with pleasure, she caught Crow's arm and said, "Let's lie down."

Crow pulled her onto the blanket. He put his arm around her, and they sat listening to the woods around them.

"I heard something," Crow said, pulling back.

Sophie looked startled and turned toward the river. She was sitting with one leg up, her chin resting on her knee. Her skin downy white with a mole beside her ear at the hairline. To Crow, looking at her, nothing seemed diminished, nothing seemed small or uninteresting.

"I'm just kidding." He tousled her hair.

Sophie stretched her neck like a cat about to purr.

"You want to go on down closer to the river?" he asked.

"No." Sophie touched his leg.

"You want to stay here?"

Then she did something Crow had not imagined her doing, or rather imagined himself doing for her. She began to unbutton her shirt, fumbling. She leaned forward and removed it, unhooked her bra. Pieces of white cloth moved down her arms. She seemed like someone in a movie, her glossy hair, the line of her cheek. The wind scuttled through the trees, riffling the leaves. Crow could not believe her skin shining in the dark. For a moment he did not move, then she reached to unbutton his shirt.

Crow's chest and arms were big-muscled. He wasn't handsome, but he had a strong, manly appearance that made girls hum with pleasure when they saw him for the first time.

Sophie settled into a comfortable position.

They kissed each other carefully, as if handling a glass object. He pulled her skirt off, and as he kissed her breasts, her nipples grew hard.

"Sophie," Crow whispered. Her hair spread on the ground, her face open, his hand on her breast. Then he rose above her. "Sophie. Sophie." He shuddered with desire.

"I know," she told him, but she looked uneasy. "Have you ever done this before?" Her voice sounded shaky.

"Not really," he told her. "I mean, not like this."

She didn't ask what he meant.

The only other time Crow had had a woman was down by the railroad tracks when Tom, Casey, and Bobby paid for Eileen's services on his fifteenth birthday. They gave him five condoms. The woman was thirty-something, and she cost fifty dollars. He hadn't liked it as much as he thought he would, but he liked it enough to think of her every night for two weeks afterward. The best part being that his friends knew he was no longer a virgin. He wouldn't tell Sophie about Eileen, but he was glad to feel the confidence of experience.

"Have you?" He didn't think she had. He felt caught by the perfume of her body.

She let him stroke her arms and legs. She made him feel slow-witted. As Crow moved on top of her, she parted her legs slightly, willing. She did not urge him to wait or stop. He touched her thighs, between her thighs. He looked at her white, papery skin and the thick tuft of dark hair. When Crow looked back at her face, her mouth seemed edgy, and a hot-blooded certainty came running toward him like a horse.

For a long while they urged each other with odd angles of arms and legs, a wild symmetry of touch and whisperings that moved them into a mood of perfect order.

"I want to go inside you." His words were a question, but he was almost inside her already, pushing. Sophie did not resist, but then said, "Wait, wait."

"No, please. Let me. Sophie, please."

"Do you have something, Crow? Aren't you going to use something?"

"Shit." He seemed awake now.

"What?"

"Oh, shit. I think I came a little bit."

"But don't you have something?" They had talked about using something the first time.

"It's in the car. In the glove compartment."

"I think we should—"

"Okay." He cursed himself for leaving the condom behind. "I'll get it." He leapt up, pulled on his underwear. The car was parked down the street in a church parking lot. No one had parked in the Fairchilds' driveway.

"Hurry," Sophie said. She looked trembly, but determined.

"I will." He laughed and slipped on his shoes. "I will." He left his shirt, pants, and wallet in a pile on the ground.

"Your shirt," Sophie whispered. "You forgot your shirt."

"It's okay," he said. "This won't take long." Sophie covered herself with his shirt.

Crow hurried through the woods toward the parking lot. There must have been ten cars parked there. He found his car, opened the glove compartment, and grabbed the package of condoms. For one brief instant he wondered if they should go through with this. He already felt foolish. But Sophie was waiting for him. Her hair and mouth, her skin that smelled like oranges. He started toward the woods.

But at that moment he heard a pickup drive into the lot, a group of girls laughing. He ducked down beside the car. When they laughed, he thought they had seen him in his underwear, were going to make fun of him, but they were only teasing each other. They got out of the truck and lit cigarettes. He was going to have to stay until they left. He recognized their voices.

The girls took their time. Crow cursed his bad luck and waited. His legs began to cramp from squatting. The girls laughed louder, lit more cigarettes. Sophie would wonder what was taking him so long. After what seemed a long while, Crow decided to risk embarrassment; but just then one of the girls grew impatient and began to urge everyone toward the house.

Crow stumbled into the woods. He pictured Sophie's face, her long legs. He could hardly wait to touch her again, and grew excited even while running. But when he got to the place where they had been, Sophie wasn't there. He called to her. No answer. He called again. Then he saw something, something white, further in the woods, and walked slowly toward it.

"Sophie?"

She didn't answer but moved slightly.

"Oh, shit. Oh, Christ. Sophie, is that you?"

He heard her moan, and as he stood over her, he saw that she had blood on her legs and hands.

"Damn." She seemed to be unconscious. "Sophie? Sophie? What happened?"

But before he could lean to touch her, he heard a police siren and a car pull up near the house. Blue lights flashed in the driveway; men headed through the woods. The silky murmur of night birds was dying down. *They'll think I did this,* he thought. *I'll just tell them. I'll say I just came back and found her.* He reached for his shirt. He wanted to look dressed. He heard them enter the backyard, talking, asking questions, coming toward him.

"Sophie?" he whispered. "Are you awake?" He shook her slightly and she moaned.

The flashlights moved deeper into the trees. "Sophie?" he said. He struggled to put her clothes back on—her panties, her shirt— then began to run. He ran fast, his legs paddling themselves on the marshy ground. When the flashlights and voices reached her, someone yelled, "We found her," and as he ran Crow heard a jumble of exclamations.

She'll be okay, he told himself. *They'll take care of her.*

But what had happened? He had been gone only twenty, twenty-five minutes. Or was it longer? His first thought when he saw her was: *Did I do that?* He knew he hadn't, but still it was his first thought, and the thought hit him like dropping a stack of plates—they all broke. "Shit. Oh shit."

Crow ran toward the river, toward the subaqueous life of its silty edge. He could barely hear their voices anymore. He thought of finding her lying there, and he couldn't think of her name. Sophie. He could not imagine leaving her there; even as he left, running away from her, still he could not imagine himself leaving her.

He went past trees. His bones formed waves of heat and fired his body. He grew giddy and sick. Limbs reached down to pull hair from his scalp. He ran, and became older running. In just a few moments he would be far away, and he would not have to explain anything to anyone.

When he got to the river, he heard someone running behind him, still far off, but behind him, so he went into the water. His pockets filled with mud. He swam underwater to hide behind bushes. In a few minutes flashlights scoured the bank, and Crow stayed very still. They had not seen him. After they left, after the voices had died away, he came out of the water and fell on the bank. He waited—he didn't know how long—until the Fairchild house turned dark; then he went to his car and drove home.

Crow entered his house through the back door and removed his clothes in the mudroom; he walked in his underwear to the outside spigot to wash himself. When he looked up, his father stood at the back door.

"What the hell is going on?" his father asked, flipping on the kitchen light.

Crow jerked away from the hose. "I fell in the river," he said, his voice calmer than he imagined it could be. "Some of the guys were kidding around and pushed me in."

"Come in here. You know what time it is?"

"No sir." Crow didn't move.

"It's almost three o'clock," his father said. "We got a call. Something's happened to Sophie Chabot." He watched Crow enter the house. "Police found her in the woods behind the Fairchild house. She was unconscious and a wallet was found near the place where she was. About twenty feet away, they said. It had your stuff in it."

Without thinking, Crow reached for his back pocket, even though he wore only underwear now. "I was with her tonight," he said. "We went to that party. But when I left I thought she was going home, I mean . . ." He felt like a ventriloquist speaking. "She's all right, isn't she? Maybe I should've taken her home."

"Maybe you should've." They gravitated toward each other, and Carl Davenport put his hand on his son's shoulder. "What's that on your leg?"

Crow had a gash on his leg from running through the woods, falling. The blood formed moist clots.

"Get that cleaned up. I'm thinking we should call Raymond Butler. I think there's going to be trouble. Don't say anything now, and don't tell your mother anything at all. Let me handle her." He paused, thinking.

Crow wanted to ask questions, but he was afraid of appearing guilty. He wanted to ask why they needed a lawyer.

"We'll call Butler at home. Go on to bed, and here, give me those clothes."

Crow lay in bed now and tried to imagine Sophie, and why he felt the need to lie. He remembered kissing her, but she became faceless as he remembered. His mind refused to bring in anything but a black bed of cold leaves and her mouth—too small now.

He rushed to the toilet to vomit, bringing up small pieces of meat and corn in white slime. He recognized portions of his dinner that evening, which he'd eaten before meeting up with Sophie. That seemed years ago now. He vomited again, until there was nothing left but his own gagging reflex. He didn't want to stop; he wanted to throw out everything that had happened, let it land in water and be flushed.

He slapped water onto his face and rinsed his mouth; he rinsed until the water no longer tasted sour, then glared at his reflection in the mirror over the sink. His face appeared normal. Normal. He had lied to his father and wondered if he would have to continue lying. Sophie entered his head like a catastrophe and filled him with dread for morning. He told himself that she was in the hospital, that she would be okay.

His father's reaction astonished him; his words had not been angry, and his expression had been more of fear than anger, or else just cold resignation.

Lying in bed, Crow pulled the sheet to his hip bones, leaving his chest bare, his heart exposed. He let the sheet hit lightly on his legs and feet, lifting it high and letting it fall softly on him like a leaf— something gentle and final, signaling the end of a season.

If someone came into the house tonight to kill him, stab him in the chest or neck or head, he might feel relief, because now he didn't care what happened to him. If he got through this, he pledged to never be a coward again, because the payment for cowardice was this: a person no longer wants the life that he has saved for himself.

A few hours ago he had hid in the black river behind some bushes, breathing hard after running. Waiting, he had seen stars in the water, and the shadow of the person he was now. The water's lapping had covered the sound of his breathing. The light of the moon, as well as police flashlights, had washed around him, and he had waited. He was alone, the fluttery rags of bats above him. He stepped onto the bank, dripping, and saw the stars again as he waded out. He had believed he was safe. And then he saw, or thought he saw—so quick it was at the edge of his eye, so thrifty of turn—a bright ribbon of snake going past him, near his foot, a movement that entered his head like a wire.

Two

FORTY-FIVE MINUTES EARLIER Carl had just leaned back into his
favorite chair, drinking a scotch and water, when the phone rang.
He jumped to answer it. Helen was in bed.

"Yes?" He recognized the voice of Sheriff Mike Evans, who
told him that Sophie Chabot had been hurt. "And they found your
son's wallet at the scene," he said.

"His wallet?"

"We wondered if Crow was home." The sheriff hesitated. "And
if you could ask if he's seen Sophie tonight."

"I'm sure he's in bed by now," said Carl. "I know he's taken her
out a few times, given her a ride home, you know, stuff like that."

"Yeah." The sheriff sounded nervous. "I'd like to speak with
him, if I could."

Carl knew that Crow's bed was empty. He'd checked both boys'
rooms when he got home from work a little while ago. The two
empty beds, all made up, had given him a moment of panic. But
then he remembered that Crow was off at a party, and young
Johnny was away at survival camp for four days. Now that flash of
panic came back. "Listen, Mike," Carl began. "Why don't you let
me bring Crow in tomorrow morning early. He can tell you anything he knows. No sense in getting Helen upset."

"Yeah, well." The sheriff's indebtedness to Carl Davenport's
campaign contribution was not forgotten in this conversation. That

money got Sheriff Evans elected. Carl didn't mention it; he didn't have to.

After the sheriff hung up, Carl set his drink down. What kind of teenage scrape had Crow gotten into?

He went into the bedroom, where his wife lay sleeping. "Helen." He shook her awake. "Helen, wake up."

"What? What's the matter?" She opened her eyes partway. "Carl, is something wrong? What time is it?"

"Almost three."

"My God, Carl. Is Crow home?"

Carl paused for a moment. It seemed wrong to get Helen all riled up before he knew what was going on. "Yes. He's in his room."

"Are you just getting in?"

"Yeah, the accounts at the mill are a mess since I let that CPA go. I had to get things straight."

Helen moved her legs in one sweep to the floor.

"Crow went somewhere with Bobby, then he was picking up Sophie Chabot. Some kind of party, I think."

Carl took Helen's arm as she put her feet into slippers. "Sophie's in the hospital," he said.

"What happened?" She put both hands on Carl's shoulders. "Is Crow hurt?"

"They found Sophie in the woods. Sheriff Evans said she was hurt pretty bad."

Helen pulled back as if she had been scorched. She looked lovely in the middle of the night. She looked best without makeup, open and fresh. "But Crow's all right? Let's wake him up."

"Wait, Helen."

"He's not back yet, is he?" Helen turned her head toward the window, trying to think. The night air smelled like rain. She grew panicky, then saw something outside. "There he is. I see him." She moved to go downstairs.

"Wait! Don't. I'll talk to him. Helen, please." Carl took hold of her arm. "He'll say more to me, I think—about this. Just let me talk to him and see how much he knows. Look, you can see that he's fine. We'll sort this out in the morning." Helen agreed, but she looked ruined.

Until the day Carl first saw Helen, he would not have described himself as a religious man. In fact, he thought he was too smart for religion. He would soon take over his father's mill, his life's work already decided. Prayer just wasn't necessary. Then he had seen Helen in the park, leaning to check the tightness of her dog's collar and leash, and the moment he saw her he prayed.

Please let her look over here. Let her see me. The words came into his mind just that quickly, and he felt embarrassed at himself. But then she looked up, even called for him to come over.

Carl pointed to himself, not understanding. "Me?" he mouthed.

She motioned again for him to come quickly, and Carl saw how the dog's collar pinched its neck—a large brown dog, mixed breed, strong. She couldn't make him stand still long enough to take it off. The dog was beginning to panic and choke. He even snapped at Helen's arms as Carl held him.

She managed to loosen the collar, and the dog ran around the park, barking. "He was choking. It scared me." Helen stuck her hand forward in a businesslike way. "I'm Helen Parker," she said.

Carl stood dumbly looking at the woman who would first break his heart, then marry him, continuing in small ways to break his heart, before he broke hers. Her hair was shiny blond, midlength, her face thin. She looked ethereal but strong-willed. And in this one moment Carl thought that some God, some Where, had brought this woman into his life and had made him walk to the park—which he had not planned to do—and then, at this moment, to see her. That God had made her dog choke on a collar, so she would call for Carl to help her. He was as sure that this sequence of events had been brought about by God as he was of his own ability to make money.

During the long autumn of that year, they went to the park often. Helen failed to notice how she bloomed along with the season of leaves, and when Carl finally kissed her, she surprised herself when she said, "I thought you'd never get around to kissing me, Carl."

"I thought you wouldn't want to," he said. "I mean, I wasn't sure."

And Carl woke the next morning thinking that this woman beside him was not the real thing, but just something he had imagined. He had had girls before, but Helen was not the kind of girl he usually attracted. She was religious. She was smart and had a strong sense of who she was. The confidence he had, or thought he had, paled beside her sense of herself.

They continued to see each other through the winter months, but in the early spring Helen's father suggested that she travel to Europe. Helen didn't want to go. Her sister, Ava, had spent a year in England and had loved it so much that she stayed for another year. The family wanted Helen to have the same experience. They had put aside the money. Helen bargained with her father by promising to spend the money on graduate school in the fall. She wanted to study literature. They agreed on Emory in Atlanta.

The separation Carl anticipated left him sad and wishing to marry Helen quickly. They had not talked about marriage until a few days before Helen left for school.

"We'll see each other most weekends," Helen said.

"I don't want most weekends," Carl told her.

"What do you want?"

"I want most days, as well as weekends."

"Like we've had?"

"No," he said, with some frustration. "Like we're going to have when we get married."

"That's some proposal," she teased.

"I don't want you to go to Atlanta," he said.

"You think I'm going to find someone else?"

"No."

But by Christmas Helen was behaving differently toward Carl, and when she came back on December 20, he asked what was wrong.

"Nothing's wrong, not really." Her nonchalance made Carl uncomfortable. She couldn't even bear to look at him. They exchanged expensive Christmas presents before Helen went back to Atlanta.

Carl threw all his attention into the business of running Davenport Mills. In January he purchased more land and began construction of a new mill. Helen came home less often, and whenever Carl questioned her she told him not to worry so much. But her phone calls came only a few times a week instead of every night, and when Helen returned in May, she mentioned that she would not be going back in the fall.

"Why not?" Carl asked. He felt pleased, though puzzled, by her new determination.

"Don't ask," she said. "Just don't ask. Maybe you shouldn't come around anymore."

"What's going on, Helen?" He felt sick and dizzy, as if he'd been told that somebody was dying.

"I want you to go now."

Carl left, but he continued to call her. Helen refused to answer or return his calls. If he came to the house, she sent her mother to the door.

He finally gave up.

By the end of summer, rumors began: Helen was pregnant and had been pregnant for almost four months. Carl heard the news first from a friend of Helen's. She told Carl that Helen had encouraged her parents to think that he was the father.

The late-September sun was hot, though leaves were beginning to turn. This was the month he had first seen Helen a year ago. Carl walked to the house. Helen's mother opened the door, made a lit-tle sound in her throat as she told Carl to come in. He could see by her expression that she believed he was the father of the child.

"Helen's in the kitchen," she told him, and as she said it, Helen stepped into the hallway. She had on blue jeans and a man's plaid shirt. Her face glowed when she saw Carl, but she didn't smile. She waited for her mother to go upstairs, then led Carl to the den in the back of the house.

Before she turned around to face him she said, "You heard?"

Carl nodded. "Can you do anything about it?" he asked.

"I'm too far along," she said sadly. Then, "I don't know if I could do that anyway."

"Whose is it?" Carl's voice had an edge, a steeliness that Helen would come to know well.

"Oh, Carl," she cried. "It's somebody I don't even care about. I was such a fool. He doesn't even know, and besides, he's married."

Carl didn't look at her. He could hardly believe her words. "Why?" he said. "Why would you do that?"

"I don't know. It was so stupid. He was my professor. He does this a lot, I think."

"I'm sorry, Helen." He tried to have sympathy for her. She looked beaten down, not like herself.

"Don't be. I deserve what I'm getting. You're the only one who . . ." She stopped and took his hand.

Carl pulled his hand away. "I'd about given up." He walked to the window and turned his back to her. He didn't want her to touch him. He could see the swelling beneath her shirt.

"I shouldn't have told you this," said Helen.

"I already knew."

"I wish it were yours. I wish you were the father."

He could hear the beginning of tears in her voice and turned to face her squarely. Still, he did not stand close. "Let's make it true then."

"What?"

"Let's say it *is* my child. Everybody will believe us. Your mother and father already think it's mine."

"I know."

"Then let's say it is."

"What do you mean, Carl? What are you saying?"

"I mean we could get married. Look, you don't want to raise a child by yourself, and I still love you. We'll get married and have the baby. All this will be forgotten soon enough."

"You make it sound so easy, Carl."

"It is. Believe me." His face softened, even looked relieved. "Helen, I've loved you from the minute I saw you. You know that."

Helen had a look on her face that Carl had wanted to see for months now.

Crowell Elias Davenport, named after Carl's uncle, was born five months after the wedding. Helen's labor lasted twenty-six hours, and she became so weak that the doctor began to worry.

Reverend Moss led the town in prayers for her, and for the child. When the baby finally emerged, bruised and misshapen, many brought flowers and baby presents.

They walked by the window where Crowell Elias Davenport's name tag and tiny cubicle held a red, ugly child, splotched—tired from being born. Already they liked him. Already they thought of him as a fine young man.

Three

HELEN LAY IN bed for almost an hour before rising and going down the hall toward Crow's room. She would not ask Crow any questions; she just wanted to see him. As she came in, she saw that his eyes were closed; she went to open a window; but as she raised it, a thought as strong as a voice came into her head, telling her to find proof of where Crow had been that night. Carl had told her that Crow had been drinking at the river. She would go there.

When she turned, she saw that Crow was awake. She leaned to kiss him and noticed a musty odor on his body. The small cowlick at the crown of his head lay flat, as if he had been touched by a palm pressed down.

Helen went downstairs, closing her robe around her nightgown and putting on one of Carl's raincoats. She picked up a flashlight beside the door, stepped out, going directly into the woods. She stumbled through low brush in her bedroom slippers. A wide section of river lay only a short distance from her house, and as she approached, hearing its sound, she searched the ground for evidence that Crow was telling the truth. For the first time, she sincerely hoped that he'd been drinking at the river.

She imagined she knew what had happened to Sophie. She imagined that Sophie had taken a mix of drugs and alcohol and had to be rushed to the hospital. She hoped her son was not to blame. She circled the flashlight on the path in front of her, and could hear thunder in the distance. She could smell the approach of rain.

Helen knew where the boys had built a fort when they were younger, and she looked there for beer cans. When she found a pile of empties, she lifted a few, cradling them like a baby.

She shone the flashlight at the cans and bottles, and could plainly see what had not been clear in the dim light of the forest: these cans had been there for many weeks, maybe years, some of them already busted and broken. Her evidence was no evidence at all. She dropped the cans and went back home.

Helen tried to think of what else to do. Rain began to fall, and her thoughts split themselves into smaller and smaller pieces. She felt reduced to a bundle of distinct vibrations. The thought that her son might have to go to jail was not reasonable. She began to run. The rain stung her face and arms; her arms flailed like strings unhinged from their instrument.

Her heart struggled against the idea that Crow might be guilty of something terrible. She prayed hard. As she entered the house, she prayed—demanding that God let this go, demanding that Crow not have to go to jail, that Sophie would be good as new in the morning, and that the whole matter be dropped. She spoke to God as if He were a houseboy.

And she prayed all night. In bed she prayed aloud, until Carl's patience broke.

"Stop it, Helen! Just stop! You're making me crazy!"

So she held her prayers in, releasing them only through a long sigh or a frenzy of short breaths. She dreaded morning, though before this day she had always loved morning. Even as a girl she had come alive at sunrise, feeling in it a realm of indistinct possibilities. Her arms and legs felt airy, and she wondered about all the things she thought were possible. But now, in bed, she felt the burden of day.

By six o'clock she was asleep, but she woke up at seven, hearing Carl in the kitchen with Crow. She pictured both of her sons downstairs with their father, then remembered that Johnny wasn't due

home until Tuesday night. That survival course offered to seventh-
and eighth-graders would keep Johnny away for a few more days,
and maybe things would be sorted out before his return. Helen
didn't want to upset Johnny. She brushed her teeth, pulled her hair
on top of her head, and went downstairs.

Carl had made coffee and caught the toast as it popped up. He
handed it to Crow to be buttered. Helen observed from the hallway
their easiness together, their way of pretending not to think about
police cars and lawyers soon to arrive. She felt as though she observed them through a glass, a grainy glass, until Crow saw her.

"Mom?" he said, his face a puzzle, his eyes deep sockets. As
she came in, he touched her shoulder absentmindedly, innocent of
her panic. She pushed her lips against his hair.

"I've made coffee," Carl said, wanting praise, wanting anything
but what was to come. Everything about him seemed transparent.

"Who called?" Helen asked. She had heard the phone ring.

"Raymond Butler. He's coming at nine."

"Crow?"

"Don't make him talk, Helen. Let's just have breakfast. Don't
make him talk."

They did not turn on the TV, not wanting to hear the news.

"We'll get through this all right," Carl said, putting cereal on the
table.

Helen brought orange juice and a pitcher of milk. She needed to
select her words carefully. "We will?" she asked. She looked for a
hole in his words. "Will we?" Were things worse than she had suspected?

"I promise you." He spoke above Crow's head, not averting his
gaze.

When Crow went upstairs to shower and dress, Helen asked
Carl, "What is it? What are you not telling me?"

"Sophie was hurt real bad. Raped, Helen. She was raped."

Helen gasped. "Well, you know Crow didn't do *that*. Carl, can
you get him out of this? Can you do something?"

"I can," said Carl. He knew he could apply political pressure. He knew how to manipulate the system with money. He waited a moment before saying, "You think I should?"

"Yes," said Helen, her prayer released. She didn't believe Crow had done anything wrong, and she hoped to protect him from punishment. She wanted Carl to make it right. If that could happen, if Carl could make this right, then Helen's vow to God would be this: *I will bring You my heart. And I will overlook Carl's indiscretions, as well as my sister's. I will forgive my sister.*

The last time her sister had visited them, Carl's affection for Ava was less hidden and Helen found herself hating him. *I will overlook that, as Carl once overlooked the way I hurt him.* Then she added, *If this can be made right, I will do anything.*

Helen refused to let herself imagine what might come from this moment. She shuddered, not knowing if she could forgive anything. But she felt relief as she heard Carl's promise, and she let her mind forget his confused plea: *You think I should?* And then her own, unqualified *Yes.*

From the kitchen window she could see the different pitch of the roof next door. The odd angle and the drip of rain made the air uncertain. Now she had come crashing into the middle of a life that did not resemble her own.

"I love you," she told Carl. The words, not having been said in a long time, solidified and hung in the air. Carl had not said those words to her either, and he did not say them now, but he heard her voice and felt the force of what he had to do.

A year ago Helen had caught Crow sneaking out of the house in the middle of the night, running toward the woods, but stopping short when he heard his mother's sharp call. As he came back toward the house, she saw tall figures retreat, long shadows moving into the woods. Had they been waiting for Crow to join them?

"Where were you going this time of night?" she asked, as he walked back into the kitchen.

"Nowhere."

"*No*where? Tell me what's going on." She could see Crow's head lift toward the stairs, listening for his father's footsteps.

"He's not awake," Helen said. "I just happened to be downstairs because I couldn't sleep. He'll have some questions of his own, though, I'm sure of that."

"Mom, don't tell him. Please."

"Where were you going, Crow?"

"I was meeting Bobby and Tom." He looked at her with a lusterless gaze. "And Antony, probably Casey." Helen did not like Casey. "We were going to ride around for a while, then come back." His words sounded cagey but true. "Bobby had his car."

"At two in the morning?" She searched for an answer in the web of his words. "Ride around and do what?" She hoped she sounded formidable enough to provoke honesty. "Johnny wasn't with you, was he? You didn't take Johnny." Johnny was four years younger than Crow.

"No. No. He's still asleep."

"What were you going to do out there?"

"They were drinking beer." He shuddered involuntarily. "Don't tell Dad. Please don't."

"I think he'll have to know," Helen told him, though they'd kept things from Carl before.

"He'll ground me for weeks," Crow said.

"And what do you think *I'm* going to do?"

Then Helen watched as Crow pushed the heel of each shoe off with his thumb and threw the shoes into the corner of the room. He sat in a kitchen chair as Helen mulled over whether to wake Carl or assign punishment herself. "I have some work you can do around here," she said. Her words sounded like a promise.

"Okay." Crow nodded.

Helen told him with both concern and remonstrance that to be in the woods at night with boys who had no business being out at that hour could land him in trouble that would be too big for anything but the police.

"Your dad and I can punish you," she told him, "but if you have to be punished by the law, their way of listening to your explanations will be very different. And they won't show the leniency that I'm showing you now."

"What do you want me to do?" he asked, his voice arched with hope.

"You can start Saturday. Use the ladder and clean out the gutters. Mow the lawn. Clean out the garage. There's plenty to do. Maybe some physical labor will make you tired enough to stay in bed at night."

Crow stood, and she leaned into him close enough to feel his body's warmth. His face wore a mask of resignation. He poured himself a glass of milk before going upstairs. Helen sat for a while, despondent, though the event did not seem to require despondency. When she returned to bed, Carl was snoring and she climbed in beside him. She needed to find new ways to inhabit the world. She knew that the singular memory of waking into a day, any day, its particular joy, was lost—though it might be learned again. Her restlessness disturbed Carl's sleep.

"What's wrong?" he asked, sleepily.

"Can't sleep." And Carl put both arms around her.

Helen dreamed that night as Carl held her, as she held him. She dreamed of a flurry of birds headed for a mountainside. The night was dark, and the moon dropped a milky smoke over the mountain and the birds.

In the dream she wanted to warn the birds, thinking they didn't see the mountain's craggy edges, thinking they might fly straight into its side. But she knew the sensing mechanisms for birds were good, reliable. The moon's milkiness grew brighter, and though it was still nighttime, she thought it was day. She thought she was awake, but she had only awakened in her dream. As the birds flew toward the mountainside, she began to shout, and her shouting woke Carl. She awoke just as she rescued the birds.

"Helen, you're shouting." Carl shook her. "You're having a nightmare. Helen!"

That was the night Helen began to believe that the cell of Crow's life was taking shape, and that he was becoming someone she didn't know anymore.

As she settled back into sleep, she envied the birds their easy rescue.

Four

WHEN THE SHERIFF arrived, Raymond Butler was already waiting at the Davenports' house. Before Crow came downstairs, he heard his mother crying, a sound like small birds or the squeal of wind coming around the edge of an old door. He stopped at the bottom of the stairs and could see her, dressed now, her hair undone around her shoulders. Her long skirt made her look like a saint. When Crow entered the room, his mother walked out.

"They have to take you in, son," Carl told Crow. "I wanted to keep you out of jail, but you'll need to stay there tonight. Sophie's mother signed a warrant, and the D.A.'s bringing charges against you. I'll post bail tomorrow."

"We can't do anything now, Crow. Because it's Sunday." Raymond Butler wore a suit. "I'm fairly sure we can set a preliminary hearing tomorrow afternoon, then you can go home. Even if they find probable cause, you can go home."

Helen came back into the room to protest.

"I'll take care of this, Helen," Butler told her. "Don't worry."

Two policemen approached Crow with handcuffs, reading him his rights.

"Don't handcuff him," said Helen. They did anyway. She followed them out to the car.

"What's this?" one of the detectives asked about the mud in the mudroom.

"I went fishing the other day," Carl said. "Helen refused to clean it up. Said I should do it myself." He hugged Helen as though this was all a big joke between them. She whispered something to Carl, which he ignored.

"Don't worry," he said to her. He got in the police car with Crow. "We'll get this settled."

Raymond Butler drove his own car to the station. Helen turned and went to the sunroom. A shudder went down her back as she heard the police car pull away.

The road where Crow lived was in the best part of town. The Davenport sawmill had passed from grandfather to father, then to Carl, and the land surrounding it had become valuable. Anyone who lived on this land benefited from its prestige, their credit lines quickly approved.

The road had been carved out through a thick forest, and the house overlooked the Tennessee River, with a view of the mountains. Part of the road remained unpaved, but homes crept in, parcels of land sold off one, two at a time. Helen had urged Carl to sell some land and start a trust fund for both sons.

"I don't want to stay here," Crow had told his mother. "I don't want to live in one place all my life."

"If you leave," she warned, "you might not be able to live as well as you do now."

"Maybe I want to live a different way. Maybe Johnny will want to take over the mills." His younger brother had always been more willing to please.

"Fine for you to say now," Helen countered. "You haven't had to struggle yet."

"I've struggled," said Crow, but under his breath.

Crow dreamed of far-off places, tempted even by the posters that advertised the navy or marines. He wanted to fly planes. His friend Tom had a brother who was a navy pilot, so he took that as a reason to believe that his own dream could take shape.

Until he was thirteen, Crow had built model airplanes, and he could identify even the most obscure fighter jets, such as the Grumman Wildcat, or bombers such as the B-47. As a child he liked to watch a plane until it was almost out of sight, until he became not the one watching, but the one flying. On his tenth birthday his father took him in a small plane piloted by a friend. Crow sat in the pilot's seat for a short time and steered the plane left and right. He felt the thrill of taking charge of something so much larger than himself. And even though, after landing, Crow vomited on the tarmac, he could not wait to get back inside the plane, to take off and veer into a cloud.

"If these boys want a good start, they can help me at the mill." Carl could not stifle his desire to turn the business over to his sons. "Let them run it with me." He hated the thought of a stranger taking it over.

"Johnny might be interested," Helen had told him. "But not Crow. You're going to have to face that, Carl."

"I'm not sure Johnny's capable, Helen."

"Stop. Just stop it, Carl."

"I've tried. You know I've tried." Carl gave his wife an accusing look. He still thought of her as beautiful. Her skin was warm and when he touched her he felt the natural heat of her body. Her neck was white and smooth, and he thought of putting his hand on her shoulder, but didn't.

Carl was cheating on her. Helen could see it in his body—his swagger, his shoulders at an angle. She had almost confronted him several times, but could not imagine what life would be like after a confrontation. Helen used to think she was courageous. She didn't think so now. Except when they lay in bed, mostly asleep, he hardly ever touched her anymore.

Over the last few years, the mood between them had grown sullen, argumentative. What lay so large between them was not anything they said out loud. Maybe it wasn't even the time Carl spent with Ava. But the frustration of secret anger grew, enlarged into a shadow, so that awkward politeness replaced their previous teasing. They both found it hard to imagine how they could get their love back to what it was.

By three o'clock on Sunday afternoon Crow was in a jail cell. He had denied repeatedly the accusation made by the district attorney, though he acknowledged being in the woods with Sophie. When they finally left, Crow asked his father, "How is she?" He had asked before, but no one answered him specifically.

"We don't know," Carl told him. "She hasn't said anything."

Crow stood up. "Has anybody *asked* her?" He thought she might still be unconscious. "Can't she say anything?" He wanted her to tell the truth.

"No. She's awake. She'll be all right. She's just not talking about what happened to her."

The cell was small and smelled of urine and mildew, yet they talked as if they were sitting in somebody's living room.

"Do they know who beat her up like that?" Crow asked.

"It was more than that," his father said. "It was much worse."

Crow waited a long moment before he said, "Listen, Dad. I think I should tell you something."

"Raymond Butler says the hearing is at one o'clock tomorrow. After that we can post bail, then you can come home."

"Listen—"

"No. Don't say anything. I don't want to hear anything."

"It's not what you think."

"Won't matter what I think. Just shut up, son. Just shut up now." Carl had tears in his voice, if not his eyes. An emanation swept over them like continents crashing against each other—father and son moving, fracturing, then tearing apart. "I've got to go. I'll need to tell your mother what's going on. She'll want to come see you tonight."

"Here?"

"I'm sure of it."

"But I don't want her here."

When his father left, Crow felt ill from the sour odor of the cell. The overhead light would be turned off at ten, but he wished it could be turned off now. He didn't want to see anything. He wanted to pretend he was somewhere else. But when the lights finally went off, he wished for them to be on again, the darkness proved so pervasive.

"I didn't hurt Sophie," Crow had told Butler earlier. "I would never hurt her. Ask her, she'll say I didn't do it. Did you ask her?"

"As of this moment she's not saying anything," Butler had said.

That night Crow imagined himself running. His feet could not carry him away fast enough. He didn't know that hunger could be translated so quickly into shame. He didn't know that life could spiral down so fast.

Maybe tomorrow he would discover that what happened had not really happened at all. Maybe what happened would melt away. Everything seemed wrong now, whereas yesterday everything had seemed right. Could it change back again? If only he could rewind his life back to the moment when Sophie took off her blouse, to when he ached with desire.

Crow turned his head to see the stars through the small, high window—their remote breath coming toward him. He wanted that ice light to get here. He wanted to be waiting somewhere beside water, and to see that starlight fall to its spongy end.

Five

ON SUNDAY MORNING, Judge Aurelia Bailey stepped out onto her porch. She wore a bathrobe she had worn for ten years. She had opened the tall windows in her house to let in morning air. Wind chimes in the yard drowsed in a mild breeze. She stood on the porch steps and let the sun seep into her, tilting her head to get more, her eyes closed. She had knocked on Bobby's door to wake him, but he didn't answer. She had thought he wanted to go fishing this morning.

Aurelia loved the sun in Tennessee, knowing it was different here than other places—as were the river, trees, and broad wings of hawks. When she saw these things in other settings, they seemed like pale imitations of what she had already seen here. On a map the town of South Pittsburg might not be noticed; even driving through on Main Street, a visitor might not stop, or comment. But Aurelia's bones were full of the dust of oak, woven with red clay. She knew this, believed it, without mentioning it to anyone.

When she opened her eyes, she felt polished, shiny for the day. A light sweat formed on her forehead and lips, between her breasts. She missed having a man in her life, though she never mentioned this to anyone either.

She clipped her hair back and went to Bobby's room to try again to wake him. She opened the door. A pile of dirty clothes blocked her path, and she lifted them into the hall. An old Labrador beside the bed gazed up, uninterested, and curtains

swung easily across the desk. Clothes and shoes lay strewn everywhere. Bobby slept with his Atlanta Braves cap turned sideways
on his head. He often slept in his cap.

Aurelia stood a moment watching Bobby breathe. His feet hung
off the end of the bed. She decided to let him sleep late. She
couldn't remember when he had grown so long.

The dog raised himself with a sigh and a shake and followed her
to the kitchen, where she filled two stainless steel bowls with water
and food. "I'll tell you what I think, Dog," she said. Years ago they
had named the dog Dog. "I think maybe it's a good thing that I'm
still alone. What man could stand my long hours? My not-
cooking? That's what I think."

Dog turned away, embarrassed by her lies. He ate voraciously,
then scratched on the kitchen door to go out. Aurelia watched
him do his business and made a mental note to remind Bobby to
clean up the yard. Dog ambled back in and returned to Bobby's
room.

Sometimes Aurelia missed Robert. After all these years she still
felt shame over her abandonment of him; though at the time nothing had seemed harsh enough. The evening she had left with
Bobby in her arms was now a strange memory; and as she dressed
and showered she thought how much easier it would have been if
Robert had just had an affair, just cheated on her in some regular
way.

She sipped her second cup of coffee, letting the Sunday morning grow wide before she left to put in a few extra hours of work at
the courthouse. A blue Buick pulled into the driveway, and she
knew the car belonged to Roland Dunphy, the postmaster.

"Brought some mail for you, Judge. You hadn't checked your
box in a while."

"Roland, I could've gotten that tomorrow. You didn't have to
come by on Sunday." Aurelia took the pack of letters from him.
The car was full of kids, one a classmate of Bobby's. "Hello,
Lester," she said, nodding to him in the backseat.

"Hey, Judge Bailey." Lester sounded friendly, but he didn't look at her; his friendliness seemed false. He did not ask about Bobby.

Years ago, Lester played catcher on the Little League baseball team, and he often came to the house with Bobby and Crow. Often Aurelia would walk in to find Lester and Crow leaning into her refrigerator.

"Can't find anything to eat," they'd say, without embarrassment.

"Look in the pantry." Aurelia usually bought extra food for them, but as they grew into teenagers and switched their focus from baseball to rock music, she couldn't keep enough on hand. They could finish off a family-sized bag of Doritos in minutes. She loved their gangly bodies pushing at each other.

"I'm on my way to church anyway." Roland Dunphy was a Catholic with a large family, and they went to mass on Sunday morning.

Later, in her office, Aurelia would wonder what Roland knew, or what Lester was hiding, but on this morning she waved as they drove off. She had a strange feeling about the day, a mood she couldn't shake off, a bad feeling. She had always been superstitious—recognizing intuitions, premonitions. She thought that Roland had almost said something to her but held back.

She went to Bobby's room again and lifted the cap from his head. "Bobby?" she whispered.

"I want to sleep," he said, and turned over.

"I thought you and Crow were going fishing this morning," she said. "Are you sick?" He looked sick.

"I don't feel good," he admitted.

She checked his head for a fever.

"Don't." He pushed her hand away.

"I'm going to the office in about an hour," she said. She closed the door, lifting the pile of clothes to take to the washer. Everything smelled of mildew. She washed two loads before she left the house. It was still early. She didn't think about Roland and Lester anymore until she went to her office and saw a rash of messages and memos—all of them urgent. She called the district attorney.

"Jeb, what's happened?"

"Sophie Chabot is in the hospital, Judge," Jeb told her. "She was assaulted."

Aurelia took in a breath.

"The Davenport boy was placed under arrest. He came in this morning, early. The police are talking to other people who were at the party in the Fairchild house. Did they talk to Bobby yet?"

"No." Aurelia couldn't think straight. The accusation of Crow Davenport had to be a mistake. Crow and Bobby were best friends. She knew Crow as if he were her own. If Crow could be accused of something, then she had to consider the possibility that Bobby might also be accused. She didn't know how any of it could be true. "Crow's in jail? Now?"

"Police got a 9-1-1 call about one o'clock this morning. Male. He told us someone was hurt, and where. Didn't identify himself."

"How's Sophie? How bad is it?"

"She's conscious, but she's not talking. She was raped, Judge."

"She won't say what happened?"

"I don't think she remembers."

"They did a rape kit, then?"

"They did. Rita is livid. Wants to sue the Fairchilds. Wants to crucify Crow! She won't let anybody touch her daughter. Sophie screams if anybody touches her."

"Well."

"We know that Crow Davenport was with Sophie last night," said Jeb. "We know that. And the thing is, they found his wallet near her. And a blanket."

"My God, Jeb." Aurelia found it difficult to stay in the mode of judge. She felt simpleminded, confused. "They pick up anybody else?"

"They're looking into it. A lot of kids were at that party. Half the kids in town, probably." Jeb cleared his throat. "We're looking at the possibility that this was done by more than one person. What my guys found at the scene indicates multiple attackers. Maybe some men who like to hang around the high school. We've suspected they're selling drugs. It's just another angle to look at."

The judge waited a moment, then said, "I guess the media will be all over this."

"Already are," said Jeb. "They're playing up how such a privileged boy could get caught in something like this. The whole town's riled up." Jeb sighed. "And there's something else."

"What?"

"Sophie has bruises on her arms and thighs, her face. It's obvious that somebody went after her pretty bad."

The impact of his words proved stunning, hard. At that moment Judge Bailey thought something monstrous was moving beneath the skin of the town, and that it might change the appearance of everything.

"Why didn't somebody call me last night?" She sat down in her high-backed judge's chair. "I know these people. Why didn't somebody call me?"

"Crow admitted being with the girl and even said they left the party and went to the woods. He said they'd been kissing, but that he didn't hurt her. He swore he didn't hurt her."

Aurelia cursed under her breath.

Jeb spoke again. "His dad's hired a lawyer. Raymond Butler. We asked Crow a few questions, but his lawyer wouldn't let him answer any more."

"Raymond Butler's such a slick bastard," she said. "But he's sure good in the courtroom, if it comes to that." She waited a moment. "I hope this doesn't go to trial, Jeb."

"Yeah, me too."

The judge didn't speak for a long moment, and Jeb thought the line was disconnected. "Judge?"

"Yeah, I'm here." Then she asked, "What time did this happen?"

"About midnight, we think. You can't serve as judge on this case," said Jeb.

"You're right about that," said Aurelia. Aurelia was a powerful woman in this town. It was difficult to think of another judge stepping in to fill her role as protector of the community, but given the fact that Crow was Bobby's best friend, there was no way she could take this on.

"I'll call a county judge from Jasper," said Jeb. "We should have someone who doesn't live here, don't you think?"

"Absolutely," said Aurelia. "But will you call me after the hearing tomorrow?"

"Sure," said Jeb.

Judge Bailey set in order the papers on her desk, made a few more calls, then dialed her own number. "Bobby?" she said when he answered in a sleepy voice. "You up?"

"Yeah."

She had no idea how to say the next thing.

Six

JOHNNY DID NOT hear about Crow until his father called around noon on Sunday. Carl soft-pedaled the news. He urged Johnny to stay in the north Georgia woods to finish the course. Carl had helped finance the course for the school, though he did it mostly for Johnny. Carl had always worried more about Johnny than Crow.

"But I want to come home," Johnny said.

"You can come home with the rest of the group," Carl told him. "On Tuesday."

"Why does Crow have to stay all night in jail?"

"We can't post bail on Sunday, son. Don't worry."

"I want to see to him," said Johnny.

"Wait until Tuesday."

"I'm coming home," Johnny insisted. "I'll get somebody else to bring me home."

"Okay," said Carl. "I'll come get you. If you have to leave, I'll come."

On a full moon in late July, Johnny came into this world, and Carl gathered his pride around him. He had the boy he wanted—though Helen had prayed for a girl.

"I carried this child so high," Helen said. "I thought if I carried a baby high, it'd be a girl." She couldn't hide her disappointment.

With Crow's birth, Carl hadn't shown this much pride. He couldn't help thinking how Crow had come from another man; and though he'd grown to love Crow as his own, had given Crow the family name, Johnny was his blood son.

"Look at him, Helen!" He was yelling. "Just look!" Carl held the red-splotched baby out to his wife. "I can't believe it!"

The baby took Helen's breast. His tiny mouth searched for a nipple and began to suck. Helen had not seen Carl this happy in years.

"Where's Crow?" she asked.

"He's with Louise and George. Antony wanted him to spend the night, so I said yes."

"But I want to see him. I want Crow here."

"C'mon, Helen," Carl urged. "Let's enjoy our son."

Helen had never heard Carl refer to Crow in this way. He might say "son" or "your son," but never "our" son. He'd been saving this phrase for the right moment. Helen felt sad for Carl, and sad for herself and Crow.

Johnny's sweet breath and affable charm made him adored. As a baby he lay in bed for hours, not whining, his eyes open, satisfied with life.

Johnny belonged to them, clean and simple. Carl favored him without apology. But as Johnny grew older, Carl grew impatient with his son's reluctance to play ball, or to engage in anything competitive. Johnny always preferred activities that kept him alone.

"When he goes to school," said Carl, "I want things to be different."

"They will be." Helen tried to be reassuring.

Crow bought his brother some robots and a G.I. Joe, thinking his dad might approve of these toys. Johnny liked the G.I. Joe, but by the age of six he preferred to be with his mother in the kitchen.

"You're turning him into a goddamn sissy, Helen."

"Don't say that."

"I'll say whatever I want."

Johnny did love being near his mother. She spoke to him in a way that made him calm, secure. What he needed from her was her nearness, her presence around him. Even at six or seven, if she was in the kitchen, Johnny asked to help measure or stir whatever she was cooking. She pulled a kitchen chair to the stove so he could stand beside her, be almost her same height, and see what she was stirring.

"We'll make fudge. Want to?"

Johnny nodded.

She showed him how to level a cup of sugar with a knife. He kept everything separate in white bowls, until she told him what to mix first, what to mix second.

The first time they made fudge he stuck his finger into the bowl of cocoa and the bitter taste on his tongue brought tears to his eyes. He thought he had somehow ruined the chocolate by putting his finger into the silky powder.

Helen explained that when sugar was added to the cocoa, it would taste the way he hoped. She pointed out to him the word *unsweetened* on the can, and the word seemed so large in his mind that he planned to mention it at school.

"Don't tell Daddy we made fudge," his mother said.

"Why not?"

"He doesn't want you to be inside all the time."

"I know. He thinks girls do this stuff."

"Yes."

"Did you want a girl instead of me?"

Helen stopped and wiped her hands on her apron. "No. Of course not." Her balance became precarious. "*You* are what I wanted, exactly what I wanted."

She lifted him up. He dangled a long spoon dripping chocolate onto the floor. Johnny squirmed because her fingers tickled his sides. When she put him back onto the chair, he stirred the bubbly mixture. He could not make his eyes leave the dark boiling liquid. He stirred, trying to calm the roiling, keep it from burning.

"I like to be here with you," he said.

Helen didn't know what to do about her love for Johnny. Looking at his face pricked her heart and made her insanely proud.

Johnny's favorite moment was folding a tablespoon of butter into the chocolate as it cooled, seeing the yellowy clump dissolve into the chocolate mixture. He swished the yellow around, making concentric designs, until the butter had disappeared. They waited for the fudge to cool; then his mother began to beat it. Johnny liked the flopping sound of the spoon against the thickening chocolate. To him, it was the sound of making fudge.

His mother let him pour the fudge onto a white platter. Later he would cut the candy into small pieces and pile them into a high design on the same plate.

One night, after Johnny's eighth birthday, Carl suggested that Johnny go off to summer camp.

"Some of the guys at the mill say their sons go away to a camp in the North Carolina mountains. They have competitions and give trophies at the end. Hell, they say everybody wins at least three ribbons. I think it'd be good for him."

"How long would he be gone?"

"There you go, Helen. See? You hold on too tight."

"How long, Carl?"

"Eight weeks."

"Four."

"Six then. Eight next year."

"Let's see if he likes it."

So at age eight Johnny went to Camp Cherokee. As he packed to leave, he insisted on taking some books and a sketch pad to draw plants and birds.

Carl objected. "Listen, son, you're not going to have time to do any of that stuff. If you take it, you'll just go off by yourself. Why do you think we're sending you?"

"I still want to take it, just in case," Johnny said. "I'll do all the other stuff too, Dad."

"Suit yourself." Carl acquiesced. Everything about Johnny looked like Carl. Their hair, arms, and walk were identical, but their temperaments were markedly different. Carl wanted Johnny to be more like himself, more like Crow. He worried about Johnny's ability to fight for himself. The idea that anything might happen to him made his knees weak.

On the day Johnny left for camp, Carl sent him off with a hale and hearty goodbye, waving largely from the yard. Then he went back into the house and closed his study door. Johnny could see his father's head on his desk before riding off on the camp bus.

He called to his mother. "Tell Dad I'll be all right," he said. Helen nodded, waving.

Johnny felt that he had two selves: one outside and another moving beneath his skin. Whenever he remembered the inside boy, as he liked to call him, his heart and chest throbbed with delight, but the outside boy could not follow the clues given from his heart. His outside self always seemed to be walking down strange streets, seeing odd Stop signs.

On Sunday night when Carl picked up Johnny from the survival trip, he continued to downplay the seriousness of Crow's ordeal. He said only that Sophie Chabot had been hurt. He did not mention that she was in the hospital.

Johnny felt the worry in his father's voice and could not imagine why it was more important for him to climb a rope and spend another night with a group of guys than to come home when things seemed bad.

"Why do you treat me like a mental case?" Johnny asked.

"I don't. I don't do that."

"You worry about me because I'm not like you."

"I just worry." Carl's voice had an edge.

"I won't break just because I'm different," he said. "I'm doing it all, Dad. I'm hiking, rope climbing, camping out all night, getting bit by mosquitoes, the whole bit. I'm keeping a journal. You can read about it."

Carl didn't know what to say to this son. He had always wanted to make Johnny more like him and Crow—but now he wasn't sure exactly what Crow had done, and though he knew how to apply pressure where it could be felt, he wasn't sure if he could get Crow out of this trouble.

"I'll be all right," said Johnny, trying to be adaptable.

Sometimes, in Johnny's dreams, an animal figure appeared, small and birdlike. He recognized the gentleness of the figure; but he knew, even in the dream, that this creature would not have an easy life.

Seven

WHEN SOPHIE CHABOT awoke in the woods, her underpants felt cold and the voice she heard did not sound like her own. She had awakened several times already, falling back into a haze. Somebody was putting clothes on her, covering her. Once she had heard Crow's voice calling to her. She had seen him. Was it Crow? She knew she was hurt.

A male and a female police officer leaned over her. "Don't you worry," the man's voice said. And the woman officer kept telling her, "You're all right now. We're getting you to the emergency room."

Sophie was told later that when she saw the two police officers, she began to scream and did not cease screaming until the doctor tranquilized her. She didn't remember making any noises.

When she awoke those times in the woods, striations of light fell through the trees. Was it light from the moon? The ground was wet and she felt rocks beneath her back. Her leg felt numb and she kept thinking that she had been in an accident. She wondered if she was paralyzed.

She knew that when Crow had kissed her, a wave of something (was it love?) had risen in her chest. She couldn't speak. Even the first time she had seen Crow in town with his friends, she felt a turn inside her, a small whirling that kept on returning. Before she even knew his name, she knew he was somebody she wanted to be with, and she began to sketch his face in her notebook.

Sophie hadn't believed Crow would ask her out, since she was two grades below him. But he had, and for a month now he had walked everywhere with her. In the cafeteria he sought her out, he walked her to classes, and after school he drove her home, or to town. When someone teased him about her, he made a noise through his nose.

"*You* wish!" he said.

Tonight had been Sophie's idea. She hoped they could go off somewhere alone, and when they got to the party, she suggested they go out behind the house. They took a blanket.

In the woods Crow touched Sophie, and when he did, she told him to lie down on the leaves with her. He hesitated.

Sophie had been instructed by other girls about ways to touch a boy, ways to kiss. Since she had arrived in South Pittsburg in January, Nikki and Stephanie stayed close to her, making her their good friend. They were both juniors and didn't usually hang around with younger students, but Sophie's unusual beauty made her popular with the older boys. Her large dark eyes always looked wet. She was competition, even though she was young, so the girls befriended her, instructed her, told her whom to date.

Sophie touched Crow through his pants. She had thought about this night so many times in her room—imagining how she would make him love her. In her mind he told her he loved her, said she was beautiful. In her mind he came unraveled with love. She had not thought she would let him enter her, but their kissing lifted to a pitch of desire she hadn't expected to reach.

When Crow tried to go inside her, she urged, "Not all the way." She was trying to be careful.

"Okay," he said. "Okay." But they went too far and she told him to stop. He was breathing hard and didn't hear her, then when he heard her he pulled out.

"I came a little bit," he told her. "I don't know if . . ."

"Do you have something?" she asked. And he remembered he had left the condoms in the car.

"I'll be right back," he said and got up, pulled on his underwear. She laughed.

"You're going like that?"

"It's not far," and he ran off.

Sophie covered herself with Crow's shirt. She watched him disappear and heard the crunching of his feet evaporate. Night sounds filled the woods, leaves rustling. She heard some voices, but they seemed to be coming from the house. "Crow?" she said. "That you?" Then she saw them, or the shadow of them.

A heavy darkness clung to the uneven surface of their faces. They looked craggy, mountainous. One cursed under his breath and another stood back, in the shadows of the trees. A word or sound passed between them. A direct word, then a quiver around the mouth, a flinch at something rooted, or unrooted, between them.

Sophie didn't remember the exact moment or exactly what happened, but as someone fell on her—wrapping the shirt around her head, knees hitting the ground beside her—another held her down. No one spoke. The only sounds Sophie heard were feet shuffling to get into position, and a tiny distant humming in her head that promised to take her far off from this moment.

She jerked suddenly, trying to push someone off; but he clamped down harder, holding her with his legs and knees. He held her arms flat on the ground. She heard his breathing. She heard her own voice calling to Crow, but the shirt was pushed tightly around her mouth so that her voice was muffled. She wanted for Crow to come back, to fight them, to pull them off.

"Please," she cried. "Please, don't!" Her voice sounded dry. She could barely hear herself. She felt the blanket beneath her. Her bra lay beside her head. Then she felt someone inside her, pushing. She struggled, then grew still, extremely still. She felt dizzy, wishing her dizziness might dim the pain.

Someone jumped up, and another was on her. He made a sound

but she didn't feel him enter her. She didn't feel anything, though he made sounds as if he enjoyed what he was doing. She tried to beg him to stop when someone jerked her head and cut her neck against a rock. When the last one pressed himself against her, he put his head next to hers and whispered words she didn't understand. She felt stickiness between her legs. She was stinging and something deeper inside felt ripped.

This last one had long hair that fell in her face. She could feel its heaviness even through the shirt that smothered her—strings on her forehead and cheeks. She tried to get up. She tried to lift herself, but he knocked her down. Then he went in, tearing her more. She kicked, but any movement hurt, so again she lay still. Then gratefully she went unconscious.

Sophie woke finally, completely, hours later in the hospital room. Just before she woke she felt her mother's hands bathing her arms and legs with a soft, soapy rag. She heard the nurse, Louise Burden, speaking.

"Has she said anything yet?" Louise asked.

"No," said Rita.

Louise, the head nurse at the Marion County Hospital emergency room, had treated most of the white kids in town. She knew them as well as she knew the blacks. Louise had always been friendly to white people. She nursed their children through strep throat, broken arms, pinkeye, stomach pains, influenza. And as they grew older she helped them through alcohol abuse and what she called "frying their brains with drugs."

"You think this was somebody she knows?" Louise asked.

Rita couldn't answer. She'd been sitting at her daughter's side for hours. She hadn't eaten or slept. She shivered involuntarily, then saw Sophie's eyes open.

"Shhh," Rita said. She stood, leaning. Louise and Rita both leaned, as if they were looking into a deep hole.

Sophie could not discern their words, but their faces hung like fruit, like something able to nourish. She closed her eyes and began to tremble, every nerve and vessel shivering.

"She's back in the world," said Louise, placing two fingers on the pulse at her wrist. "If she's trembling, she's back in this world."

Eight

E. G. HOLLIS, a tall man, thick and uneven like a tree trunk, stood in the kitchen stirring some soup when he heard knocking at the front door. He wasn't expecting anyone, and a visitor after dark usually meant bad news. Hollis, a teacher in the local high school, had already heard the news, and it was bad. He knew all the students and had taught them, or would teach them, American and European history. He leaned his large head to look out the window and saw Charlie Post's truck parked under the pecan tree. Charlie liked to have pecans fall into the truck and would even shake the tree to make them fall into the bed.

"You could just ask me for a bag of pecans, you know," Hollis once told Charlie.

But Charlie shook his head. "It's better this way."

Hollis opened the door and motioned Charlie in. "Want to have some soup with me?"

Charlie wiped his hiking boots on the mat and stepped inside. "What'd you make?"

"Beef vegetable."

"Sure."

The two men took bowls and spoons and bread to the kitchen table. After tasting it to see if it was seasoned well enough, Hollis ladled the soup into two bowls and put a spoon into each one. A big man with wide shoulders, Charlie sat gingerly on a kitchen chair. The chair let out a creak as Charlie edged it closer to the table.

"Raining hard?" Hollis asked. Water dripped from Charlie's cap and drops hung from his chin.

"Yeah," he said. "Might hail." He spooned soup into his mouth. He and Hollis had been friends for nearly eighteen years. They had coached Little League for ten years. The boys still called Charlie "Coach."

"Did you hear about Sophie Chabot?" Charlie asked. "And that Crow Davenport's been charged?"

"Yes."

"What do you think?"

Hollis's fingers drifted to his scalp. He had grown slightly bald over the past year, and during that time, he'd picked up the habit of rubbing the smooth part of his head whenever he was deep in thought. "It'll be hard to convince me that Crow did something like that."

"I don't think he did. Even though the evidence seems to—"

"I don't care what it shows. It could have been anybody." Hollis couldn't think of many students who would be less likely to attack a girl. "Anyway, I think the sheriff should be looking for those men who've been hanging around the school."

"It's about time they looked into that. I've made formal complaints to the police about those guys. I've seen three or four of them lurking near the practice field in their leather jackets and badass construction boots. I've tried to talk to them, but they always wander off when I head in their direction. You can bet they'll be brought in for questioning." Charlie slurped his soup.

"Good," said Hollis. "And we should ask the kids at school what they know about these guys. Could be selling drugs."

"Could be," said Charlie. "Smizer, down at the station, told me that Jack Canady was jobbing in some extra workers to finish up the new hospital wing on time. Which might explain why they're in town, but *not* why they're hanging around the high school."

"How is Rita?" Hollis asked. Charlie and Rita had been together now for over a month.

"She's hardly herself. She won't even speak to me if she thinks I'm sticking up for Crow. She's blind with rage and can't think of anything but blame. No matter if she might be wrong."

"She is wrong."

"That's not something I can tell her."

"So we'll stay alert to anything the students might tell us," Hollis said. "Keep our ears open."

"Yup." Charlie poured himself some more soup. "This is good. Didn't Lila used to make soup like this?"

"It's her recipe."

They could hear hail bouncing off the porch and roof. "Where're your dogs? Better get them in. It's getting bad out there."

"They're in the shed," Hollis said. "They're fine." He looked out the back window. "I'll check on them later."

"You going to the jail tomorrow?" Charlie asked. "To see Crow?"

"I'll be there," Hollis said. "Crow needs to see us there."

"My thoughts exactly." Charlie drank the dregs of the soup from his bowl. "They're questioning all the boys—Tom, Bobby. They went to Antony first."

Hollis stopped eating, seething. "They went to Antony because he's black." He lifted a cigarette from the pack on the table. "They go to Louise Burden's house?"

"I guess."

"Damn."

Charlie carried his bowl to the sink and rinsed it. "I better get home," he said.

"If you pray at all," said Hollis, "this might be a good time to do so."

When Hollis was a young man he had struggled with the idea of becoming a priest, but then he met Lila and married her, choosing instead to teach. But since Lila's death ten years ago, his lifestyle did not seem so far from the priesthood—the students being his congregants; this house, his abbey. Most days, it seemed enough.

He had wept when they married in the Methodist church on a bleak winter afternoon. Only a few members of his family came to celebrate the wedding, some cousins and a sister. Most had wanted him to become the priest he had promised to be. But Hollis had not wept at Lila's funeral. Three weeks later, when the empty house made him believe completely what he had lost, the tears had come. From that time on, he had poured his love and care, his attention, onto his students—a benefit for those who grew up in South Pittsburg.

Every night he came home to his small house outside of town and cooked vegetables or made a thick soup. He rarely ate desserts but kept oranges and apples in a drawer at school. Often during a free class period, if he didn't keep study hall, he could be seen peeling an orange and eating the sections one by one, filling his mouth with juice, working his tongue into his cheek, or cutting an apple into slices rather than eating it whole.

He read science in his spare moments, not as a precise study, but in order to understand patterns occurring in the natural world, to see how those patterns compared to rhythms in history and even human interaction. He was usually not disappointed. He used analogies, as he understood them, to explain historical changes to the students.

Students teased him about this practice, but they usually remembered the comparisons. Even years later they reminded Hollis of something he had told them about azimuth, or gravity, or magnetism. They liked him. He was attractive in a craggy, Ichabod Crane way. His skin appeared slightly pocked from early years of acne, and his eyes, round and gray, looked huge in his face. His gaze could pierce, like a shot, into the heart of a boy or girl who told a lie.

The year Hollis arrived in South Pittsburg, Charlie Post had just built a hardware store, Post Hardware. Hollis went into the store his second day in town, to find tools and materials to repair his porch. He also asked where he might find some fishing gear. Their friendship began because of a shared love of fishing, but they soon discovered how closely their values, their thinking, coincided.

Now Charlie sat in his truck, not starting it, not wanting to leave yet. He was sorry he had mentioned Antony. "I feel something coming," said Charlie. His hand flew up into the air. "Besides this storm."

Hollis felt it too but did not say so.

"Just a brewing in the air," Charlie said. Then he laughed, thinking of a way to change the subject. "Did you know the boys signed up for that competition in Knoxville? The Battle of the Bands?"

Hollis nodded. "They've got their hopes up too much, I think."

"Maybe that's good," Charlie said. "I'm just wondering though, have we taught them how to lose?"

Hollis smiled. "We taught them. I don't know if they've learned it yet. Last year they were all excited about the Gulf War, you remember? They talked about it like it was a show on TV. They wanted to go over there, be heroes."

"The way they're looking at this Knoxville thing, they think they're gonna get rich. They think they'll be famous!"

"Who told them that?" Hollis shook his head.

"Damn! Who needed to tell them?" Charlie reached to straighten his side mirror, and it came off in his hand.

"When are you going to get a new truck, Charlie?"

"This one's still good." He put the mirror on the seat beside him.

Hollis smiled at his friend. "We better prepare those boys for something other than the unmitigated success that they expect."

Charlie turned the ignition. "Thanks for the soup," he said.

Hollis went back into the house and opened the curtains to see Charlie's lights move down the driveway toward the main road. A black roach made its way from beneath the pantry door into the kitchen, and he watched it scoot across the floor before he stepped on it.

Nothing in this world had prepared Hollis for the affection he felt for his students. Laughter could be heard coming from his classroom; a lively undercurrent of interest could be felt just by passing the door, even if the door was closed. Other teachers experienced the energy that spilled out into the hall; some grew jealous of Hollis's popularity. They claimed that the students liked him because he gave high grades. He did.

In fact, the students worked harder to earn their grades from him. They spent more time on his assignments. No one wanted to disappoint him.

After Charlie left, Hollis took food out to the three hounds, then stayed awake trying to think of a way to speak with Crow the next day. A zip of dread pulled down his spine. As he thought of visiting Crow in jail, he knew he could not let a modicum of fear show. He knew that the young lived their lives in a compartment and did not see the appearance of shadows in the corner; but a shadow had come in.

Another roach scuttled across the floor. Hollis washed the empty bowls, wrapped the bread in tinfoil, and put the leftover soup into the refrigerator. He dried his hands and shuddered.

He stayed awake long into the night preparing for class, a man with his books, trying to imagine discoveries, maybe just *one* discovery or some new question about history: trying to explain slavery, or the anger between Indians and white men—the scalping of heads, babies dashed against rocks. He dreamed of discovering the cause of civil and uncivil wars, the onslaught of epidemics, the Great Depression. Then, if he could only take back Hitler's orders, release the cold starved bodies of Jews from the ovens, understand the Vietnam massacres, warn the students against the love of war.

Hollis tried to imagine what had happened to Sophie Chabot and why. He could not believe anyone could do it, not even the

Walker brothers, who had been caught breaking into Smizer's Mobil station. It was easier to picture those strange men in town as the culprits, bringing dark destruction to their good, simple community. He wondered if the parents in South Pittsburg had been warned about this new danger. No girl should be out after dark alone until this had all been sorted out. That night Hollis fell asleep in his chair amazed, disheartened by the thought of all he would not understand.

Nine

ON THE DAY Crow went to jail, Louise Burden drove to Helen's house in the late afternoon. The sheriff had already talked to some boys who had been to the Fairchilds' house. Antony had gone to that party, and rumors of drugs and heavy drinking were circling the town. Louise hoped Helen would be alone, and was glad when she saw Carl's car gone.

Helen saw Louise get out of her big gray Chevy and ran to meet her. "Oh, Louise." They walked back into the house and stood in the hallway. "I needed somebody today." Helen seemed about to fall over—as though if someone had pushed her with one finger, she might topple.

"I was at the hospital when Sophie came in last night," Louise said. "I wanted to call you, because rumors were flying around like crazy."

"How is Sophie?" Helen asked, keeling to the left, then balancing herself on a hall table. "I wanted to call Rita Chabot this morning, but wondered if I should."

"Nobody knows exactly how Sophie is, not really. I mean, she's bruised up, but she's not saying anything about what happened. Or can't remember. Breaks my heart to see that girl."

"Oh, Louise."

"Don't worry about Crow, Helen. I know he's not in on this. I don't care what they're saying, I don't believe it. I've been watching him grow up for a long time, him and Antony. Now, I can think of some other boys who might've done something like this, but I swear, Helen, no one with any sense could think it was Crow. Oh, God. That poor girl."

"Crow can't quit talking about Sophie. All he wants to do is see her." Helen began to cry uncontrollably. "Don't let me cry," she said. "I don't want to be crying when Carl comes home." They walked through the dining room into the kitchen. "Come on, I'll make us some coffee. Louise, you are the answer to a prayer."

Louise laughed through her nose.

"How's Antony?" Helen asked. She wanted to speak of something different.

"He's working at the diner, washing dishes. His hours, they're not regular. I never know when he's gonna be working, or gonna be home."

Helen stopped, her back to Louise. "I'm so worried, Louise. I don't know what to do."

"Listen, Helen, Crow wouldn't have the *ability* to do something like this. I know it as well as I know Antony wouldn't be in on it."

"Who mentioned Antony? Did someone say something about Antony being there?"

"He went to that party." Louise plopped down into a straight-backed chair, as if she had walked the whole way to Helen's house. "Just being black could make them blame him."

Louise and George were raising their grandson as a son. Their own son had left town, leaving Antony with them—not returning. "I just hope his bad luck has run out," she said. "You know how good luck can run out? Well, in the case of Antony, his bad luck could use a break."

They had talked in this kitchen before. Antony was three when his father left, and from that day these two women had come together to talk while their boys played ball in the yard.

Helen reached for some cups in the drainer. She measured coffee. "You still like it strong?"

Louise nodded. "Where's Johnny?"

"Carl's gone to get him at that survival camp. He wanted to come home." She turned the coffee grinder on, and the noise drowned out their voices. They waited for quiet.

"Louise, why do you think Sophie's not saying anything?" She measured the coffee and water and sat, waiting for it to drip. "Why won't she talk about it?"

"Sophie's scared." Louise was thoughtful. "I'm thinking her mind won't let her remember. She's in shock. Or maybe Rita just doesn't want to push her too hard." Louise shook her head. "One thing I know, something ugly has reared its head in this town. That girl won't feel safe for a long time."

Antony had not felt safe for years after his daddy took off. Louise had to promise him every day that she and George wouldn't leave him, would never leave him. Louise had been on the porch when her son drove up with Antony. He kissed her and said that his wife, Antony's mother, was at work and that they would pick up Antony later in the afternoon. He waved from the truck, and a flicker of sadness came over his face, just a fraction of a second of sadness—then he was gone. Mother and father, both gone.

Louise snapped her fingers. "Something can happen just like that." She snapped them again. "And everything's different."

Helen poured them each a cup of strong coffee and pushed cream and sugar toward the middle of the table. "Now, Helen, Antony's a friend of Crow's. Part of that rock band and everything. And when suspicion falls on Crow, it falls on my Antony too, more than on the other boys." Louise looked at Helen with her neck drawn back slightly, as if she might be preparing herself for some unexpected onslaught of racial bias.

"Louise, that makes no sense."

"Listen." Louise's voice was stern. "I've seen it time and again. Things can turn on a dime when you're black."

"Don't even think about that, Louise," Helen told her. "Don't even let that worry come in."

"I do worry," said Louise. "And you should too. I heard that Rita was pushing to get the D.A.'s office to go after Crow, get him convicted. She's afraid somebody might accuse Sophie, you know, say she asked for it because she'd been drinking." Louise leaned in. "Helen, I came here to ask about Crow, but I'm here, too, to say if Antony's accused of anything, you got to help him."

"I've got to help Crow first, Louise," said Helen. She looked as though she might stand up.

"You and Carl can help him." Louise was not listening to Helen. "Antony won't need any more bad luck in his life."

"I don't believe in luck," said Helen. "Good or bad. Just things happening and God looking over all of it."

"Where you think God was when Sophie needed help?" Louise spoke, her anger spitting out. "If you take care of sick people like I do, if you see people come in in all kinds of torment, a person begins to wonder who's in charge. I know you have a strong faith, Helen. I used to have it too, but things come in sideways and take it away. And if something happened to my Antony, I think I'd curse God."

"No you wouldn't."

"Yes. I would. I would do just that. I would fight tooth and nail for that boy."

"He's not in trouble for this, Louise."

Louise drank the rest of her coffee; she didn't look comforted. "Sometimes I can't tell the difference in a misfortune and a blessing. Sometimes it seems like one thing, sometimes another. Like my own big son leaving his baby boy and not coming back. Saying he's coming back, telling his boy he's coming back, but not doing it. Was that a misfortune or a stroke of good luck? Hard to tell from where I stand. Sometimes I get ashamed thinking about what he did—leaving in a truck, smiling like he was a good person, a father. Damn him. George won't even say his name in the house, but that's less from any anger and more from just being hurt. I haven't said my boy's name in thirteen years, Helen, not out loud. I say it sometimes in a whisper though. Just let my mouth form his name soft, like I'm kissing him."

"I know, I know," said Helen. But she didn't know. "God's ways aren't always known to us."

Louise laughed. "He does have some strange ideas about things, God does. But Antony, now, he is certainly my alternative blessing."

Both women put their cups into the sink and walked back through the house to the front door. As they opened the door, Carl drove up. Johnny got out, but someone else was in the car, a woman. Louise saw who it was, but Helen saw only Johnny coming toward her, and Carl's face. She searched it for clues.

Louise said goodbye. Helen let Carl get into the house, then held him tight. He let her hold him, his arms down at his sides, pinned, his body stiff as a tree.

A few days later Antony came home at suppertime talking about his surprise interview with Deputy Canton and what people at school were saying, and what the police were asking the other boys.

"Back up," said Louise. "Officer Canton interviewed you at school? George, put down the newspaper and listen up."

George did as he was told. "Go on, son."

"Not school," said Antony. "He came by the diner."

"That is outrageous," said Louise. "If that ever happens again, you are not to speak with the police until you get me or your grandfather down there. What did he ask you?"

"He asked me what time I got to the Fairchilds', who I hung out with, and when I left. Wanted to know did I drink or take drugs at the party, and which kids were drinking or drugging. He wanted a list of Crow's friends and a list of who's in our band. Asked me if Crow had a bad temper. How long he'd been dating Sophie and how he treated her. Asked me if I knew anybody who might want to hurt Sophie. I don't like that Officer Canton. He kept twisting what I said and misunderstanding me on purpose, saying stuff like, 'So you and the rest of the boys got Sophie to take a drink or two, right? And then you invited her to take a walk—into the woods?' "

"And what did you say?" George asked.

"I said no way. I just kept my cool, like you always taught me."

"This is exactly what I was afraid of," said Louise, a tremor in her throat. "They're singling out our Antony because of his skin color."

"Mama," said Antony. "You don't know that. Everybody who knows Crow is getting asked stuff. They pulled Bobby and Lester out of math class today and were talking to them for a long time. They talked to Sophie's girlfriends too."

Louise went behind the chair where he was sitting and put her arms around his neck, hugging him hard.

"You trying to choke me to death, Mama?" he said, making an exaggerated choking sound.

"Won't be such a hard way to go," said Louise. "Being loved to death by your grandma." She let him go as quickly as she had taken hold. "I talked to Helen the other day, and I was there when Carl came back home."

"Maybe I ought to go see Crow," Antony said.

George looked at Louise and shook his head.

"Better not," said George. "Better give it a little time. No sense asking for trouble. They'll be looking for people—other than the Davenport boy—to blame this on. Just keep to yourself for the time being."

"Why would anybody want to hurt that girl?" Louise asked no one. "I tell you, I don't believe Crow Davenport did any of it. I don't believe he could. Now, Casey or that Tom Canady—either one has enough meanness to make me believe anything."

"They're all right," said Antony. "A little crazy at times, but all right."

"Well, I know you like 'em, but that won't mean I have to."

George sat with his back to them but turned now to ask, "What're they saying happened exactly?"

"They're saying rape," Louise told them. "But the girl herself, she's not saying how it happened—can't remember anything."

"If she won't talk, then Carl Davenport probably had something to do with keeping her quiet," said George. "A son of Carl Davenport won't have to play by the regular rules."

"Well, they did the rape kit, but results won't be back for a while," said Louise. "And if that rape kit comes back positive, and Crow's involved, won't be much Carl can do. DNA doesn't lie."

Antony's eyes grew wide, and Louise instantly regretted her words.

"Antony, if you repeat what I just said to anyone outside this kitchen . . ."

"I won't!" said Antony.

"I saw somebody else over there today," Louise told George. George looked at her, guessing with his eyes. Louise nodded. "Ava. She was in the car with Carl when he came home. Carl must've called and told her to come. He went to get Johnny, then must've picked up Ava at the train."

"That's either good, or the stupidest thing he could've done," George said. "I don't know which."

"Crow and Johnny like her," said Louise. "And I think she might be able to comfort Helen."

"That's pretty hard to see from where I'm sitting," George said.

The first time Louise saw Ava was when Helen got so ill after Johnny's birth and Carl hired Louise as a nurse to come to the house four times a week. He brought Ava in to help look after Crow, who was four, and the new baby. Ava lived in south Georgia. She had no children, had never been married, and when she arrived to take over the rituals of the house, she got so comfortable she stayed for two months. Louise stopped going to the house after three weeks, but she could already see what was taking place. Carl came in the house looking not for Helen, but for Ava. Ava was lively in ways Helen had never been. She wore shorts and sun-bathed in the backyard. She wore her nightgown until ten o'clock on Saturday mornings. And she kept Crow up late, which made him ill-tempered the next morning.

Helen got better, then worse, then better, worse. Louise could see how hard she was trying to get back to her duties—so that Ava could leave. Carl began to come home in the middle of the day—ostensibly to check on Helen. He spoke to Helen, then went to the kitchen to eat lunch with Ava. Helen and Louise could hear them laughing from her bedroom.

"Maybe you need to go to sleep," Louise suggested.

"How can I sleep with all that racket?" Helen sat up in bed. "Anyway, I'm not tired. Bring the baby in here, let me hold him awhile."

Louise went into the nursery and lifted Johnny from his crib. She looked at the schedule Helen had written out for Ava and saw that it was time for Johnny's bottle. She brought the baby to Helen and went to the kitchen to get the bottle ready. Ava and Carl sat with their faces very close to each other; they seemed to be whispering. Louise's presence startled them.

"I'm just getting Johnny's formula," Louise said.

"You eaten lunch, Louise? Ava's made some tuna salad with grapes and apples." Carl seemed to be bragging.

"I've eaten," said Louise. She lifted a prepared bottle from the refrigerator and warmed it in the bottle warmer. The room grew quiet as the bottle heated; Carl seemed to be waiting for her to be finished and leave.

"I think Helen's getting better," Louise said. "I mean, I think she's gonna be up and about very soon. Very soon." She turned and gave them a smile.

"That's good," said Ava. "You think she'd like some of this salad?"

"I don't think tuna fish is the best thing for someone who needs a *bland* diet." Louise's words came out of her mouth like swords. She hadn't meant to sound quite that sharp, but as she went back upstairs and noticed that the laughter had stopped, she was glad she'd said it in just that way.

Ava had come back to town every summer since that summer of illness, and Louise, along with everybody else, had seen Carl and Ava driving around town together, eating at the diner, or with Helen going to a movie. Louise always wondered if Helen knew— if she knew and turned her head, if she knew and didn't care, if she knew and thought it would end by itself. The affair had begun when Crow was four; now he was sixteen. Ava had never married, and George liked to say that Carl Davenport's luck was going to run out one of these days.

"So you think it's a *lucky* thing to have two women, do you?" Louise asked.

"I *would* think so," said George. "If I didn't have you."

"Oh, baby, that is a *fine* answer. At least I *think* that's a fine answer."

George let well enough alone.

Ten

AVA GOT OUT of the car and brought her suitcase to the porch. She walked into the hallway where Helen was holding Carl like he was a tree. "Helen," she said.

Helen startled out of herself and turned. "Ava."

"Carl thought I should come," Ava said quickly. "He thought you might need me."

Carl jerked with embarrassment. "I'm going upstairs," he said.

Helen turned toward Ava. She let herself be held by her sister, trying to think how Ava might be able to help her. Growing up, Helen had always been the responsible one. As they climbed the stairs to the guest room, Helen carried Ava's suitcase.

During visits to her sister's house—Thanksgiving, Christmas, Easter, and several weeks in the summer—Ava worked hard to make her presence felt. She cooked and served dinner. She baked pies and cakes. Now she got busy washing clothes, and within a few hours she was folding Carl's underwear and T-shirts carefully on his dresser. She avoided talking about Crow unless Helen brought it up. Earlier, upon arriving, Ava asked Helen if she was going to visit Crow in the jail or wait for him to come home tomorrow. Helen ignored the question. She didn't even lift her head.

"You don't have to do laundry," Helen told Ava. "Ginna comes in three times a week."

Ginna, a teenage girl whose mother had a neurological problem, came after school to earn money. Helen paid her handsomely
and often gave Ginna something to take home to her mother. She
sent flowers and food, and once, after Ginna mentioned that her
mother couldn't get downstairs very well, Helen bought a tray that
propped easily on the bed.

"Well," said Ava, "Ginna will have an easy time this week. I
like to do it, Helen. I don't have anybody to take care of at home."
Ava could feel Helen watching her lower backbone. She could feel
her older sister's judgment about her choices in life.

"Seems like you could've found somebody to be with by now,"
said Helen. She began to put away Carl's clothes into drawers. Ava
sat on the bed and watched her.

"Yes, it does." Ava sighed wistfully.

"I mean, at some point, you've got to get tired of just having affairs." She turned to look at Ava. "Anybody new?"

"Not really."

"What're you waiting for?"

"Something like you have." Ava stood and strode toward the
door.

"Listen," said Helen, "you think it's all been roses? Look at
what we just went through, Crow accused of some awful thing."

Ava turned around and saw tears in Helen's eyes. She wondered
if Helen knew about the times she spent with Carl. She rushed to
comfort her sister.

"No," said Helen. "Don't touch me. I feel worse if I'm comforted."

"It'll be all right, Helen," said Ava. "Things'll get back to normal in no time."

"I don't think things will ever be back to normal," Helen said.
She pushed the last drawer closed. "Let's make some dinner. Want
to?"

They ate dinner, speaking of small things, then sat silently at the
kitchen table. "Sometimes," Helen said, "you seem to want to *be*

me, to have the life I have; but you don't know how this life is—
you see it only in your imagination. You only dream it."

Ava didn't know what to say.

Ava did love to dream. She loved dreams more than her life, and at
age thirty-five, she thought her dreams *were* her life. Helen accused her of building idle fantasies instead of trying to make real
change. She said Ava refused to grow up. Ava knew that she did
prefer her own particular state to the grown-up burdens that
seemed to come with Helen's life.

When Ava was young, she kissed men in order to be kissed
back. Helen's strategy was to wait for someone to express affection first, or to take her hand. The men in the family paid more attention to Ava because of her buoyancy and affectionate nature.
Helen stood back, beautiful but aloof.

"Helen is always so responsible," her mother said, then re-
quired her to live up to that definition. The only time Helen had
been irresponsible was when she got pregnant in college, and Carl
had come to the rescue. That was during the time Ava was galli-
vanting through Europe. When Ava returned home, Helen was already married.

Early this morning, after Crow was asleep, Carl had called Ava
and asked her to come to the house, just until things calmed down.
He told her to come for Helen, then said, "I need you here, Ava."

Ava felt acutely aware of the pleasure Carl brought her. She imagined, at times, that she could rationalize loving her sister's husband. She told herself that Carl was able to remain with Helen
because he had Ava's attentions, and that, instead of splitting up a
marriage, she was helping to keep it intact. She knew that affairs
often worked to the good in this twisted way: a man sometimes
went outside marriage to get sex, which allowed him to be affectionate toward his wife, instead of resentful; and the wife, who did
not want to bother with sex, seemed content.

Carl was the kind of man who needed a great deal of room, and Ava didn't know how she could allow him the room he wanted. But not being his wife, she didn't need to test her abilities.

Carl appeared happy to see Ava. He enjoyed the neediness of her arms and mouth, but he usually didn't want her to stay for more than a few weeks. Whenever she left town, he seemed glad to see her go. He sometimes told Ava he loved her, but usually he just said that he was "fond of her"—though he said it in a *tone* of love. Sometimes he stroked her face and hair and held her close. "You know that I'm fond of you, don't you?" He trembled as he spoke these words. Ava nodded, wanting more but not asking.

She knew every part of Carl's body: his smooth upper arms and thighs, his hairy forearms and chest, his back, with its map of moles that she traced with her finger as if connecting the dots, allowing her hand to move softly over his skin while he slept.

She had fallen for him twelve years ago. And though she had been with other men during those years, and though Carl grew jealous of those men, she couldn't make him jealous enough to say he would marry her.

He would never marry her, though he never said so. He would never leave Helen, though he never said that either. He wanted to be with Ava when he could. He wanted to love her. Still, if push came to shove, he would renounce her.

Ava would watch Carl eat, paying attention to each mouthful he swallowed. She imagined herself being his food, his breath. She couldn't get enough of him, and wondered, if they lived together as man and wife, whether her appetite might drive him away.

"I would be so easy to please," she told him one night a year ago, after they had made love. "I mean if we lived together, if we made it *not* a secret."

"You're not suggesting I leave Helen, are you?"

"I think I've been suggesting it for years." She leaned back into the motel chair and smiled weakly. "You don't believe I understand anything about marriage, do you?"

"Not about married life with children, no, I don't think you know that. I think you think of it as exciting."

"To a person who lives alone," she said. "To someone who knows what it is to come home and not have anyone there night after night, for that person to have someone come in the door at dinnertime, to laugh at a joke, to share what happened during the day—these smallest things would be exciting."

"You have men in your life." Carl turned away from her, then got up to shower. He had to go home. "Helen tells me about all the men you go out with."

"Don't even start with that," she said. "Half those men are made up, some are friends, and two are men who care about me. One asked me to marry him. So, Carl, what do you think about that?" She rose and wrapped the sheet around her. She hated what she'd just said. She knew better than to challenge Carl. He always came back with something mean.

"Maybe you should think about it," he said irritably. They dressed in silence. Carl kissed her before he left.

"It'll be all right," he said.

"I know," she said. But she didn't know anything.

Helen went to bed early. She had visited a short while at the jail with Crow. Ava offered to go again with Helen, but she said no.

"I've never seen her like this," Ava told Carl. They were both still up after Helen went to bed.

"She took a sleeping pill," Carl said. "I think I'm going to have to do the same." He offered Ava a pill prescribed by Helen's doctor. Ava refused.

She leaned against the sink. "Listen, Carl. Maybe I shouldn't be here. Maybe I should leave."

"Stay," he said. "But this time you're here for Helen. Not me."

"I thought you said you needed me here."

"You should be here for her," he insisted. Something was shifting. Carl smiled, but his body wanted enormous distance between them.

Eleven

By the first week in May the sky was blue, with clouds only on the horizon. Crow was indicted for aggravated rape, and today at the arraignment he heard the charge officially stated. He pled not guilty.

When he arrived home from the Jasper courthouse, he did not go inside. Instead, he went to the backyard. Johnny followed him with a tennis ball they used for throwing. They liked to stand in a specific spot in the far part of the yard and throw back and forth—the ball going out like a breath and landing firmly in the other's hand. They had talked like that, tossing the ball, for as long as they could remember, far enough away so their parents couldn't hear.

The trial had been scheduled for the first week in June; and though Sophie had not yet described what had happened, the evidence looked damning for Crow. His DNA had been identified from the rape kit, along with clear evidence of multiple attackers. Butler was looking hard for probable cause to investigate other boys at the party.

"Dad says that Butler thinks they don't have enough of a case," Johnny said, trying to speak about what was unspoken. "Too many unanswered questions, and not enough evidence to mess up your story about what happened."

"It's not a story," muttered Crow. "What I said is the truth." He dropped the ball and scurried to retrieve it. "I wish I could talk to Sophie. It feels bad not to be able to talk to her."

"Not much chance of that though. Right?"

"Right." Crow threw the ball and heard it smack into Johnny's palm.

"How was survival camp?" Crow asked. "You haven't said anything about it."

"It was okay. I was the best one with the bow and arrow. I was better than anybody. Dad should've seen me."

"God," said Crow. "You shouldn't do all that just so Dad will like it."

"It's okay."

The ball kept slapping into their hands.

"Somebody made a 9-1-1 call Saturday night," Johnny said. "Called to say that Sophie was hurt and where she was. Was that you?"

"No."

"They have a recording."

"It wasn't me. I ran off. I saw the police coming."

"Maybe that will be a good thing for you," Johnny said, hopefully. "That somebody else called. Maybe they'll find out who it was. I heard Dad talking on the phone last night about those construction workers of Mr. Canady's—they have an alibi?"

"Yeah," said Crow, grinding his teeth. "Butler told me they were getting drunk at a bar in Chattanooga. Ten witnesses can back them up."

"Still," said Johnny. "It's not a strong case, right? They still can't get Sophie to accuse you."

"I wish I could talk to her," Crow said. He had tried to call Sophie several times, then hung up when her mother answered. And he had seen Sophie once, coming out of the drugstore, almost not recognizable, her hair greasy and pulled back tight. Actually, she saw him first and stopped. He thought she almost waved to him before hurrying off in another direction. He thought she almost spoke.

"Will she be at the trial?" Johnny asked.

"Butler thinks she'll be there with her mother, but she probably won't testify." Crow sucked his teeth, feigned indifference. "I'll probably have to testify though."

Johnny looked at his brother as if seeing a future he didn't want to see. "It won't be so bad to testify," Johnny said. "Just tell the truth."

"That's what I've been trying to do." For Crow, to stake his life on that moment of running away, to admit to leaving Sophie alone and vulnerable, was not consoling. He knew this trial would be the end of youth, if not life—the end of that marvelous way of looking at possibility and days to come. Whatever had been steadfast or good in Crow's life had changed color, had grown dark in his hands.

The wind blew in off the river near the house, a common thing. But today the breeze sent a chill into Crow's body. "Let's go in."

"And stop having all this fun?" Johnny said, smiling, trying to lighten their mood.

As they walked toward the house, both boys felt a damp, wild foolishness; for Crow, even the stones in the yard seemed to be saying goodbye, the trees losing the flavor of earlier times.

Crow was afraid of the trial, and for the next month he would tremble from dreams every night in bed—but on this day, when he had heard the charges read in court, he tried to imagine his whole life. He tried to picture what would come.

That night when spring rain came in a downpour, as if from huge barrels over the door, he had a tremendous thought—imagining his life as a secret train. If this part of his journey was a reaction to that strange time of running away, if the cowardice he knew about now was just his own darkness rising up, then whatever happened would go hurrying down the track on which he was solidly lodged. And even if everything failed, even if he were found guilty, he would persist—but not by running away, not ever again by running.

The threat before Crow enlarged his capacity to wait. Even the light of the day looked to him like waiting—the sun waiting to set, the moon to rise.

Twelve

THE COURT BUZZED and crackled, packed with people from town. Reporters stood on the courthouse steps, and in the parking lot visitors kept a curious vigil. It was the day that Crow would testify. The June morning was filled with clouds but remained bright. Stray dogs and cats sniffed the ground searching for food.

Inside the large courtroom Crow Davenport, his young body tall and tender-faced, sat at the long table next to his lawyer. From time to time they leaned to speak to each other, Butler's bald head nodding toward Crow; they looked expressionless, waiting for the judge to enter the room.

The jury sat very still, their faces ready for anything, anything at all, to be written on them. Aurelia Bailey and her son, Bobby, sat in the back row. Sophie had not yet come in, but everyone watched for her.

As Crow readied himself to testify, he found it hard to breathe. His head felt strange, light with anticipation. He had been coached about what to say when he took the stand, had rehearsed, but Raymond Butler had warned him not to make his answers sound planned. Crow was trying not to plan anything, trying to keep all hope in abeyance.

The day before, Crow's mother cornered him in the kitchen. "Have you prayed about this, Crow? Maybe you should."

He lifted orange juice out of the refrigerator and drank from the carton. She handed him a glass, but he didn't take it.

"I don't know." Crow shook his head. He had prayed but didn't want to admit it. His mother's eyes bored into him like a beam of light. He had no secrets, but the space inside his head began to create hidden pockets. Her face pleaded with him.

"Maybe I should leave prayer up to you," he said. He didn't want to hurt her feelings.

"Well." She lowered her head. "Johnny wanted me to ask if you minded him being in the courtroom tomorrow. He wants to be there when you testify." Crow had not wanted his younger brother to attend the trial, but now he thought Johnny's presence might bring comfort. "He wants to come, Crow. He wants to be there, but if you don't want him to . . ." She laid her hand on his shoulder. They were alone in the house. "I know things are going to be all right," she said. "I just know it."

Crow couldn't imagine how he, how he himself, could ever be all right.

He had gone to bed feeling nauseated, his belly rising as soon as he lay down. Even though he was ready, prepared carefully for taking the stand, still he couldn't picture it. He looked at the clock every hour, until four-thirty or five, when he fell into a hole of nightmare: his lawyer's face floated like someone offstage, and Crow recoiled at the necessity of telling the truth. ("I left her. I put clothes on her and left. I got scared when I heard someone coming. I was afraid they would blame me. And they did.") This is what he had to say, but even in his dream he couldn't speak the words.

He woke to hear his parents arguing downstairs. Their voices sounded emphatic, interruptive.

"I think it's going very well, Carl," he heard his mother say. "I don't know why you say that. I think the jury believes he's innocent."

"It *is* going well, Helen. And Butler has a good chance of proving reasonable doubt. He says the prosecutor was crazy to let Sophie's mother and the mayor's office and the local papers hound them into a trial before they'd nailed down those multiple attackers. That's why they keep coming to us with this plea-bargain idea. Crow rats out his accomplices and they lighten the sentence."

"But he had no accomplices!" Helen roared. "He didn't do it!"

"Stop shouting," said Carl, his throat tight. "I know that. But you asked me how I think it's going and I'm telling you. The testimony today will cinch it. Crow has to do this right."

Crow lay in bed, something sour-tasting rising in his throat. He forced himself to swallow. He pulled himself out of bed and threw water on his face several times, rinsed his mouth. His face, swollen and dark-eyed, had a hard look that terrified him. He looked older than his sixteen years, and after today he would feel older.

He pulled on his T-shirt and shorts to go downstairs, but his fingers felt huge and trembly, as though he had on gloves.

"What do you mean 'do it right'?" Crow stood in the doorway of the kitchen. Johnny sat at the table eating a bowl of cereal.

"You have to *sound* right, son," said his father. "To sound sincere."

"But I didn't do it."

"Yeah, like that." He clapped his hands.

Crow hated that his father thought he was practicing.

"I'm going today," Johnny said. "I'm going to be there, unless you say no."

"Naw, man. I do want you there."

Helen smiled and touched Johnny on the back of the neck. "I told you he wanted you to come, honey." She turned to her husband again. "Carl, you want eggs?"

"I'm just saying," Carl continued, "that even though everything's going well—I mean, hell, not even the victim's saying anything against him—I mean not so directly against him, since she doesn't remember—and even with that, when Crow gets on the stand, he's got to sound innocent."

They spoke as if Crow were not in the room.

"Tell me what you're talking about," Crow said. He remained just inside the doorway of the kitchen, feeling unwelcome.

Helen turned quickly. "But—" she said.

"Let me finish, Helen. You never let me finish. He has to hold his head up, look people in the eye. He has to get up there and say how awful he feels about what happened to Sophie."

"I *do* feel that way," said Crow.

"Just keep your voice low." His father turned to him now, motioned for him to sit down and eat something. "I mean, don't get mad at anybody, son. No matter what you do, don't get mad at anybody. You hear?"

"Yessir."

Helen asked Crow if he wanted some eggs, but Crow shook his head and poured cereal into a bowl. "I've practiced with Mr. Butler," he said. "He told me what to expect."

"Just come across as *hum*ble," Carl continued. "You have one strike against you already because we're wealthy, you know. That doesn't help."

Crow didn't say it, but it was a strike he had been dealing with since he was very young.

"The papers are having a field day with that." Helen pursed her lips as though she might spit something out. "And we've done so much for this town."

"We can't even think like that, Helen. We're on our hands and knees with this one."

Crow wanted to ask his father if he had bought off any of the jurors. He only thought this because of the way his father kept reassuring everyone, even the lawyer—though today, for some reason, he was not reassuring anyone.

Carl picked up the paper and handed the sports section to Crow and Johnny. Helen made eggs for herself and ate quietly, until Carl announced, "Be ready at nine-thirty, everybody."

As Crow showered and dressed, he heard his parents arguing

again, his mother saying that everything was going to be fine and urging Carl not to be pessimistic.

A few days earlier Raymond Butler had told Crow, "Your reputation at school is good, academically and socially. You're from a good family. You've never been arrested or even been in trouble. All these things will build on a presumption of innocence, and the circumstantial evidence will seem misplaced, wrong." He spoke as if he were already in court, as if he might not believe all he said but was trying hard to believe it. Even in a restaurant or in a small room, Butler's voice could take on an air of fortification and rightness. It was just the way he was.

"And we know," he said, "that because of the evidence of sperm, there were multiple attackers, and that complicates the prosecution's case considerably."

Crow's face worked and stretched for a moment before he said, "Isn't my dad making sure that they get DNA from . . ." He couldn't crank out any names.

"Your dad was pushing hard for that," said Butler, "but parents are making it impossible. Even Judge Bailey put up a big fuss about civil rights and privacy issues. I don't think it's going to happen."

Crow looked at the wall charts Butler had posted next to the desk, showing who had attended the party that night, timelines and cross-references about boys unaccounted for, kids who were drunk and stoned. Even Crow's best friends were angry, complaining about Butler's questioning, as well as the investigator and Hollis, who would not get off their backs.

Crow brushed his hair back from his face into a neat, preppy look, and wondered if he should have cut his hair shorter. His blue eyes looked large, his nails bitten to the quick. He did not wear a suit or even his best shirt, opting instead for a crisp blue button-down shirt and navy tie. Unassuming, he thought. He practiced looking humble in the mirror, but most of his expressions seemed merely sad.

"You okay?" Johnny asked. Johnny was a foot shorter than Crow.

"I don't know why they haven't found somebody else to arrest," Crow said. "What've they been doing? Have the police already decided it was me? I mean, what's going on?"

"What do you mean?" Johnny said. "They've been questioning everybody. I still think it's those guys that were hanging around the school."

"They had a pretty good alibi though," Crow said. "I mean, they weren't even in town that night."

"They'll find who did it," Johnny said.

"It wasn't me."

"I know that."

"I'm scared. I am so scared." He sat on the bed.

Johnny didn't respond.

Crow leaned to put on his shoes. "No. Okay." He looked up. "I'll just do what Butler says. Anyway, I think Dad probably bought off some jurors."

"Shit," Johnny said. "That's why he wants you to be *hum*ble." A hint of a smile crossed Johnny's lips.

Crow laughed for the first time in several weeks. He wondered how long laughter would feel unfamiliar to him.

The judge came out of his chambers and everyone stood as court was called to order. E. G. Hollis and Charlie Post sat near the front on the right-hand side. Crow heard Mr. Hollis clear his throat as they stood. He turned and both men nodded to him. They wanted to offer the solidarity of their presences.

Coach Post leaned to speak to someone sitting behind him, and though Crow saw the two men out of the corner of his eye and wanted to acknowledge their presence, he didn't. He felt that any extra movement might cause his body to break.

He had seen Bobby and his mother in the back of the room, and he had seen Sophie's mother sitting near the prosecutor's table, next to an empty chair for Sophie. Rita Chabot, who was normally a shiningly beautiful woman, did not look like herself. During the last two months her face had become gray and fathomless, her posture stooped, her eyes black. She wanted to make someone accountable and hoped Crow would help her to that point. She held her arms across her torso and kept her lips tightly closed.

Sophie had slipped in a side door and stood near the back by a window. She kept looking outside, as though she might bolt. She had collapsed in the hallway of her house twice before arriving at the courthouse. The judge agreed to let her stay in the back if she wanted.

Sophie could not say that Crow had hurt her, but she knew her mother wanted her to say it. Sympathy and outrage fought inside her. "It wasn't Crow," she had told her mother that morning.

"Don't, Sophie."

"It wasn't," she said. She didn't know if she could watch the D.A. question Crow. She wanted to take back the accusation forced on Crow by her mother, but she wasn't strong enough.

Yesterday rain came in a downpour like any spring day, and today had a bright-washed look. Sophie used to like the day after a rain—the clearness of it. Now she felt that any kind of clearness could not be part of her life. She wanted weather that matched her mood.

Raymond Butler summoned Crow to the witness box.

Carl and Helen sat in the front row, very still, not turning their heads or moving. Their attire was tasteful, but they were not overdressed. They looked like stick figures in fine clothes. Johnny sat between them, fidgeting nervously. He kept his hands between his knees.

"Do you know Sophie Chabot?" Mr. Butler asked.

Crow nodded. He imagined himself confident. "Yes. I do."

"How do you know her?"

"For about a month we'd been going out."

"Were you seeing her, that is, going out with her, at the time she was assaulted?"

"Yes. But it was the first time we'd gone to a party together."

"But, as it has already been established"—he cleared his throat—"you had seen her often before that night?"

"I'd been to her house, and we went places after school and sometimes to a movie."

"You saw her every day?"

"Almost. I liked her. I liked being with her."

"And your feelings for her were reciprocated?" Butler asked.

Crow looked puzzled.

"She liked you? Did she show affection toward you?"

"Relevance, Your Honor," the district attorney interrupted.

"Your Honor, I want to establish a friendship, an affection, between these two people."

"I will allow it."

"Did she say how she felt about you?"

"She said she liked me from the first time she saw me, and that she'd wanted to go out with me."

"She told you that?"

"Yes."

"And did your relationship become physical?"

"Sometimes we kissed in the car after a movie, but we'd never had sex before."

Someone in the courtroom made a sound. When Crow looked to the back of the room, Sophie was gone.

"Before that night?" Butler sounded at this point more like the district attorney. The jurors squirmed.

"Right. We talked about it, but I wanted to wait until she was sure." Crow looked at the jurors when he said this, and a few of them smiled at him. Crow knew most of the people sitting in the jury box.

"And she was sure that night? The night of March twentieth?"

"Yes."

"How did you know she was sure? Did she say anything to let you know this?"

"Yeah. Like, when we went to the woods to be alone and started kissing? Then she said, 'Let's lie down on the leaves,' so we did. And, like, we started to touch each other."

"She touched you?"

"Yes."

"Where?"

"On my legs," he said. "And here." He cupped his crotch. The courtroom was quiet, and Crow blushed.

"Had she touched you like that before this night?"

He couldn't look up at the jury or the lawyer. "Yeah."

"What happened next?"

"She started taking off her clothes."

Someone coughed. It was Rita. She cocked her head to one side. She did not take her eyes away from Crow's face.

"She removed her own clothes?"

"Yeah, well, I was taking some of them off and she was taking off some of mine."

"She removed some of your clothes?"

"She helped me pull off my shirt and unzip my pants."

"Go on."

"And we started having sex then, but somewhere in there she said no. She said to stop. She said, did I have something."

"What did she mean?"

"She wanted to know if I had a condom. We'd talked about that. I said it was in my car. In the glove compartment of my car."

"So what did you do then?"

"I told her that I'd just be a minute, and she covered herself up with my shirt. I said I'd be right back."

"And were you?"

"I put on my underwear and my shoes. I did it fast, then went to where the car was. It wasn't so far away."

"But far enough that you didn't hear anything." Butler had taken great pains to go over this next question with Crow. He hesitated, then asked. "How far was the car from where Sophie waited for you?"

"About a hundred yards. About the length of a football field. Only it was through the woods. It was the parking lot of the First Baptist Church."

"So you ran through those woods to your car."

"Yeah, and I was about to go back when some girls drove up in a truck. I thought they would get out and go on to the party, but they stayed and smoked. They just stood around their truck, laughing. At first I thought they saw me, that they were laughing at *me*. I ducked down and waited. I didn't want anybody to see me, you know, running around in my underwear. Anyway, the girls took a long time. I almost left."

"How long were they there?"

"Seemed like probably twenty, twenty-five minutes. I kept wondering what Sophie was thinking. I was afraid she might have left, gotten mad, you know?"

"And when the girls left?"

"I ran as fast as I could, and when I got to the spot where Sophie had been, she wasn't there. I called to her, then I saw her farther back in the woods. I thought she was asleep until I got close. Then I saw."

"What did you see?"

"Something real bad had happened. She was hurt. I got scared. She was unconscious, I think. I tried to wake her up, you know. I put some of her clothes back on her and—"

"Why did you do that?"

"Because I couldn't stand to see her just . . . I had to put something on her. I thought I would take her to get help. Then I heard police cars pull into the Fairchilds' driveway. When I heard that, I ran away."

"You tried to help her first."

"She wouldn't wake up. And I was afraid the police might think I had done this to her, so I ran. I knew they would take her to the hospital. See? She needed help, but I was afraid they'd think I did it. I ran off. I wish I hadn't."

"And Sophie Chabot was unconscious, or at least it seemed that way to you."

"She looked pretty bad. There was a lot of blood."

"So you ran away?"

"Yes." His lips said the word.

At the back of the room Judge Bailey gazed at Crow as if she were trying to make up her mind about him.

"Did you ever, even for one moment, think she was dead?" Raymond Butler rubbed one hand over his head.

"No. I knew she was unconscious. She made a sound, like a moan or something. She was hurt, but I knew she wasn't dead." Crow looked out at everyone. "I wished *I* was dead though, at that time. I wished it was me."

Butler returned to the long table now. He was almost through.

"I'm sure anyone in your position would have felt the same way."

"Your Honor," Jeb Wall objected.

"Withdrawn." He motioned to the judge to indicate that he was finished.

Rita Chabot was crying, the cords of her throat worked themselves, swallowing, then swallowing again. Coach Post went to sit behind her, and light from the courtroom windows ballooned around them.

Crow's face, as he waited for the questions from the district attorney, looked like a mask that could not be allowed to flag.

Jeb Wall stood now and paced slowly toward the jury box. He began his questions to Crow, but he faced the jurors.

"So, you ran away. You left Sophie Chabot there."

"But help was already there. I knew the police would take care of her." Crow felt helpless and looked to his lawyer. Raymond Butler appeared calm, and he smiled, gave one slow nod. "The police were already there."

"The police were there, but not before you ran away. Isn't that what you said?"

"Yes."

"And did you see anyone, I mean, besides the police? Did you see anyone else in the vicinity?"

"No. And, see, I was afraid that everybody'd think I did it. And that's exactly what happened."

"They found semen from several different men. What do you say about that?"

"I know I came a little, then I stopped. Sophie wanted me to use something . . ." Crow couldn't finish.

"She told you to stop. You and your friends."

"Yes," said Crow. "No, wait. What friends? It was just me and Sophie."

"So you got mad, frustrated, and you—"

"No. I stopped. I left to go to the car, and when I came back, that's when I found her."

"You found her beat up, and you ran away," said Wall. "But you didn't go to your car then, did you? You had just been to your car, and you didn't go back there?"

"I ran. I wasn't thinking. I just ran. I couldn't believe what'd happened. I ran into the river."

"But you picked up your clothes, didn't you? Before you ran, you gathered your clothes?"

"I guess." His voice came out muffled.

"You *guess* you gathered your clothes?"

"I did!" yelled Crow. "I picked up my shirt and pants and ran. I didn't even know what I was doing." He was sweating. A terrible shame split his head and stung the tips of his fingers. He looked dumbfounded. Sweat formed at his temples.

"Maybe you didn't know what you were doing when you beat her up. When you raped her." Jeb Wall let these words sink in. "Maybe you didn't know what you were doing then either."

"Objection."

"No." Crow's voice cracked. "I cared about her, and she cared about me. I didn't hurt her." Crow was crying, his face in his hands.

"Though you *did* leave her there."

"Yes," said Crow, though he was shaking his head no. "I'm sorry. I told you. The police were going to take care of her."

"What time did you get home?"

Crow didn't answer.

"Would the judge instruct the witness to answer?" Wall said.

The judge leaned toward the witness chair, and Crow, working through a band of intricate thought, said, "About three o'clock, I think. My dad was at the door. He told me the sheriff had called and that Sophie was in the hospital."

Wall straightened his shoulders. "We already know there was underage drinking at this party. How about drugs? Were there drugs too?"

Crow wasn't ready for this question. He had thought about his answer, but when the D.A. asked him he wasn't ready. He hesitated. "No."

"At this party, there weren't any drugs?" The D.A. kept restraint in his voice.

"Some, I guess."

"Some, you guess." The district attorney faced the judge.

"Did you take any drugs yourself?"

"No."

"Did Sophie have anything to drink? How old is Sophie Chabot?"

"Fourteen."

"Did you get her drunk before taking her to the woods?"

"It wasn't like that," Crow objected.

Raymond Butler stood. "He's badgering the witness, Your Honor."

"Cool down your tone, Mr. Wall," the judge said.

"But she had been drinking that night, is that right?"

"I guess she'd had a little." Crow could not look up, could not lift his head.

"How much?"

"I don't know, but she wasn't drunk. I'll swear she wasn't drunk."

"If you'll remember, you're swearing to everything here." Wall ambled back to the table as though he might be through, then quickly turned. "If there was so much affection between you and Miss Chabot, then explain why there was evidence of force found. How did Sophie get those bruises?"

"He's badgering the witness again, Your Honor."

"I'll rephrase." Wall turned again to face Crow. "Sophie's body had bruises and evidence of rape. We have pictures showing the state of her body. Are you saying that you did not penetrate her?"

Crow put his face in his hands again. "I didn't hurt her. I didn't do anything to hurt her."

"But you did have intercourse with her."

Crow really wasn't sure if he had.

"You've already testified to that."

"We went too far," said Crow, "and I had forgotten the condom, so I went to get it."

"But you had already had intercourse by that time."

"Just barely. I mean hardly at all."

"One more thing, Mr. Davenport."

At the mention of his name, Crow looked up.

"Did you happen to see anyone else there, in the woods? Did you see anyone from the party there?"

"No." Crow hadn't appeared to even try to recall whether he had seen someone.

"You sure?"

Crow looked toward his dad, who was not moving, not even blinking. "Yes, I'm sure."

That was all.

Crow was allowed to step down, but as he walked back to the defense table, he shuddered. Aurelia Bailey breathed heavily, seeing Crow step out of the witness box, a gloomy mist emanating from his body. She tried to read the jurors' expressions, but their eyes stayed level. Their body language revealed nothing. Crow coughed before sitting down, and a weak rattle could be heard in his chest.

The jurors were dismissed and the courtroom emptied, but as Crow went through the side doors, he half turned to look at Judge Bailey and Bobby, a wide sharpness in his face. Aurelia saw the alert grief in him, and she felt the heat of Bobby beside her.

As they left, Bobby nodded to his friend once, in a military way.

Thirteen

BOBBY HAD NOT seen Crow for several weeks, not since it happened. He didn't know what to say. But Aurelia kept insisting that he go over to the house. "He's your best friend, Bobby."

But Bobby did not go. He couldn't talk to Crow but found some reassurance in talking to the other boys who were being questioned by the police, comparing what they were asked and what they had answered.

Lester and Tom closed the gate to Bobby's yard. Dog came barreling up to greet them. They sat in swings from a childhood swing set that was cemented into the ground. Their legs dragged in the dust.

"Deputy Canton ask you a lot of shit?" Bobby asked.

"They asked everything," said Lester. "Hell, they accused me of helping Crow attack her. I ended up yelling at them."

"Me too," said Tom. "And they tried to make me say that we got Sophie drunk so Crow could get laid."

"They're going after everybody the same way," said Bobby.

Aurelia came out the back door and went to the side garden with a basket of tools. She dug out a few weeds.

"What does your mom say, Bobby?"

"Not much."

Lester's determination had grown unstoppable. "I hope they find the sons of bitches," he said. His mind couldn't take in what was done to Sophie. "They can't pin this on Crow."

Tom nodded. "How's Crow doing anyway? Anybody talk to him?"

"Not yet," said Bobby.

Aurelia stood up. "You boys ought to go over there. All of you. Stop avoiding him. It doesn't matter what you say. Just go."

Bobby and his mother had come to Tennessee from Washington, D.C., when he was five, almost six. His father was gone, a car accident, his mother told him. Bobby only half believed that. His head, even at that age, buzzed with doubt. He had never seen his father's dead body, and he remembered no funeral. The funeral was private, his mother explained. Bobby had stayed home with a babysitter. Within a week they moved to Tennessee.

In South Pittsburg, Aurelia Bailey, not yet a judge, placed Bobby in first grade. On his first day at school he sat at his desk in shorts, a new shirt, and sneakers, his spine very straight. He held a teddy bear with both hands. No one spoke to him at first.

At recess the teacher, Miss Sweet, who had a mean voice, introduced Bobby as the "new boy." The first person to speak to him was Crow Davenport. He asked Bobby to get the softballs out of the locker and said he could play ball with them, if he wanted to. Bobby ran to gather up softballs and a few bats, struggling to carry everything to the makeshift baseball diamond, where the bases were rocks painted yellow.

"You go first," Crow said. "You be first bat."

The pitcher lobbed the ball across the plate. Bobby hit it high and halfway across the field. All of the kids swung around to stare first at the ball in the air, then at the boy who hit it.

For the next few weeks everyone chose Bobby for their team and treated him like a treasure. Crow told him, "I knew you could hit it. I knew you could hit the ball like that."

On that same day, when Tom Canady mentioned his big brother, who was then in high school, Bobby bragged that he also had a big brother, but that his brother lived in Florida. "I didn't see him in a long time," said Bobby.

"You mean your brother never lived with you?" Tom asked.

Bobby hated being an only child. The world felt saddest when he woke early and knew he was the only one in the house awake. He had Dog, and sometimes Dog was enough. But he thought about having brothers and sisters around, waking each other. He imagined peeking under the eyelids of a brother, there where the waking-up started in the skull's base and moved up like smoke in the wide trees of the brain. Whenever he imagined other children in the house he felt "on fire," his dreams coming true in a moment, then, just as quickly, the wind blowing and blowing until all the smoke was gone and faces disappeared in the shadows.

"He lives in Florida, I said," Bobby told them. "He's a lot older."

For much of the first year his classmates believed him, and at night Bobby sank into the ease he felt when he thought of himself with a brother. He felt lucky to have a big brother, he said, and claimed that his brother had taught him how to hit a ball. Everyone knew Bobby's father was dead, so Bobby never mentioned him.

Some mornings Bobby woke and vomited before school. He was popular and even had a best friend, Crow, but he felt constantly anxious that his lie about a brother might be exposed.

The inevitable moment came the summer before the boys entered second grade. The boys were swimming at the river, and only a moment earlier Crow had swung from a rope and landed in the water. As he swam back to shore, Tom yelled at Bobby that he didn't believe he had a brother at all. "Your father's dead, and I heard your mama say that you were her only child."

Bobby managed to control his tears by standing very still. Aurelia Bailey went to stand between Bobby and Tom. "What's the matter with you two?" she yelled. She had heard the boys arguing.

Tom repeated his accusation.

Aurelia looked stung. Now it was abundantly clear to her why Bobby kept a framed picture of his older cousin in his room.

"So he doesn't have a brother at all," said Tom. "He can't have one. He just told a lie. Are you a liar or what?" Then he yelled, "Liar!"

They stood in a circle and Bobby covered his face with his hands. Aurelia leaned to touch his back, but he pulled away from her. The river shuddered under the sun as Crow emerged dripping, wiping his face with a towel.

"I've seen his brother," said Crow, and Bobby put out his tongue and tasted his tears. "I saw him one time."

"Yeah?" said Tom. "Where? What's his name?"

Crow looked at Mrs. Bailey.

"His name's Vincent," Aurelia said, and Bobby's sad white features lifted. "His name is Vincent, but we call him Vinny."

Crow held his towel in midair. "Yeah," he said.

Tom walked off. He still didn't believe it, but couldn't go against Mrs. Bailey.

Crow smiled at Bobby. Both boys smelled like mice.

"Wanna swim?" Crow said. Sun and shadow dappled the ground, and the river played havoc with midday light. The world was wild and suddenly beautiful.

"Sure." They ran into the water laughing and pushing each other.

Aurelia Bailey wrapped her arms around her waist and took a breath. She wanted to laugh out loud at the shenanigans of boys, but a gnawing sensation kept her from it. She stood haunted, trying to smile, caught up now in her son's wish for a different truth. She didn't know how that different truth might expose itself.

In mid-January Bobby had driven out to Mr. Hollis's house. The three hounds barked as he knocked on the door.

"That you, Bobby?" Hollis yelled. Hollis thought Bobby had come by to get his present. He'd turned seventeen on New Year's Day. "Come on back. I'm in the kitchen." He sat at a table, blue Formica with white specks, chrome-and-vinyl chairs from the fifties. He was reading. "You want something to eat?" The hounds encircled Bobby, who was usually very affectionate with them. Today he ignored their friendly welcome, gently but firmly pushing them away.

Bobby threw the letter onto the table.

"What's that?" asked Hollis.

"It's proof," said Bobby.

"Of what?"

"Just what I thought was true. What I came here to ask you is this: Did *you* know?"

"What the hell are you talking about, Bobby?" asked Hollis, but as he lifted the envelope with the return address of Robert Bailey, he paled.

"Well," he said.

"You *do* know."

Hollis ordered the dogs out of the kitchen and closed the door. "Where'd you get this?"

"I went by the post office to mail something for my mom. Mr. Dunphy gave me our mail from our P.O. box to take home. I didn't even know we had a P.O. box."

"Roland Dunphy doesn't know about this. Nobody much knows."

"Well, I sure as hell didn't. Why didn't somebody tell me my father was alive? All these years living somewhere." Bobby stood very still, as though if he moved, he might hit someone.

"What does the letter say?" Hollis could see it had been opened.

"Read it." Bobby picked up the letter and threw it at Hollis. "It says I have a dad who went to jail and that he's out now. It says he wants to see me."

Hollis took the letter and read it.

Thursday, January 15
Dear Bobby,

At the start of this New Year you turned 17, and I have some news for you. I hope it will be good news. You've believed, until now, that your father was dead. The reasons for that are complicated. The truth is I am very much alive, though ashamed of much of my life. I was in jail for ten years, but I've been out now for two. I have a wife. She has two children of her own and we live in Kentucky. I'm rebuilding my life, Bobby, and I want to include you. I hope your mother will give you this letter.

Years ago I behaved in a stupid way. I was caught up in a scam and the final responsibility was laid on me. I was not the only one guilty, but I became the scapegoat. This is not a complaint, finally. Just a fact. I was guilty and if you feel anger towards me, I don't blame you.

I can only imagine the shock you feel as you read this letter. I cannot guess what effect it will have on you, or even if you will be allowed to read it—but you are my son and I still love you. Can you believe that? I have a picture of you on my mantel—of you and the whole Little League team. It was sent by E. G. Hollis when I was in jail, and even though the picture is old, I feel proud every time I look at it.

You can call me at (502) 555-9377. I have dreamed of seeing you, Bobby.

Love from your father,
Robert Bailey

"He didn't want you to know he was in jail, Bobby."

"But I thought he was *dead*." Bobby held on to the back of a chair. "I thought he was fucking dead! Is that better than knowing he was in jail?"

"I guess your mother thought so." The smallest hound let out a mournful howl at the door. "Knock it off!" Hollis yelled. He took his plate to the sink.

Bobby spoke in a quieter tone. "You knew all this time?"

"I didn't have any say in the matter, Bobby."

"But what did you think? Why did she tell you and not me?"

"I knew your dad. I did urge your mother to tell you, but I couldn't say anything without her permission."

"Right."

"What did she say about the letter?"

"I didn't tell her. I'm not going to either. Why should I?"

"You have to. She needs to know."

"Why? I just came to you to see if this was a hoax or something."

"It's not a hoax."

"Hell, I can hardly believe it now—I always thought he was alive somewhere, and even though I've read the letter and I know he wrote it, it's still hard to believe."

The image that came to Bobby's mind over and over, a day he had grown not to believe, was this: his father bringing home a yellow Lab puppy that they named Dog. His father laughing with admiration at the name. Bobby could close his eyes and hear the sound of his father in that moment, his laugh that had the round shape of a bowl. And he could hear the praise that followed.

"Perfect," his father had said. He had lifted Bobby up, pulling him to his chest, nuzzling. His father's smell was strong, like cigars. "A perfect name. Straightforward, nothing fancy. I like it." Then he turned to Bobby's mother. "The boy named the dog Dog. Perfect."

Then he had put Bobby down, and the eager puppy licked their arms. Bobby's mind that day became a happy sea, as he chased Dog in circles, then ran around in waves of delight. As they ran across the yard, birds flew up, and later that night the dog slept beside his bed. The arc of a moon swung low in the sky. Cloudless. Bobby dreamed, and later when the puppy cried and wanted to sleep beside him in bed, he pulled Dog up, as his father had lifted him, and in sleep he became the father, a small velvety ear under his chin.

Hollis wiped the blue table, lit a cigarette, and motioned for Bobby to sit down. The vinyl on the chairs was cracked and torn. These chairs had been part of Lila's kitchen, and Hollis kept them as they were. Even though Hollis had slept with women from other towns, he had never subjected them to more than a few days of his affection. After that, he wished to be alone, became impatient and began to long fiercely for his wife. His kitchen looked as though Lila might still live there.

"Listen, Bobby. I know you're angry. You're mad at me, your mother, everybody probably, though hardly anybody knows about this."

"Coach Post? Did he know?"

"I told him."

"Shit."

"Listen, you can let this be a good thing." Hollis walked toward Bobby. "Just because you veer off course doesn't mean you're going to crash. Remember in class when I talked about azimuth?"

Bobby rolled his eyes. "Yeah, yeah." He had grown tired of Mr. Hollis's science analogies. "I've got to go," said Bobby. He didn't want to hear anything hopeful.

"Come back later, if you want," Hollis offered. "And think about talking to your mother."

Bobby did not tell his mother about the letter, but he told Crow.

"I took the mail from Mr. Dunphy and he asked me something about Lester, and that's when I saw on top a letter from Robert Bailey addressed to me care of my mother."

On the steps of the post office that day Bobby had held the letter a few moments before opening it. He had read it slowly. Then he had read it again. He had read it once more later in the car, trying to memorize the words, as if they could disappear.

"Man, that's great!" said Crow. "So he's not dead?"

"His name's Robert. Like mine."

"Cool. You gonna write him back?"

"I don't know."

"Let me see." Crow reached for the envelope. Bobby took out the letter and gave it to him.

Over the next few days Crow appeared envious of this mysterious new figure who might show up in Bobby's life. "Have you written to him yet?"

"No."

"Why not?"

"I'm just getting used to the idea."

"You always wanted a dad; now you've got one. But you don't do anything about it. Hell, if it was me—"

"It's not you, Crow."

Crow stopped asking, except in offhand ways. At lunch or after basketball practice, he'd say, "How's your dad?"

"Okay, I guess." Bobby would smile. One day he said, "I wrote to him finally. I told him that my mother didn't know I knew anything yet. He wrote me back, care of Mr. Hollis. He said I could handle this any way I wanted to."

"That's cool."

A few days later Bobby bought a gun. A Glock nine-millimeter pistol. He kept it in his room under his pillow. No one knew he had it. Bobby himself didn't know exactly why he had it. He liked the feel of it under his pillow. It had a sweet silver odor, like the moon or a cake of blood. And with it he slept the sleep of the ocean, safe, rocking like a fish. He hadn't loaded it yet, had only six bullets, but he liked the feel of the cold handle and the square look of it in his hand. He thought his father might be proud of him.

It was the beginning of the second semester, and rumors were being spread about a girl who had moved to town with her mother. They moved in a few doors down the street from Bobby, and they would be coming to dinner tonight.

II

Old Ground

Fourteen

As THE MOVING van came around the corner, Rita Chabot called inside the house to her daughter, then rose from the front steps to stand in the yard and wave down the monster white truck. This was the first move she had ever made without her husband, and memories of Ben rose up like crickets, insistent, familiar, and brought in the full force of his absence. How long had it been since she felt voluptuous?

"They're here!" she called. "So-phie, they're here!"

They had left Montana four days ago and stayed in a motel until the van arrived. They seemed ready for a new life, but this morning just before dawn, when the light was only a thin pencil line on the horizon, Rita read again the newspaper article she kept folded in her purse. The clipping described her husband's death.

Ben had been a forest ranger in Glacier Park when they met. She had never imagined anything would happen to him. She'd believed they would be together in old age. She read the article, wanting to bring him into this new adventure, keeping a razor-sharp control on her emotions. She noticed how she was losing that stoic quality she had counted on.

She allowed herself to take out a picture kept tucked in her wallet: Ben standing beside her, his arm around her waist, her skirt billowing around her legs. How long would her mind feel these ragged edges? Ben faced the camera, but she had turned to look at him. Her desires then appeared simple.

The van slowed and pulled up to the curb, then backed into her driveway, blocking part of the narrow street. Two men climbed down from the cab and handed Rita the papers itemizing everything she owned. She called Sophie again, and hoped they could be civil to each other today.

For the past nine months (since Sophie had turned fourteen) civility had not been part of their repertoire. Before that, they had argued in predictable ways. Rita didn't know if the change in mood stemmed from the move or Sophie's hormones.

Sophie came out of the house in jeans and T-shirt. "I love not wearing a coat in January." She held her arms wide to the sky. "Radio says it'll be sixty-five degrees today. Hey! When can we get a phone?"

One of the men approached Rita, holding out a sheaf of papers. "Lady, you want to look at this list? Check off the things as we bring them in?"

The morning was moist, with warm sunlight coming through the clouds. Rita tried to imagine what this move would force from her, hoping some kind of inner order might be achieved. She stood in the yard and heaved a sigh as the two men opened the back of the truck, making a sound like thunder.

"What's wrong, Mom?" Sophie asked, standing beside her.

Rita laughed. "I'm just thinking . . ."

"It doesn't feel normal, does it?" Sophie's expression looked surprised but not worried. "I mean, it doesn't seem right yet." Her hair was long and pulled up on top of her head. She was excited and ready to work, but she was thinking of Montana—the place she had always called home.

When they'd left Montana, a furry, feathery snow covered the ground. Ben had taken them skiing every February, and Rita thought of that now. Neither Rita nor Sophie had skied since his death two years ago. When Rita suggested they move to the South, Sophie hadn't liked the idea, but Rita could see that she enjoyed telling her friends that she might move away. She liked hearing them beg her not to leave.

Rita had never lived in Tennessee, but she had visited the mountains and liked it there. Hot summers and long lazy springs would be welcome but unfamiliar. Maybe Ben's presence would not feel so strong there. For days, as they approached their new home, Ben's face had lingered over them like an illusion, but now it began to vanish with the business of the day, as the movers brought out a long narrow table, a rug.

"Show them where to put things," Rita told Sophie.

All day they made quick decisions, putting sofas, beds, tables, and chairs in expected places. The sun began to run the thermometer up to almost seventy degrees. A neighbor brought over a pitcher of peach tea and a batch of chocolate chip cookies, still warm. It was the town's judge, Aurelia Bailey.

She shared the cookies with the movers, and though they ate three or four each, a full plate remained. The aroma of cookies had preceded Aurelia Bailey into the house, and Rita liked her immediately. Her face was round and full, her hands strong like a man's. She asked about Montana. "I noticed your license plates," she said. Her questions were direct and without excess curiosity.

Rita told Aurelia about Ben and his job in Glacier Park. She placed a bronze plaque on the mantel—one that honored Ben and his courage. Judge Bailey read the plaque, then ran her fingers over the letters of the name, etched into the smooth bronze. After a few moments Aurelia said, "Why don't you and Sophie come over for dinner tomorrow night?" She moved toward the door. "I have a son who's a little older than your daughter. He can introduce her to his friends."

By five o'clock all the furniture was in and placed—suitcases in the bedrooms, clothes hung in the closets, plants scattered around in odd places, and Sophie's books, sketch pads, charcoals, and paints neatly arranged on her bookshelf. Rita ordered pizza. The pitcher of peach tea sat with two glasses. The only thing in the refrigerator was ice.

"Should we go to the grocery store tomorrow or tonight?" Rita asked. "Are you tired?" Rita rubbed her neck, trying to ease a knot that had developed from a day of lifting.

Sophie stood up. "I'll make a list."

Rita gazed at her daughter's face, a bloom of color and petal-like skin. Sophie kept redoing her ponytail to keep hair out of her eyes. Her legs were muscular, and her breasts in the last year had doubled in size.

Someone was barbecuing chicken and hamburgers next door, and Sophie thought of buying a grill. She wrote "grill" on her list. "Who ever heard of anybody grilling outside in January?" she said.

The pizza arrived and they ate all but one piece. Rita lifted the last slice from the box and wrapped it in the Saran Wrap taken from the cookies. Sophie loved cold pizza for breakfast.

As they rode to the store, Rita noticed a group of boys near the movie theater. They turned to check out the unfamiliar car and saw Sophie in the passenger seat. Rita rolled down the window to inhale short breaths of cool air. *How strange,* she thought, *to be able to taste the air.*

One boy waved to them. Rita smiled at his boldness. "We might like it here, huh? It might be friendly."

Rita hoped that she herself might find someone, and though the prospect of going out with a man had not much appealed to her, she imagined it more easily now. She had already tried it once.

The previous fall, on a Friday night, Rita had suggested that Sophie go next door to a friend's house for the evening. Sophie thought her mother was going to a movie. She often went to the movies with her friend Ginger.

"You'll be back by nine, won't you?"

"Well, honey, the truth is, I have a date," Rita said, her tone confessional.

Sophie smiled, an unexpected response. "Who with?"

"Ted Farrell." As she spoke the man's name, she hoped he was not the father of one of Sophie's friends at school.

Sophie kept smiling.

"Ginger introduced me to him. She said we might like each other." Rita sounded as though she was making an excuse, trying too hard to explain.

"Okay," Sophie said.

"So you'll go next door?"

"Sure. What's your curfew?"

"I don't have one."

The whole scene turned out better than Rita expected. Her conversation with Sophie had been playful, teasing. Her first date went well, and the more she went out with Ted, the more Sophie teased her.

"Has he kissed you yet?" Sophie asked.

Rita wouldn't answer.

"I guess that's a yes."

"Does it bother you?" Rita asked. "I mean, because of your dad?"

"I don't think of this guy as a replacement," said Sophie. She paused. "Anyway, he's got a great car."

Rita shook her head.

"His car is really hot, Mom."

Rita swept the floor thoughtfully, pushing crumbs into a dustpan. "What kind is it?"

"It's a Mercedes, E-class. Mom, you've been going out with him four months and you didn't notice?"

Rita threw the crumbs into the garbage and tied up the bag. "Take this out, will you?"

She stopped seeing Ted within the next few weeks, both of them losing interest.

Rita and Sophie spent an hour unloading and putting away their groceries. They threw away the Pizza Express box, and helped each other make up beds. Then they went to their separate rooms, putting away clothes and calling back and forth to each other to ask where something was.

By eleven o'clock they were both in bed. Rita had already fallen asleep when she heard Sophie call from down the hall.

"Go back to sleep," Rita said.

"I can't. I'm wide awake."

"Go to sleep, honey. I'm tired."

They heard a car pass on the street, slowing, then moving on, then another car, then quiet.

"I'm wide awake," Sophie yelled.

"We sound like the Waltons." Rita laughed. "But not as pleasant."

"Who?"

"Nothing."

"Can I come in there with you?" Sophie asked.

"Come on."

Sophie entered her mother's room and climbed into bed, quietly grateful. "I kept hearing strange noises," she said.

"Different houses have different sounds," Rita told her. "We'll get used to it."

"Did you lock the doors?"

"Front and back." She held Sophie in her arms and felt her relax. "Are your eyes closed?"

"No."

"Close them." After a few moments she said, "Are you still scared?"

"I wasn't really scared," said Sophie. "It just felt strange."

"I know."

In a few more minutes Rita heard the slow breathing of sleep and felt the small twitches of her daughter's body fade into a perfectly designated slumber.

The next morning Rita woke to an empty bed. She could hear the shower running in the hall bathroom and, as she sometimes did, imagined that Ben was up before she was—showering. In only a few moments he would wake her by shaking his wet head over her face, then touching her, tickling. A bump of grief pulled her back to the hollow of her bed.

During the weeks before moving to Tennessee, new thoughts had come into Rita's head: of beginnings and hope, of weakness and dread, of assessing the world differently, of assuaging a barely drifting edge of sexuality as it began to enter her bones again.

Rita loved waking last night, feeling the small delicacy of her daughter's breath on the pillow. Sophie had spread herself across the bed, leaving little room for her mother, but they had made it through the first night in the new house. Now Rita would get up, make French toast, and cut up bananas and fresh pineapple. She would allow Sophie to play her music loud as they worked to unpack boxes and put order to the house. Later she would take Sophie to see the school she would attend. The second semester was about to begin. Rita felt the form of her life taking shape again. She suspected this day might be one they would keep in their memory for years, but she wondered if their memory of it would be the same.

Fifteen

Sophie worried that moving from Montana might cut her off from memories of her father. She felt that, by leaving, she might even forget him. She tried to say this to her mother, but her mother couldn't listen.

"You'll like Tennessee," she told Sophie. "It'll be different. A kind of adventure."

"Don't you like Montana?" Sophie asked.

"Oh, honey."

During the Thanksgiving holiday they went to look for a house. They flew to Chattanooga, rented a car, and drove to South Pittsburg. "If you don't like it, we won't move there," Rita said. "Okay?"

"Okay."

The day they bought the house on Mulberry Street, the temperature was fifty-five degrees. "It'll be spring before you know it," said Rita. The house was two stories and had a guest room for friends or relatives who might want to visit from Montana. They imagined themselves living there, deciding where to put the sofa and which room would belong to Sophie. By the time they left, they felt connected to it, eager.

Sophie pretended to be happier than she was, but she did like the countryside, the weather, and the chance to start a different life. "It's just that I won't know anybody."

"I won't either. We'll meet people real fast, though. You'll see."

"I want a rug in my room," Sophie said. "One with an Indian pattern."

"And I'll have a garden." Even after returning to Montana, they thought of where to place things in the new house. They were already beginning to move there in their minds.

"Can we afford this?" Sophie asked. "Will you get a job?"

"Maybe," said Rita. "But your dad left us in good shape, honey. And the insurance money paid for this house. Now pick out a color for your room."

"Light yellow. But that slanted wall, I want that purple, or red."

"Fine, baby. You've always had a good eye for color."

Everything Sophie did brought her mother's approval, and Sophie knew this had to do with her willingness to move away. Their life now seemed about to lift off, and they both trod softly on each other's turf.

"Are you going to take all your clothes with you?" her mother asked. "I mean, sometimes the styles are different somewhere else. We could just get rid of a lot that we have, I think."

"I like my clothes. I'm keeping them."

"What about all these ski clothes?"

"It's not going to help," said Sophie.

"What?"

"Getting rid of these things, moving. Nothing's going to make us miss Dad any less. Don't get rid of *his* clothes. You haven't, have you? You haven't gotten rid of his clothes!"

"It's been almost two years, Sophie. I can't keep hanging on to them forever."

"Then *I* will. I'll keep them in my closet. Don't get rid of anything of his. I want them. I want to be able to go back to them."

"So, we're taking this stuff with us?"

"Yes." Sophie snapped her head up. "Don't worry. I'll make space for it. That house has plenty of room."

Rita sighed.

Sophie started to turn away, then she said, "You think if you get rid of the clothes that we won't miss him as much? You think what we feel is ever gonna go away?" Her words stunned them both.

"That's not what I meant."

Stillness hung in the room like a shadow. Flecks of gold reflected in Rita's eyes. Those blank white days in the hospital came back in, then weeks followed by rituals and casseroles and hams, cakes and pies brought in, not eaten, thrown out, frozen. People thought Rita had been given a drug to help her stay calm, but it was not calm at all—just a daze, a numb, stun-gun look. Sophie did not want that look to return.

"Listen, it's gonna be all right," she told her mother. "We'll move to Tennessee the way you want. We'll take Dad's stuff, the way I want."

Those words forced Rita to choke in her throat. "You're pretty smart," she said. Tears welled in her eyes.

"Yeah, I am."

"Sometimes I think my mother is alive again in you, you know that? Sometimes she comes out in the words you say." She cleared her throat.

"I guess that's good."

Sophie, only fourteen, carried patterns of old life in her bones. She looked at the woman who was her mother and often wondered what was to become of them. Today she felt good about their life.

Rita picked up the car keys. "I'm going to tell some people goodbye. Wanna come?"

"No."

Sophie watched her mother pull out of the driveway, seeing her turn to look at the house before she sped off. Then Sophie wandered the house, looking into boxes half packed and stacks of clothes. She lifted two of her father's shirts and smelled them. The odor of him still lingered, though she wasn't sure if it was actually there or if it was just brought back by the act of burying her face into the sleeve or collar. She rubbed the shirt's softness onto her face and what she smelled was her mother's perfume, so she knew her mother had been dwelling with these shirts, that she too kept searching for ways to bring him back.

Sophie sat down hard on the floor, heaving a huge, blank sigh into the cotton, letting the sigh move down into the floor, then up toward the ceiling, rising through the walls to the roof and out into the dark winter air of a vast Montana sky.

The day Sophie arrived with her mother in South Pittsburg, she saw Crow Davenport in front of the movie theater. She didn't know his name then. He was thin, tall, with short hair that brushed forward and up in front, as if a dog had licked his forehead. He was with three other boys, one with long hair over his ears, one tall and dark-haired, and one with glasses. When her mother drove by, all four boys checked out the new car in town. They stood together, their arms and legs moving as though they felt dangerous, even to themselves. And Sophie saw this moment as a lucky sign in her new life. One boy waved, and the others continued to watch as her mother pulled into the Kroger parking lot.

"Did you see that sign in the hardware store?" her mother asked. "It said 'Help Wanted.' "

"For me or you?"

"Me."

"You're gonna work in a hardware store?" Sophie swung open the car door. "You want to do that?"

"It might be perfect," Rita said. The grocery-store doors slid open, and they could smell a deli and bakery all at once. "Mmmh, let's get something good. You pick it out." Rita took a basket and gave one to Sophie. "Something chocolate, okay?"

They separated, each having a list of items. When they met at the register, both of their baskets held items not on the list. As they placed their groceries on the rolling counter, they shared a conspiratorial grin. "We're going to eat with our neighbor tomorrow night," said Rita.

"That judge lady?"

"Yeah. She has a son she wants you to meet."

Sophie hoped the judge's son proved to be the boy with dog-licked hair. If she hadn't seen the boys a moment ago, she might be less willing, or less curious, to join her mother at a neighbor's house. Now she felt like she had already met these boys, and that they already liked her. Now she had a plan. On the way home they passed the movie theater again, but the boys had gone.

The next evening they entered the judge's house with a bottle of wine. Bobby answered the door, and Sophie thought he might be one of the boys she had seen the day before. She was immediately struck by how handsome he was. Most girls liked Bobby immediately, and she saw how easy he felt around girls. His dark hair and brows set off light blue eyes, and he looked slightly mischievous. When she saw him, Sophie let her lower lip fall into a slight pout. She had practiced this look in the mirror: her dark eyes large, her mouth slightly puckered. She usually wore her hair pulled up in back, but tonight she let it fall around her shoulders. Bobby's long glance indicated that he liked what he saw.

"Bobby plays in a band," Judge Bailey said, introducing him to Sophie and Mrs. Chabot.

"Please, call me Rita," Rita insisted.

"What do you play?" Sophie asked, the pout still in place.

"Rock, blues mostly." Bobby wore a Braves cap and pulled it forward with one jerk on the bill.

"No, I mean what instrument?"

"Oh." He laughed. "Guitar."

"He's good," said his mother. "He plays lead guitar. They're entering a statewide competition this summer."

Bobby motioned for Sophie to move out of the kitchen into the backyard. They wanted to get out of the range of mothers.

"What kind of competition?" Sophie asked.

"One that, if we win, we win big-time," he told her.

"Like what?"

"A contract from a recording studio." He smiled. His whole body looked confident.

"Really."

"If we win, you could hear us on the radio. We call ourselves the Bandits."

"Really."

"We're kinda famous. We've played all over the state, even went to Knoxville once. Listen, we're practicing tonight. Want to come?"

"Depends on where."

"The band's practicing at Casey's house. You could meet everybody."

"Maybe."

Bobby could not stop looking at this new girl, and he could not believe his bad luck. He had meant to break up with Stephanie a few weeks ago but aside from dropping a couple of hints to test the waters, he hadn't done much about it. Now he wanted to be free. Sophie's mouth was a perfect bow. He watched as she pushed out her lower lip.

"Are you French?" he asked, excited by the suggestion. "Your name is French, isn't it? Sha-bo."

"Most people say 'Sha-bot,' you know, saying the *t* sound. You said it right. My daddy was French Canadian."

"Can you speak French?"

"Yeah. Some."

"I thought you might be French," he said, slapping his leg. "That's so cool."

After dinner Bobby mentioned taking Sophie to hear the band practice and meet some of his friends. Judge Bailey urged them to go.

"Don't be late," Rita said.

"What's late?" asked Bobby.

Judge Bailey frowned. She thought he sounded rude.

"I just want to know what time she has to be home," he said.

Sophie felt like a child. She shot her mother a look: *Don't embarrass me.*

"She knows her own limits," Rita said. "She can judge the time." Rita shot back a look of equal demand.

As they left, Sophie turned to see her mother carrying dishes into the kitchen. Rita was laughing, but she watched Bobby's truck pull out of the driveway. Bobby drove a truck so they could carry their equipment from town to town when they played.

"You heard of the Doors?" he asked her. The question came out abruptly.

"I think so."

"They're the best. The whole sound is so different, you know? Well, Antony, our singer, can make us sound just like them. And we write our own songs."

"You do?"

"Yeah, me and Crow write most of the songs. Crow's my best friend. He plays rhythm guitar. I play lead."

"That's what your mother said."

"Oh, yeah."

Before she could ask about the others in the band, Bobby turned onto a dirt road and Sophie could see the lights of a house behind the trees. "That's it," he said, too loudly. His eyes, restless and worried, kept something secret behind them. She hadn't seen it until now—a moment that showed the hidden piece that shone like metal around his body. She suddenly had an image of him as a robot. She didn't know why.

"That's Casey's house," he said, pointing. "He's our drummer. He's really good. We practice in his old man's barn. Me, Crow, Tom, Lester, and Casey. Antony on vocals."

"No girls?"

"Not yet. You play anything? Hey, can you sing?"

"Depends on what you call singing."

"Guess that's a no." His legs were so long that his knees hit the steering wheel. Sophie thought he must be an athlete. He walked and moved like an athlete. He turned the wheel into the driveway.

"We saw you yesterday in the car with your mom," he told Sophie. "You were going to the store, I guess."

"Was that you?" She spoke with a nonchalance that no one would have believed.

"So, you've already seen most of the band. Crow, Lester, Casey, and me." Bobby laughed, and again Sophie saw a piece of him she didn't understand—a way he shifted, turned his head, something that seemed false. "Tom and Antony are the only ones you haven't seen. Antony's our singer." He laughed again.

Sophie laughed too, even though she didn't know what was funny.

Bobby pulled the truck onto a grassy lot beside the house, honked the horn twice, and jumped out to take his guitar and speakers into the barn. "Wanna help me?" he said cheerfully, the hidden piece back in like a turtle drawing in its head and legs, tail and feet.

As she helped him with the equipment, Sophie hoped some girls would be there, someone to talk to while they practiced.

In the house a specter of a woman came to the door, her slim body seeming to float. She waved toward the barn and went back in, closing the door behind her.

Three girls stood on one side of the barn drinking beer. Bobby waved to one of them. They steered themselves away from Sophie, because she was new, maybe contagious.

Sophie spoke to each boy, not seeing Crow until Bobby said, "She's French," as though he owned her. "I mean, she's really French. Not from France, but . . . her name is Chabot." That was when Crow looked up.

She didn't know what to say, so she walked toward the girls. She had never been shy about meeting new people. She knew that most people liked to have someone introduce themselves, so that they didn't have to make the effort. It made them feel pleased, chosen. The girls offered Sophie a beer. They probably thought she was older than fourteen. Sophie looked older. She was beautiful, and the girls weren't sure if they wanted to like her.

Lester walked over to them, nodding at Sophie. "We saw you yesterday," he announced.

"Yeah, I know." She liked his face immediately. He wore glasses. He looked open and without guile.

Crow stared at Sophie but never approached her. Bobby kept telling everyone, "She's French, but not from France. Her dad's French."

"C'mon, Bobby, give us a riff. Let's get started." Crow and Tom called him back to practice.

Bobby didn't want to leave Sophie with the girls. One of them, Stephanie, burned a look into him.

They played several songs, but Antony wasn't around to sing. "Where's their singer?" Sophie asked.

"He can't always come," said Nikki. "He's black, and his mama's strict. She's a nurse."

The other girl hung around Casey, standing near the drums.

Crow kept looking at Sophie as he strummed his guitar. She grew embarrassed by the intensity of his stare but didn't turn away. His muscles looked stringy and hard, and he swayed with the music. She felt sure he would speak to her before the night was over, but as he finished playing, he did not look at her again. They packed away their instruments, Bobby coming over a few times to ask how she was.

At ten forty-five Sophie asked if anyone could take her home. Bobby offered to leave, but the other guys wanted to stay, so Nikki volunteered to drive her home.

"I have my car," she said. "Come on, girls, and Sophie, you ride up front."

"Where do you live?" Stephanie asked.

"Three houses from Bobby," she said.

Stephanie rolled her eyes. "Watch out for Bobby, Sophie. He's trouble."

"He is trou-ble," said the girl who hung around Casey. "Good-looking as hell, but trouble."

"Bobby's still taking you to the movies, right, Steph?" asked Nikki. She wanted to inform Sophie that Bobby and Stephanie were a couple.

"I guess," said Stephanie. "He said he was."

Sophie guessed the tension. "I only met Bobby tonight," said Sophie. "We hardly know each other."

"That's all that'll go out with him now—the ones who don't know him. God, his hands go everywhere." Stephanie's voice was tight. "We've been going out since September, but we're about to split. He just got so bad." She looked teary as she said it.

Casey's girl leaned toward the front seat. "*I'd* go with him." She sighed.

"Yeah, but you're a slut," said Stephanie.

They laughed.

"Lester's good though," said Nikki. "Lester's all right." They were telling her which boy to go out with, informing her politely of her choices.

Stephanie squinted. "I bet Lester calls you, Sophie. I saw him checking you out tonight."

"Listen," said Nikki. "You really French?"

"Sort of. My dad was French Canadian. He used to speak it a lot." No one asked where he was. "He's dead now," she offered. "He died in a forest fire two years ago."

"What year are you, Sophie?"

"Ninth."

The girls looked at each other. Everything they did made them seem older.

They dropped Sophie at her house, and Nikki told her to look for them at lunch on Monday. She said they would be on the steps by the east door. "You'll see us," she said.

Sophie thanked them for the ride. As they drove away she heard them laughing. "She's all right," Nikki's voice rang loud. "C'mon, y'all. Don't dis her just because she looks good."

None of the girls had said a word about how Sophie looked. They had not promised to like her.

Sixteen

THE DAY AFTER Bobby had introduced the French girl to his friends he went to her house. He felt excitement and a kind of ownership. He imagined that Sophie liked him, and his step grew light and fast.

Rita answered the door. "Oh, Bobby, I was expecting the plumber. Sophie's out in the backyard. She can't believe that it can be so warm in winter."

"She sunbathing?" asked Bobby.

"Better let me tell her you're here," Rita said.

Sophie came into the house wearing one of her father's shirts over a pair of shorts.

"Hey," said Bobby. "I'm glad you heard us play last night. You like it?"

"Sure," said Sophie. "And the girls were nice. Nikki said I could meet them for lunch on Monday."

Bobby nodded. He wondered what the girls had told Sophie about him. "What'd you talk about, in the car?"

"Nothing. Just about school and stuff." Bobby felt nervous around Sophie, and Sophie found that she didn't like his nervousness. "Listen, I got to go."

"Sure. I'll come by tomorrow. We'll go somewhere."

"I don't know," she said.

"I'll come by anyway. Maybe."

"Okay."

He came by every day for the next week, until one day Sophie told her mother to say she wasn't home.

"You want me to lie?" Rita said, with Bobby waiting in the kitchen. "Why don't you like him?"

"I do. I just don't want him to come by the house every single day."

"He's smitten. That's for sure."

"Well, I'm not."

"I don't know why. He's certainly handsome."

"Well."

"I'll tell him you're not here. But at least let him come by later."

"Might as well see him now then." Sophie went into the kitchen. She couldn't tell if Bobby had heard what they said, but his face looked expectant.

"Wanna go for a ride? I can show you around?"

"Okay."

Bobby took her to the Dairy Queen and they bought some hot dogs and cones of chocolate-dipped soft serve. "Wanna walk down to the river?"

"Sure."

They ate their cones as they walked, and then Bobby turned to Sophie and said, "My heart is pounding so fast." He lifted her hand and let her feel his heart. "Feel that?"

"Don't," she said.

"Why are you so uncomfortable with me?" he asked. His experience with girls had been easy until now.

"You just seem kinda stiff or something. You—"

"Well, you got that part right." He laughed. "The part about being stiff."

Sophie didn't laugh.

"What's the matter with you?" he said. He wanted to kiss her. He pulled her to him.

"Stop, Bobby. Stop it!"

"Okay. Okay." He released her, throwing his hands high into the air. "I'm just trying to tell you something here." His voice grew soft again. "I'm just trying to tell you." He leaned to kiss her, not touching, just leaning to kiss her cheek. "I think about you all the time." His breath was hot, and Sophie found herself both flattered and scared. "One kiss," he said. "Let me kiss you one time, then we'll go. It's not so much to ask." He was sweating, and the sweat on his face made him more handsome. He was the best-looking boy she had ever seen, but still she wanted to leave.

"One." She could not imagine that one kiss would hurt anything. So he kissed her. She had not been kissed in this way. When he let her go, she felt dizzy.

"Okay," he said, happy. "That's all I wanted. Just a chance, you know?" He treated her with caution all the way home. The whole outing had been strange, and Sophie was glad when it ended. Bobby seemed happy, satisfied, and she was going back home. "Want to go hear us practice tonight?"

"No," said Sophie. "I can't go tonight." She got out of the car and waved to him. He sat until she had gone into the house and closed the door.

Seventeen

ONE EVENING IN late January just before Charlie Post was closing the hardware store, a tall woman in a hooded coat came in the door and the bell, tripped by a small wire over the door, began to tinkle. The woman's sudden appearance out of the near-dark night made Charlie think of a ghost, or possibly a monk. He felt startled until she threw back her head, releasing the hood from her face.

Charlie had already heard about the woman who moved in down the street from Judge Bailey, and he was vaguely curious. He stood behind the cash register and watched her brush off her coat. He couldn't remember what people had said her name was.

Her hair fell in long, bright red ringlets around her face and neck, and her face was wet with rain. "I got here just in time," she said. "Looks like you were about to close." Her words lost themselves in the room and Charlie could still hear the bell's high sound and the slam of the door, as if he had not caught up to the present moment yet but lagged a moment or two behind. He said nothing.

"I'm sorry," she said. "You want me to come back tomorrow?" She moved toward the cash register. "I know what I'm looking for, and if I can get it now, I won't have to make another trip."

"Of course," said Charlie. He turned and pretended to wipe off a shelf behind him. "I wasn't ready to close anyhow."

She called to him from behind one of the high shelves. "Are you Charlie Post? The owner?"

"Yep," he said, feeling an opening. "And you moved in near Judge Bailey, right?"

Rita emerged from the back shelves carrying faucet fixtures, a few pipes, a small array of washers, and the best wrench in the store. Charlie laughed. "Better make sure you have the right pipe size. You have to—"

Rita interrupted. "They're right," she said. "I've done this before, lots of times. My dad was a handyman and taught me how to repair houses and cars, even plumbing. I've been doing this since I was ten."

"Oh," said Charlie. "Sorry. Does that house need a lot of repair?"

"More improvement than repair," she said.

Charlie liked her, her wild mop of hair, her big eyes, her purchases. He told her to come back anytime and asked what her name was.

Rita did come back several times that week. She even asked him about the help-wanted sign in the window. He thought she was kidding, but when she asked again he said, "Are you serious?"

"Are *you*?" Rita asked.

"Well," he said. "I only want part-time, two or three days a week."

"That's all *I* want."

The bell above the door announced someone's entrance, and Charlie looked up, startled by the intrusion.

"Lester," he said, waving Lester to the back. "I've been expecting you."

Lester had come to bring scholarship material to Charlie— envelopes and forms. He wanted a personal recommendation from his coach. He had plenty of people to recommend him academically. Charlie took the material from Lester. "Where is it you want to go? Yale?"

"Let's just see who's gonna take me."

"Anybody would."

Lester pulled Charlie into the back room.

"What's the matter?" Charlie asked.

"I'm going to ask out the new girl. She's French. I'm asking her today."

Ever since Little League, Charlie had advised Lester about girls. It had started with MaryLou Adams in the seventh grade, moved on to Cindy Harbison, then Annie and Jill Wright, who were sisters. None of these had turned out well.

"She'll probably say yes."

"Right." The muscles in Lester's jaw tightened.

"I know what you mean," said Charlie. "I've seen her mother."

Lester laughed.

By the end of January, Rita was working three days a week at Post Hardware. Her presence brought in more customers, both men and women. The men came in to see Rita, let her sell them something, hear her talk about pipe fittings and wrenches. Women came in to look over what the men were flocking to see.

Most days Rita wore jeans and a T-shirt. Her figure was trim, her manner businesslike and friendly. Her face, though, glowed with excitement, with knowledge about hardware, and she moved through the store with a smooth grace.

Charlie sold more merchandise in the middle of the week than he did on weekends. And though at first the women who came in didn't like Rita, she spoke to them as though they could install anything themselves, as though they didn't need a man to help them. So they left the store liking her spirit, trusting her.

Tuesday through Thursday Charlie grew used to having her around the store. He grew used to her voice calling him from the storeroom, used to bending over the counter with her looking through catalogues as she pointed out new items he might want to order.

As she talked, his eyes roamed her shoulders and plump breasts beneath the cotton T-shirt or sweater she wore. At times, while she talked, her nipples grew hard and he could distinguish the particular lilt of her breasts. Even through her jeans he could see the musculature of her thighs and buttocks, and he let his mind move his tongue around those hard nipples, between the white inner softness of her thighs, her legs opening for him.

"Listen," she said, as she closed a catalogue. Charlie jumped. "How would you like to come to my house for dinner on Friday night? An old friend of my husband's sent some salmon he caught in Montana, and I want to share it with somebody."

Charlie backed up, knocking over a stack of brochures. Probably the phrase "an old friend of my husband's" caught him off balance.

"My husband died in a forest fire," she said, helping Charlie restack the brochures. "Maybe you didn't know that. He was a forest ranger and was killed in one of the fires. It's why we left Montana, came here." She took a few steps back. "Anyway," she said.

"I knew about your husband," Charlie explained. "I didn't know what happened to him. But yes, I'll be glad to help you eat salmon. I'll bring wine, and I make a good apple pie."

Rita smiled and touched Charlie's arm. Charlie felt as if he should apologize for the intimate thoughts he'd been having a moment ago. He wondered if she could read his mind, if the longing he felt maybe had a strong odor to it, or something visible had told her the thoughts in his head. He smiled at her, and Rita prepared to leave for the day. She picked up the purse she kept behind the counter and rushed out the door as a man wearing soiled work clothes walked in.

"You leaving?" asked the farmer. He had come in to buy something from Rita.

"I'll help you, Jake," said Charlie.

"Okay." Jake sighed. "Won't be as good, but okay."

Eighteen

LESTER DUNPHY DIDN'T know love could happen so fast. He didn't know it could come in like a wave and knock him down, the undertow being worse than the knockdown. The first time he saw Sophie she was in a car, passing at a slow pace, her mother driving. And though all of his friends had turned to see, and though he didn't know her name, he knew she was looking straight at him. The next night he saw her at Casey's house. Bobby brought her, but she didn't seem interested in Bobby. She hung out with the girls all night. She watched the band rehearse. Lester noticed that she held a beer but didn't drink it. He had wanted to take her home that night, but Nikki and the other girls left with her before he could offer.

Every day at school he watched for Sophie. He saw her in the cafeteria, learned her class schedule. Sometimes he walked with her to social studies. He waited for her everywhere.

After trailing her around the halls for almost a month, Lester finally worked up the nerve to ask her to the Spring Dance, always held the first weekend in March. Most of the other girls had a date, but since Sophie was new in town, he planned to take advantage of this lucky break. He might not get the chance again.

Her long hair was piled on top of her head, messy and sexy. She didn't wear makeup, her skin shone smooth—a rosy glow. Lester walked with her down the hallway telling Sophie about Mr. Hollis.

"In history class he closes the door so he can smoke cigarettes." Sophie laughed, and when she laughed, Lester blurted out his invitation.

"Wanna go to the Spring Dance with me next week?" He tried to make his words sound offhand, as if he had just thought of it.

"Sure," she said, and slipped quickly into her classroom as the bell rang.

"Okay," said Lester. *Had she said yes?* "I'll call you," he yelled. He didn't know her number. *Shit!* He felt stupid. *She'd said yes, hadn't she?* He'd never before gone out with a girl who looked like this and couldn't imagine the event actually coming about. He hoped his father would let him use the car.

On the evening of the dance Lester picked up Sophie in his father's Buick. He parked at the far end of the school parking lot, so that everyone would see him arrive with his date.

The sky turned deep gray as he walked with Sophie toward the school. Music from the band floated through the high windows out onto the air, and a streak of pink brushed across the sky in one low sweep. Edges of cloud rose up, like the feathers of an enormous bird. As they walked through the gymnasium doors, they hardly recognized the room as a place even connected to the school.

"It's like this every year," Lester said proudly. "In fact, I was the one who thought up the jungle theme for this year."

A transformation of huge paper flowers sprouted in various shades of yellow, red, and blue in each corner of the room. Long lengths of crepe paper hung low to create a ceiling effect of soft splendor. Each strip twisted with sprinkled glitter so that the colors of the flowers reflected in tiny sparkles. Big knots of red ribbon hung on the basketball hoops, and girls in pale silk, voile, and crepe glided across the floor. The band played at the far end of the room and music echoed into the gym's rafters. Each member of the band wore a purple sequined jacket.

"I love it." Sophie sighed. She looked like a girl in a magazine. Her navy blue dress exposed her shoulders and legs. Her breasts pushed up slightly from her tight bodice.

In the middle of the gym a hanging mirrored ball was lit by colored spotlights shining from two sides of the room. The lights seemed to make the ball revolve on its string. Bits of light and sparkles circled the room. The girls wore short black dresses with meshy tights covering their legs, or long pink silk dresses, or blue crepe. The light split from the glass ball and landed on their hair, legs, faces, and shoulders. Sophie smiled, and Lester could see how pleased she was.

Large papier-mâché animals hid behind the flowers. Tigers, alligators, rabbits, and squirrels looked over the tops of bushes and trees. Colorful birds looked poised for flight. Elongated boys, sleek in their tuxedos, prowled the floor. Their hair glimmered under the diamond spell of the evening, and the room appeared to be floating.

Lester asked Sophie to dance. He saw Bobby follow them with his eyes. Crow motioned a thumbs-up with both hands to Lester. Bobby, even while dancing with someone else, glared at them.

Acne scars had left their mark on Lester's face, making his skin leathery. Still, his features were chiseled and manly. Each spring he rode the crest of popularity as the catcher on the baseball team, and he was a great clutch hitter. His excellent grades brought only cruel teasing, but playing baseball balanced out his good grades.

Tonight was his, because the girl everyone wanted to be with was with him. Stephanie and Nikki hovered around Sophie, hoping to identify with her newfound popularity. They pretended to be happy for her.

"They should've let your band play tonight," Sophie told Lester. "You were really good. At least what I heard was good."

On this night Lester's mind sizzled with the steam of hopefulness and change. Maybe his life would take a turn. He was the mailman's son. He was forced to go to mass every Sunday. He was good at baseball and at playing the keyboard, but he stayed on the fringe of Crow's tight group. Maybe now his friends would see him in a different light.

By intermission, as the band took a break, the night had begun to slacken. Bobby had danced with Sophie for almost half an hour, and if Lester tried to get her, bring her to a different side of the gym, Bobby followed. Crow urged Bobby to leave them alone, and once he tapped Bobby's shoulder and said, "C'mon, man. Don't be an asshole."

Crow walked Sophie back to Lester, but just as he was about to leave, Sophie turned to him and said, "Crow, I think I'll dance with you."

The way Sophie Chabot looked at Crow made Lester know that his time was already over. He wondered if his time had ever even begun. Bobby danced with every other girl in the room. He couldn't believe Sophie didn't want him, but he was glad she didn't want Lester either.

"She blew you off, man," Bobby told Lester.

"She did not blow me off. I told her to dance with Crow."

"She blew you off."

"Have you ever heard of the term 'open-minded'?" said Lester.

"Not really." Bobby left, going out a side door. A girl who stood on the sideline called to him.

When Lester took Sophie home, the sparkle of the night had faded into gloom; still, he kept a certain dignity in spending the evening with her. And she had stayed with him, only him, for the last fifteen minutes. Crow had seen to that. Lester's only triumph came during the last dance, when Sophie put her head on his shoulder. Whether the gesture came from weariness or affection, Lester didn't know; but he saw the grudging respect in the eyes of those standing around him, and for those few moments he felt the full-throatedness of his expectations.

He walked her to her door and she thanked him. The awkward-ness of their bodies made him feel impulsive. He trembled, a little current going through his body, and though he knew he might regret it later, he smiled and leaned to kiss her cheek. To his bafflement, she kissed him back and went into the house.

Lester stood facing the door, a stupid smile on his face. The night became appallingly quiet, and he walked back to the car, taking a quivery intake of breath before he opened the door. He started the motor. The radio was already on, and Lester swayed to the music. His heart would be broken, but it wasn't broken yet.

Not yet, he thought. And he imagined her in a vague bedroom, his hands exploring her neck and breasts, her hips twisting, floating toward him. He imagined crushing her tight, her skin warm against his, her head falling back. She would love his touch.

The next day everything went sour.

Crow came to Lester's house. "Hello, Mrs. Dunphy," he said. Mrs. Dunphy leaned to take care of the baby. Lester's house was full of kids. Younger brothers and sisters, and a new baby.

"Come in here and let me see you, Crow Davenport." Mrs. Dunphy liked Crow. She liked him more than she liked the other friends Lester brought to the house. Bobby and Tom, she said, had "narrow, squinty eyes." She didn't trust either one of them. "But that Crow Davenport. He's a good boy." The baby began to cry. "Lester!" she yelled. "He'll be right here," she told Crow and held the baby out to let him see. When Lester came, she left the room.

"Hey," said Lester, moving reluctantly toward Crow.

Crow threw a ball to Lester. "Think fast," he said. Crow liked to have a ball in his hand—a small orange ball that he threw to people. Usually his friends were prepared, but Lester was not prepared, and expressed impatience at the ball's sudden appearance. It bounced onto the sofa.

"Shit, Crow." He lifted the ball and held it, turning it slowly in his hands.

"Bobby was an asshole last night," Crow said, trying to sound friendly.

"I know that."

"I talked to him."

"Won't do any good."

"He's messed up, man. You hear what he did?" Crow took the ball from Lester and threw it into the air.

"No."

"He tried to pick a fight with me."

"No shit?"

"He came to the house and took a swing at me."

"When?"

"Told me to leave Sophie alone."

"Looked to me like Sophie was going after *you,* not the other way around."

"He took a fucking swing at me," Crow said. "I couldn't believe it. He's my best friend."

"What'd you do?"

"I swung back. Hell, he's messed up."

"What's the matter with him?"

"He said he brought her out there the first night. Said you shouldn't have asked her out."

"He's crazy," Lester said.

"Yeah, if anybody should be mad, it's you. That's what I told him."

"Well, you know him better than anybody." Lester put on his jacket and followed Crow out the door. "Where're we going?"

"Who cares?" Crow said. "Get in."

They got into the car and turned on the radio.

"Sophie doesn't care about him," said Crow. "She didn't even want to dance with him last night. That's what made him go off, you know? The one girl he finally couldn't get."

"I know." Lester paused. He reached to take the ball from Crow. "Sophie went after you though."

"The hell she did," Crow said. "It wadn't my shoulder she was sucking on during that last dance."

Lester laughed. "No, but all the way home she asked questions about you. Saying how great you were."

Lester felt suddenly too tired to think through what had happened the night before. He threw the ball up and caught it behind his back. Even sitting in the front seat he could do this trick. "Hey man," he said, rolling the ball in his hands. "Shit happens. If you weren't my friend, I'd hate you."

"You can get her back," Crow said.

"You don't get it, do you? I never had her. Anyway, I don't hear you saying you're not interested."

"C'mon, Les. What do you want me to say?" Crow held up his hand to catch the ball.

"It's like this," said Lester. "A man gets this present, and he opens it, see, and he thinks he knows what it's going to be."

"Yeah?"

"He thinks it's something he's been waiting for, but it's not. You know what it is? It's a set of fucking en-*cyclo*-pedias. If the guy wants a dog, he can look up the word *puppy,* see the *picture* of it, but it's not the same. It sucks."

Crow threw the ball into the backseat and turned toward town. "We gonna mope around all day, or what?"

"Hell no."

"Okay then."

So they were still friends, but the dream Lester carried all those days before the dance fell backward now. And when they saw Sophie come out of a store, she waved—her wave mostly for Crow, her mouth pouty—and for a moment the friendship between the boys wavered slightly. Lester forced himself to be calm. He knew the moment he let his dream of her go—the exact time was 2:33.

"Hey," said Crow. "Wanna get some fries at the King?"

Nineteen

FOR SEVERAL DAYS after the dance, Sophie hated the expression she saw on Lester's face. She avoided him, and now he refused to look at her in the hallway at school or in the cafeteria. She wanted him to be nice to her, like before. When she finally tried to speak to him, he pulled her aside and whispered in a voice she barely recognized.

"Fuck off, Sophie. You made your choice. Now leave me alone."

Sophie sat in her last class hearing his words like a mantra in her head. On her way home she decided to stop by Post Hardware, knowing her mother would be working until six. As she pushed open the door, a bell made Charlie look up to see who it was.

"Rita, your daughter's here," Charlie called. His head towered above the customers around the cash register. The store was filled with shiny coffeepots, piles of tools, shelves of weed killer and Miracle-Gro, light fixtures, fans, and cans of paint. Charlie winked at Sophie. He already felt affection for her mother and had come to their house for dinner several times. He pointed to the back of the store where her mother stacked boxes of nails and bolts. Rita came out from behind a shelf, looking like a gypsy in her long colorful skirt and white blouse. Her face brightened to see Sophie, but a closer look prompted her to ask, "What's wrong?"

"Lester just blasted me," Sophie said.

"Why did he do that?"

"I hurt him. I didn't mean to, but I did."

"How?" her mother said.

"Just not liking him. I mean, I like him, but not the way he wants."

"What do you want me to say?" Rita asked.

"Just something that might help."

"Well, Sophie, I'm sure you didn't mean to hurt him. You could call him, say you're sorry."

"Mom!"

"What!"

"I can't do that!"

"Why not?"

"Because."

"Well, I can't help you then."

"I'm going home," said Sophie. "I can't talk to you when you're like this." She turned to leave. "What time is dinner?"

"Honey, I told you. I'm eating with Charlie tonight, remember?"

"Whatever," she said.

As Sophie passed the Baileys' house, she heard music coming from Bobby's room but couldn't see anyone. Sometimes Crow was there. Sometimes she saw him at Bobby's window.

She walked across her yard, inhaling the early-spring air with its pale tinge of sulfur. She checked the mail and went into the stuffy house. She wanted somebody else to be there, for the windows to be already open. Sometimes she pretended her father was home. Sometimes she felt he was really there. But today Sophie felt alone, like something large had failed. She felt like a fraction of herself.

She turned on the hall lamp as well as the light in the kitchen, thinking how lights could not be expected to work indefinitely. Lights burned out, needed to be replaced. She supposed that even the yellow light of the sun might fade and grow dim. Surface dust that clung to the sill loosened as she opened the window.

Her jaw began to ache. Everything she expected to happen kept diminishing, and she felt skittish, like a horse. Could things diminish until she wouldn't know what to expect at all? Lester's curse, his flat refusal to talk to her, his lusterless gaze, his voice modulated and even, like a stranger on the radio—these things kept coming back in, confusing her picture of life.

Sophie heard footsteps outside, and something inside her gripped firmly. She jerked her head upright. She didn't know if it was the sound or intuition that made her turn and see Crow at the kitchen window. He waved for her to come to the door.

"What're you doing here?" she asked.

"I was at Bobby's and saw you go by," he said. "I felt bad about what happened today. I mean, with Lester."

"You heard about it?"

"Yeah." Crow stood with his hands in his pockets. "It's not like Lester. He's really cool." Crow's T-shirt fit tight over his long chest, and she could see his pectoral muscles above his small waist. He was so tall. He was the tallest boy.

"Lester wouldn't speak to me at all, then he . . ." She stopped.

"Yeah?"

"He told me to fuck off."

"Yeah," said Crow. "That was cold. I mean, it's not like you did anything wrong."

"Wanna come in?" Her voice grew shivery with excitement. At night Sophie dreamed about him, his arms around her. And she imagined him kissing her. When she opened the door, Crow ducked in under her arm. Everything they did seemed secretive.

They could hear cars whoosh by on the road. Sophie liked being alone with Crow. She'd seen him only in crowds, never by himself. She opened the refrigerator and offered him a cold drink. The red afternoon sun dwindled into evening, and light and shadow spilled across their clothes. She poured the soda into a glass with ice and handed it to him slowly, meaningfully—as she had seen women do in the movies.

Each night before she slept, she let wild thoughts roam around her mind, so that when she saw him at school she felt embarrassed enough to avoid him. When she handed him the glass she believed, she imagined, that he'd been having the same thoughts.

Sophie watched the way he sipped from the glass, his mouth, his tongue dipping onto the ice. When she suggested they sit down, he asked her out.

"You wanna do something Friday night? See a movie or something?"

"Yeah. Sure."

"We'll get dinner somewhere first."

"What time?" Her voice sounded squeaky, like a tiny girl's.

Without answering, he leaned and kissed her on the cheek, then again, barely, on the lips.

It was over as quickly as it had started, so that when he left, Sophie wandered the house, not so alone now, glad that her mother wasn't home. Later, she was afraid that maybe she'd dreamed Crow's presence there, then she found the empty glass, the melted slivers of ice. She kept the glass in her room, so that her mother wouldn't wash it.

Twenty

ON THE LAST Saturday in March, Bobby told the others to meet him by the river. He had something to tell them. Bobby got there first and built a fire. They often built a fire when they met near the quarry. Tom arrived irritated that he had to meet them. "This better be important," he said. "I had to beg the old man for a couple hours off. He's making me work construction the whole frigging weekend." He sat on the ground. "Where is everybody?" Tom was skinny, lankier than the others.

Crow walked through the trees. He looked worried. Bobby was still his best friend, but a new quality had given him jagged edges; and even though Bobby looked excited, happy, Crow didn't trust his friend's moods anymore.

The fire was burning high when Antony and Lester walked up. Lester held a bag of marshmallows and an array of sticks to use for roasting.

"Look at those dickheads," Bobby said in welcome. "Lester and Antony come in with marshmallows making us look like a bunch of fucking campfire boys. Here, give me that bag." He opened the bag with his teeth, then handed it back to Lester, urging him to push marshmallows onto sticks and pass them around.

"That's cool, Lester," said Tom. "Somebody comes around, we'll look innocent as hell."

Tom kept looking toward the woods. "Where's Casey?"

Antony took a stick with three marshmallows and held it over the fire. "What's this about, Bobby?" Antony asked. "I don't have all day."

"Where's Casey?" Tom asked again.

"He'll come when he comes," said Bobby. "He'll get here when he gets here." He took the stick Lester handed him and squatted beside the fire. "Look at that sucker bubble up."

Tom's eyes stayed intent on the woods behind them. He remained alert, his brows knitted. When he saw Casey come through the trees, he gave a slow smile. "You took your sweet time, you goddamn fucker." He waved his stick in the flames. "Casey's got some news," he said.

"I thought Bobby called us out here," Crow objected.

Casey took a piece of paper out of his pocket and held it up. "There's this band in Johnson City," said Casey. "The Mountain Boys. Anybody heard of them? I hear they're damn good. They'll be hard to beat in the competition. They just came out of nowhere, seems like."

"How'd you know about them?"

"Got this flyer at the music store saying where they're playing. Everybody's talking about them. Say they're gonna beat *us*." He held up the flyer. "Next weekend they play in Chattanooga. I figured we could go hear them."

Bobby took the flyer.

"They're not gonna win," said Crow. "Hell, I've written two new songs that really kick."

"What's going on?" said Bobby. "You not writing songs with me anymore?"

"Naw, man. Don't get crazy. You can look at them anytime."

"Jesus," said Lester. "Let it go, Bobby."

"I'd rather practice our own stuff than go hear some damn band from Johnson City." Bobby grabbed the flyer and pitched it onto the ground. "Antony, you coming to Casey's Friday night, right? You haven't practiced with us in I don't know how long."

"I'm working Friday nights," Antony told them.

"We can win this thing," Tom said. "I know we can. But we gotta practice. We gotta be ready."

"Antony?" Crow said. "You gotta come."

"I don't know."

"You got to. Hell, you haven't even heard some of the new stuff."

"What's the matter with you, Antony?" Bobby said. "Don't you want to do this?"

"I like playing the gigs with y'all." Antony shifted, uncomfortable. "But I don't know about this competition thing. I mean, it's hard enough. I mean, I get tired of taking shit about being the nigger in the white boys' band."

"C'mon, Antony," Tom said. "We'll be famous. You can take a lot of shit if you're gonna be famous."

They all nodded.

"Let Antony do what he wants," Crow said. "We need you, man, but no pressure. Okay?" He looked at everyone else.

"Damn." Bobby shook his head. "This whole thing, it's our ticket out. You know that? Lester won't need a ticket out, since he's going to Yale or some Ivy League shit-hole school like that, but me and Tom and Casey—you too, Antony—we need a way out of this town."

"What about me?" Crow said. "What am I? Dead?"

"You got the money to get out whenever you want to." Bobby didn't look at his friend. He stood and pulled a marshmallow off the stick with his teeth.

"I think we can win," Casey told them.

Lester had picked up the flyer and was looking at it when they heard a sound like a gunshot.

"Holy shit!" Lester jumped.

Bobby laughed. He held a gun in his hand. "It'll shoot," he said, and passed it around. "It's a Glock—nine-millimeter."

"What are you doing, Bobby?" Crow yelled.

Tom took the gun. "Where'd you get it?"

"From the trunk of some guy's car."

"You steal it?" Casey asked, impressed.

"Hell, no, I bought it."

"How much you pay?"

"Two-fifty." Bobby lifted the gun. "Look." He cocked it, sliding back the top part. "It has a slide."

Casey reached for the gun. "Police aren't using these so much anymore. They use a SigArms, like Special Forces. You can drop it in sand, drop it in water, it'll still fire."

"Yeah," Bobby said. "But this one's good. Just look at it." Casey handed it to Tom.

Antony got up, stood a long moment, and said, "Listen, guys, I'm leaving. I can't be found anywhere where somebody's got a gun. You know what my grandma'd do to me?"

"Well, I hear *that*," said Crow. He knew Louise Burden's fierce tongue.

"I can't be anywhere where there's a gun," Antony said again. "You didn't tell me this was about no gun."

"I didn't know," Tom said. "We were talking about the competition. We didn't know Bobby was gonna pull this shit. But go on if you have to."

"I'm leaving too," Lester said. "Antony's right."

"*Puss*-sy," Tom hissed. "Antony's mama gonna come after you too?" Then he turned to Bobby. "Why'd you buy a gun anyway?"

"I just wanted it. Shit, I know about guns. I go hunting with Hollis and Coach every fall. I know about guns."

"You hunt with a *pis*tol?" Lester said. "How many animals you kill with a pistol?" Lester began to walk backward.

"Here." Bobby handed the gun to Lester. "You shoot it."

But Casey took the gun. He grabbed it fast and shot at a squirrel, hitting it but not killing it.

"Shit, Casey." Tom took the gun, walking up to the squirrel. It was screaming. He killed it by hitting its head with the butt.

"What the fuck's wrong with you?" Bobby reached to take it from Tom. "Casey Willig, you're a sick bastard."

"We better go," Crow said. "That's two shots fired. Somebody probably heard."

"So what? We're out here roasting marshmallows, that's all." Bobby stuffed the gun back into his jacket pocket.

"Yeah, then they pat you down and find a gun in your pocket," Casey said. "Then what?"

"Then I call my dad," Bobby said.

"What do you mean?" Casey turned to Bobby. "Call him from the dead?"

"He's not dead," Bobby said. "He lives in Kentucky."

The moment was quiet before Tom said, "Bobby, you've been making up stories for about fourteen gazillion years. Vinny. Remember Vinny? Hell, Bobby."

"Yeah, but this time it's true." Bobby lifted the letter from his back jeans pocket, and his friends hovered together to read, to realize altogether that Bobby's words this time could be the truth.

They looked at him. "I'll be damn," Tom said. "Why didn't he write you before now?"

"He was in jail, but he's out now, and he wants to see me. I mean, I just found out."

They all looked at Bobby in silence.

"Cool, man."

"So why'd you buy the gun?" Crow asked.

"I don't know. I just wanted to celebrate or something. Have something to show him. I'm gonna do some target practice with bottles and crap. Then I'll be good at it when I see him."

"You think he's gonna care if you're good at that?" Tom said.

"Hell yeah. He'll care. *Your* dad would care."

"Yeah, my dad would really *like* it if I bought a *gun*." Tom roasted another marshmallow over the fire and ate it slowly, chewing even bites. He wiped the sticky sugar from his mouth with his sleeve, his eyes squinting into the fire. "We'd better bolt, before somebody shows up," he said. "If somebody asks, we'll say it was firecrackers." A soft breeze eddied down the hill and blew the flames.

"Where's Lester?"

"He left."

"Did he hear me say about my old man?"

"I don't think so."

It was getting dark. Their faces in the firelight were dark and light and young, and for a moment a cord of affection ran between them.

"My brother did time once," said Casey. Nobody knew much about Casey's family. "He talks about it like he was proud of it. Said it taught him ways to take care of himself."

"What'd he do?" Crow asked. "Rob somebody?"

"He beat a guy up in a bar in Alabama. Hit him with a board, broke his head wide open."

"Man."

"The guy lived, but my brother went to jail for about five years. Then the second time he robbed somebody." Casey stared into the fire, his forehead shining white in the early-spring dark. Casey hardly ever spoke about anything personal. He never spoke of anything but playing the drums. He moved his stick now to beat a rhythm on the ground. "That's where he learned how to fix motors and stuff, so he could be what he is now."

"Rehab." Bobby had heard his mother talk about rehabilitation programs often enough. "Goddamn rehab!" He laughed, and they all laughed with him. Their breath lingered in the air and mixed with the smoke. Leaves rustled around them and the fire flared.

Crow put the last of the marshmallows on a stick for himself. "Shit. I love these things," he said.

They heard someone coming and saw three policemen step from a stand of bushes. "What're you boys doing out here?"

Casey stepped backward. "We were roasting marshmallows, Officer." Tom held up the empty bag, grateful to Lester and Antony.

"We heard gunshots," one policeman said.

"That was us, Officer. We set off some firecrackers." Casey sounded innocent. He pulled a firecracker from his backpack. Bobby dropped his gun behind him into the bushes.

"We're celebrating because we think we're gonna win that Battle of the Bands in Knoxville."

"Celebrate after you win, boys," said one officer. "Not before. Anyway it's not until July, right?"

They checked each boy, searching jackets and backpacks until they were satisfied.

"It's too dry out here for firecrackers, guys," said one officer. "Go on home now."

They kicked dirt over the fire until it was out, until the only light was starlight. The policemen waited for them to finish. Bobby couldn't think of how to retrieve his gun. He'd have to come back later. The boys lifted their backpacks and began to leave the woods, the officers behind them.

They walked at arm's length, unruly and faithful. As they came closer to town, darkness came down like a wing, and a stir of light troubled the streets and gave a charge to their mysterious bodies. They imagined that they were on a quest, and each boy wondered what the other was thinking about.

These eager boys who thought they were, but were not yet, men.

Twenty-one

TOM CANADY LIVED on the edge of town in an old house bought and rebuilt by his father, a contractor. Their home was a show-place, not because of its size but because of its gabled entrance and large sprawling porch. His mother sat on the porch most days, cur-ing her restlessness with bourbon and Coke. She was known in town as a fabulous cook, but she had stopped having dinner parties years ago.

Tom's last image of his mother "alive and well" was one day at the beach four years ago. She had been sickly and cross for days, but the suggestion to spend a week at the beach in South Carolina cheered her and she began to prepare by washing clothes and bringing home groceries. The first day at the beach was bright and sunny, everyone in bathing suits and shorts, the wide beach littered with towels and chairs stuck firmly in the sand. Dogs ran into the water and back out again. Tom and his older brother, Peter, set the cooler down and opened the beach chairs at the edge of the water, and to everyone's surprise, Mrs. Canady—alive in spirit for the first time in months—suggested they go into the water. "Right now," she said. "Let's take a swim right now, before we eat any-thing."

But Peter settled down, scanning for girls, so Tom did the same. Over the last few years, as Tom realized who and what he was, he had created for himself the burdensome role of an impostor. He wore expensive tennis shoes and cut his hair like a jock. He wore khaki pants and large, dark sweaters. Sometimes he wore a tie and endured the gentle ribbing from his friends. He made good grades but flew into a rage if achievement was mentioned. He wanted more than anything else to be one of the gang. At every turn, he tried to imitate his brother. They both pointed to a girl with big breasts walking near the water. She seemed to know they were watching her.

"C'mon," his mother said, but they ignored her, so she went into the ocean, hesitating at first, like a child, then moving full force. Some young girls were riding the waves, and Tom watched his mother join them, laughing and jumping up to ride the surge of a wave. Her face looked suddenly younger. Jack Canady laughed at her, but his laugh sounded more like jeering. Peter joined the laughter, then Tom. She could not hear them. When she returned, her face was flushed with adventure, until she realized they were making fun of her. She was not blessed with a gift for comebacks. "I don't know why you're laughing," she told them, and plopped down defeated into the chair Jack had set up for her. She did not speak for more than an hour. No one seemed to notice.

Tom's memory of her that day brought a kind of shame to his heart, but he told himself that she probably didn't remember it. She was the kind of woman who never demanded kindness from her family and so, therefore, it was not given.

Tom blamed his mother in ways that weren't explainable. He hated to hear her complaints. If she could just take control, he thought, stop drinking and take control, then his family might be happy. If she didn't drink so much during the day, the family would be different. Tom wished his mother could protect him. Each year he felt more estranged from the world. He wanted his father to be proud of him, as he was of Peter. For as long as Tom could remember, his dad had worshipped Peter.

In gym, fifth period, Tom undressed with the other boys as they clowned around in the showers, yelling obscenities, calling each another "fag," flipping towels. Sometimes he got an erection that he tried to hide. He felt desire and tried to think of a way to blame his mother for this embarrassment. All the while his insides seemed to tear away, recoiling from the outer layer of his skin. He tried in his mind to keep the two layers connected. But he grew weary of this effort and began to think he was damaged beyond repair.

There was one story told in the family about Tom, the only story that dwelled on him as a special creature. Whenever they told it, Tom grew quiet with pleasure. And tonight, while sitting around before dinner, they told it again.

"We almost lost you in the months before you were born," his father said jovially.

"I went to bed, stayed in bed for two months," his mother added. She usually told the story, with his father and Peter chiming in. As she told it, her face became animated. "And after all those long days in bed—meals brought to me, nothing to do but sleep and watch TV, read—after all those days, I went to the hospital in the middle of the night and you were born. But it took twelve hours, because the cord was wrapped around your neck and they had to do a cesarean section. When they lifted you out, when I saw you, I screamed. Your face was so blue, purple really. I thought you were gone. I thought you might never take a breath. Then, of course, they loosened the cord and I heard you cry. And that cry pinked you up."

"The doctor came out to tell me and Peter you were okay," said Jack Canady, taking credit for something, Tom didn't know what.

"Yeah, but earlier they came out to say you might not make it," Peter added. "We didn't expect you to even be alive." Peter liked when the family focused on Tom.

"That doctor thought you were a goner. I mean, he thought you might not be all right." His mother shook her head. "Mentally," she said. "And just look how smart." She raised her arm toward Tom, celebrating his mental capabilities.

"I don't know," said Peter. "He's pretty screwy. I think that cord did something to him." Tom had grown so skinny in the last two years that his knees stuck out, and the family had begun to call him Knobs. Tom didn't mind the nickname.

Peter and Tom wrestled momentarily until their father suggested they all go out to dinner. He had completed one wing of the new hospital last week. He wanted to celebrate.

"Oh, and Tom," his father said. "You got a call from Mr. Davenport. He wants to hire you to teach that boy of his, Johnny, to show him some of your spearfishing expertise. Your bow and arrow still in good condition?"

"Yessir."

"Well, make him pay you, son. You don't have to do it, but if you do, get some decent pay. He's been trying for years to turn that boy into a man. Maybe you can do it."

Peter would be home all weekend, and Tom's favorite time was being with Peter on Saturday and Sunday afternoon as they lounged around, hair tousled, faces blowsy with naps, half dressed, a football game blaring, the blinds drawn. Their father would leave about midafternoon to check on some site. Peter and Tom stayed the course, drowsing until five-thirty or six, then they walked into town for a burger, maybe to see a movie. What would he do with himself when Peter was stationed far away? What would the house be like without his brother? Would his parents behave differently? His mother would surely continue to drink.

Tom knew Johnny Davenport, had known him as Crow's kid brother, but he hadn't really noticed him until a fire drill at school the previous fall. The students filed out into the halls, moving into the side yards of the school. The principal stood on the platform set up for the cheerleaders and announced the threat of a fire in the middle school cafeteria. Smoke had filled the halls on the first floor. He sent everyone home. Police swarmed the grounds, and an air of both menace and freedom descended upon the day.

As Tom left for home, he saw Johnny walking alone toward a

car. He saw him but did not at first recognize who it was. Johnny had grown larger in the last year, his muscles filling out. He had always seemed puny and thin, an earnest-looking boy, but since his father had sent him to a camp with a ropes course, his body had changed. Tom felt drawn to him. He didn't look at all like Crow. Had he ever been drawn to Crow?

Johnny wore ratty jeans, torn on one side. His baggy shirt looked jaunty, and he had a Band-Aid on his arm. The effect was good. His eyes were dark blue fields, small flecks of green inside, his smile pretty, like a girl's. Tom felt a strong attraction to him. He didn't want to. He didn't want to be attracted to boys. There had been one girl in the eighth grade that he thought he could like; but when he pursued her, he felt sorry for her instead. Love turned almost immediately to pity.

What in his mind was not to be possible, not to be part of his life, not even open for examination, was now skirling around in his head. Everything suddenly looked too small for this place in the world, for this town.

When Johnny waved, Tom felt embarrassed. He caught up to him and walked him to the car, where his father was waiting. Johnny got in and Mr. Davenport spoke to Tom, asking him about his hobbies and what he did at his father's construction sites. When Tom mentioned spearfishing, Mr. Davenport zeroed in on it, saying that Johnny might like to try it sometime.

"Sure," said Johnny with very little enthusiasm. "It sounds okay."

Tom waved goodbye to Johnny and imagined that Johnny held his look longer than usual, eyes bright as marbles.

A high fog hovered in the tops of trees, and birds could be heard but not seen. The day felt full of quiet promises. The thought of Johnny carrying his books in a small orderly pile, climbing into the car, overeager and shaggy, made Tom's heart open. The taste on his tongue felt hopeful. As Tom walked onto the porch of his house, he entered as if he were the ambassador of good news, his posture straight-backed, ceremonial.

"What happened at school today?" his father yelled. "It's all over the news. That fire at the school."

"It was nothing. We got out early because of all the smoke. Something in the cafeteria."

"Peter's gone," his mother said. Her voice slurry, a chuckle, an incoherent sentence, then, "He said to tell you goodbye."

That night, as Tom lay in bed, stars, cold as knives, sharpened themselves against the dark sky and a triangle of moonlight fell into the room across the floor and onto the sheet that covered his legs. Tom thought he could feel the weight of the moonlight on his arms and legs, a heaviness working over his body like quicksilver.

Twenty-two

OVER THE PAST couple of years Johnny had spent more time with his father than he imagined possible. They drove to Atlanta to see the Braves play Cincinnati. Carl took him fishing or frog-gigging. Sometimes Crow came with them. They hiked and camped out in the woods. They went hunting. Johnny came back from these excursions exhausted and bored. He hated fishing the most. He began to dread his father's call to come downstairs.

For Christmas Johnny got a bow and arrows from his father. "I've asked Tom Canady to show you about shooting at fish with a bow and arrow," Carl told Johnny. "He'll take you out on Saturdays. Tom's really good. His father says he's better than Peter at this."

Johnny made a noise of assent.

Carl tried to reassure him. "It'll make a difference to be good at something, Johnny."

"I'm good at things now," said Johnny. "I'm the best in my art class, and in math I'm second highest, and I've read more books than any of the other guys in my homeroom."

Carl smiled. "Well, I know that, and that's all fine, son. But now we need to really toughen you up. And I'm just the one to do it." Carl laughed a hard laugh. He didn't see Johnny's expression as he turned away.

"What's gotten into Dad?" Crow asked. They were sitting on the porch. "He seems frantic to take you places."

"He thinks I'm a pussy."

"He say that?"

"Not straight out. He's acting like he wants me to get over something. He hates that I like cooking and painting and stuff."

Crow laughed. "He's trying to make you like him. He did that to me too."

"But it worked with you. You didn't mind it. I wish he'd stop. Now I have to spend Saturday mornings learning how to shoot a bow and arrow—with Tom Canady."

"Je-sus, Dad doesn't know what he's doing. Can you get out of it? You want me to talk to him?"

"I don't think so. How bad can it be?"

"Listen, Tom's into drugs sometimes." Crow paced the room. "I don't want you around him. Don't go."

"I thought he was your friend."

"He is. He probably won't give you anything, but he's got a reputation now for carrying it around."

"I've never tried it. Never even smoked. Have you?"

"Well. A few times."

"What's it like?"

"Better than being drunk."

"I've never been drunk either."

"Don't take anything from Tom, hear? And if you ever want to try something, pot, whatever, come to me. I want to be with you if you try anything."

Crow stood to go into the kitchen. "Don't mention what I said about Tom to any of your friends."

"I won't," Johnny said. "I don't have any friends." He laughed. "You're my best friend, Crow." Crow laughed, but he knew it was true.

The next Saturday morning a mist hung over the ground until nine-thirty. By ten, Tom arrived at the house in his Camry. Johnny was ready, waiting on the front steps.

Tom drove several miles out of town and they walked straight to a clearing, where a canvas bull's-eye was mounted on a bale of hay. Johnny opened the car door and got out. He helped Tom carry equipment.

They hadn't talked much on the ride there. Johnny had asked Tom about his trophies and medals and Tom answered, but he didn't expand beyond the basic details, so they rode the last few miles in silence. Just before they got out of the car, Tom said, "Your dad said he thought you didn't want to do this."

Johnny nodded. "He thinks it'll be good for me." They both laughed, sharing a joke about fathers.

Tom took out his bow and handed the arrows to Johnny. "Well?" he said.

"Well, what?"

"Is that right? About you not wanting to do this?"

"Pretty much right, but it's okay," said Johnny.

"Bastard," said Tom.

Johnny didn't know if Tom meant him or his dad.

Tom showed him how to hold the bow, how to aim by resting his hand against his cheek, how to hold his shoulders in the right position. He showed him how to place the arrow on the string, how to make the string taut so the arrow wouldn't fly off. He stood behind Johnny and held his arms, letting him feel the strength it took to pull back the bow just right, then the fun of letting the arrow go, letting it fly toward a target.

"This is great," Johnny said.

"Yeah, it's all right."

They shot arrows for thirty minutes. Johnny sometimes shot without instruction. Tom sometimes instructed, standing behind Johnny, breathing into his hair. "Your hair smells like shampoo," Tom said.

"I washed it this morning." Johnny wondered if Tom might be angry because he had washed his hair, if this would seem feminine and wrong.

"Smells good," he said, smiling. "Why don't you take off your coat? It'll make it easier to hold the bow."

"Naw."

Tom pulled off his jacket, letting his shirt ride up to reveal a hard body, a tight waist. He put his jacket on the ground and turned to see if Johnny was watching. He was, and Tom smiled.

The tone between them had changed from one of discomfort to something like camaraderie.

"Are you afraid of me?" Tom asked.

For some strange reason Johnny was not surprised or jarred by the question. "I don't think so."

Tom suggested that Johnny try some arrows that had a different kind of feather. He explained how arc and speed differed from one arrow to another, depending on the type of feather. Johnny grew interested. He could smell Tom's hair oil and the odor of his skin.

Tom stood behind Johnny, pushing his body against him and pulling back the bow, letting it strain against Johnny's arms and wrists, feeling a tautness develop in both bow and string. He held Johnny's arms like that for a few seconds, told him to aim for the middle of a far tree, then release. When he did, the arrow moved straight toward the middle, hitting slightly off center. Tom kissed Johnny quickly on the cheek in congratulation, then pulled away. Johnny was startled and could think of nothing to say.

Tom put his jacket back on. "We've got to get back," he said. "I've got to go somewhere this afternoon. My dad'll kill me if I'm late."

"Okay." They hustled to pick up arrows that had gone astray.

"One's missing," Tom yelled.

"I got it. It landed in a bush."

"First lesson," said Tom. "Something's always gonna land in a bush." He smiled, but his mouth barely moved and he gave Johnny a long, serious look. "So," he said. "See you next week?"

"Okay," said Johnny. The ride home wasn't much different

from the ride there—not much talking. And when Johnny got out, Tom said, "You okay?"

"Yeah," said Johnny, because he thought maybe his dad was right, and this was how it was supposed to be. If he felt different, maybe the differentness was this. "I'm okay," and he gave Tom back the same smile Tom had given him—one that had in it the very meaning of hiddenness.

Twenty-three

BEFORE GOING OUT with Crow on that March night, Sophie had bathed and put lotion all over her body. She had seen Crow almost every day for the past three weeks, and it seemed that they talked on the phone more times a day than she talked with her mother.

"This might be getting out of hand," Rita told her. "After tonight, I want to put a limit on the number of times you can go out in one week. It's ridiculous. You are too young."

Sophie didn't want to argue with her mother. She knew what she and Crow planned to do tonight, and she didn't want to bring on any suspicion. "Okay," she agreed. "But there's this party tonight, and we—"

"Where is it?"

"At the Fairchild house. He's a doctor."

"Is Crow driving? Anybody going with you?"

"He's driving. But I don't know. We'll probably be going with some others."

"Crow's too old for you, honey. Why don't you go out with somebody your own age?"

"But I like him."

"Well, I know that." Rita softened. "He hasn't tried anything, has he?"

"Mom."

"Well, has he?"

"No."

"All you have to do is call me. If you want to come home, you call me."

"I will," Sophie promised. Her face shone, and Rita could see that Sophie's excitement was about more than a party.

"I want you home early," she said.

"I will," Sophie agreed.

That night had changed everything for Sophie, and since then her mother had kept everyone away.

"Just until after the trial," Rita said. "I don't want anyone around, except maybe Nikki or Stephanie."

But a few weeks before the trial, Sophie looked up one afternoon and saw Lester in the driveway. He did not approach the door to come in, just stood beside his car, motionless, as if he had been there a long while.

Sophie opened the door. "Lester?" Her voice scratchy, not recognizable.

Lester startled, his restless brown eyes intent on her. He took off his glasses and wiped them on his shirt, then walked to the doorway. "I was afraid to knock. I thought you might be sleeping." A soft breeze eddied against them and lifted Sophie's hair.

"How long have you been out here?" she asked.

"About a half hour." He had stood meditative, his face grim, blank of expectation. He breathed heavily. "I called your mother and she said I could come over."

"Is that true?"

"No. She didn't say I could come over."

"She wouldn't mind your being here though." Sophie grimaced, and she turned to go back inside. Lester followed her in.

"I hate what happened to you," said Lester, shuffling his feet. A gloomy mist emanated from him, and he looked about to cry. "I hate whoever did this. I want to kill them."

"Shhh." Sophie looked around to see if her mother had heard. "Close the door," she said.

He did. "Do you know who did it?"

Sophie shrugged, fixing her eyes on the blue carpet. "I can't remember anything." Sophie spoke uneasily.

"You mean you really don't know?"

Sophie released a low moan. "If I can't remember, I can't accuse anybody, but my mother wants me to." Her eyes had grown prominent in her skull. She could not help but remember how the figures had lingered over her, the musk of their sweat, the twinge before they fell off her. They thought she was unconscious when she saw them leave, not seeing their faces, but just a band of tall shadows walking away, then another shadow coming to her, the tenderness of a touch.

"I saw somebody on the ground that night," Lester said. "Did you know that I was the one who called 9-1-1?"

"Yes, I knew that."

"I didn't know it was you. I wish I had known."

Sophie's hands began to shake, and she sobbed without tears.

Rita came downstairs, surprised to see Lester. "What's going on here?" Her full face regarded them from a distance. Lester sat down in a chair, middle-aged. Rita looked for motive in his face, looked for something not to trust, but didn't find either.

"He came to see me, he's just visiting me," Sophie said.

"Well, I don't think you need any visitors yet." Rita motioned for Lester to leave.

Lester left the room without turning around, but as he got to the door he said, "I'll be back again, Sophie. Is that okay?"

"Yes." Sophie wanted her mother to hear her invite him back.

"I don't want you getting her upset, Lester," Rita said, but Lester had already gone.

Rita led Sophie upstairs, and they changed the sheets on their beds. Regular rituals around the house seemed to calm Sophie. "You want me to wash your hair?" Rita asked.

Sophie nodded.

That night Rita tucked Sophie into bed and lay down beside her. The night hung precipitously above them, as though it might fall at any moment and crush the house.

Twenty-four

CROW'S TESTIMONY HAD gone well, but on the day of summations, Aurelia awoke ready to perform the ritual she always performed on difficult days. She ground coffee and poured four cups of water into the coffeemaker. She took the special mug she always used on days she wanted luck.

Bobby came into the kitchen followed by Dog, his toenails clicking on the linoleum floor. "You using that County Fair mug?" he asked.

"I guess so." She spoke as though it didn't really matter. She felt shy about her superstitions and didn't want Bobby to tell anyone.

Bobby tossed two scoops of kibble into Dog's bowl, filled the water dish, then dropped into a kitchen chair. "You'll drink three cups, then you'll eat something, then you'll go upstairs and brush your teeth, gargle, shower, dress, and drink one more cup. Right?"

Aurelia smiled at how well he knew her. He hadn't teased her this way in how long? A year? She reached for his favorite cereal and brought a carton of milk to the table. He drank from the carton.

"So what do you think would happen if you didn't do all that stuff?" Bobby asked, wiping his mouth with his sleeve.

"Catastrophe probably." She felt happy having him in this mood. "Earthquakes, high winds, lightning."

Bobby got up, dripping cereal, and poured her a cup of coffee, implying, she thought, that he too believed in her charmed habits.

This day might go fine after all. She felt grateful for his playfulness, and wondered if he had any rituals that he himself believed
in. She worried about his sulky moods and the look of slyness that
had lately crept into his eyes.

"You'll be in court today, won't you?" She was breaking their
light banter.

He didn't answer but got up to let Dog outside. He stood with
his back to his mother.

"Bobby? You've only come once."

"I don't think he wants me there."

"Why would you think that? Did he tell you he didn't want you
there?"

"I think he's embarrassed."

"If you don't go, it will seem strange," she told him. "How can
you even consider not going?"

There were questions Bobby wanted to ask. He wanted to ask if
Crow could be found guilty. He could not imagine it. Whenever he
spoke, words started and stopped.

"Jail . . . I just don't . . . what if . . . wild . . . messed up." Simple and edgy, random words came out without composure, like
fire, then collapsed. His mouth turned downward into the mouth of
an old man, the mouth he would have as an old man. But he was
seventeen. He was still a dream dreaming itself, but lately he felt
like a nightmare inside another nightmare, spiraling until he became wide, wide awake.

"I'll probably go," he said. "He'll get off, don't you think he
will?" Bobby asked tentatively.

"His testimony went well," she said.

"Yeah," Bobby said. "There's not a chance they're gonna find
him guilty." He poured a large glass of orange juice and drank it
like it was whiskey. "You think it'll be decided today?"

"Probably not today," she said. "But soon. Maybe today." She
smiled hopefully. "I'll just be glad when it's all over."

•   •   •

At four o'clock Aurelia came home. The jury had deliberated for three hours, and Crow had been acquitted. Bobby had been there. And though Aurelia felt glad, her mind stayed riddled with doubt—not about Crow, but about the broader implications: something terrible was still out there. Something not yet seen. She had watched the judge from Jasper dismiss the jury, saying Crow was free to go. She congratulated Raymond Butler and the Davenport family, but as she left the courthouse Aurelia felt afraid of what had already entered this town. And now, as she entered her house, the rooms, the ceilings, looked different to her.

She ate dinner alone: two hard-boiled eggs, some buttered toast, and tea. She went upstairs wanting to take a bath, but as she passed Bobby's room, she looked in. She had never before snooped through his things, never had an urge to do something she thought was beneath her dignity. But tonight she began to leaf through some papers on his desk and bed. What was she looking for?

"Please, God," she said aloud. "Please. Please."

She kept saying these words, an incantation. As she lifted his covers to straighten the bed, she saw stuck between the headboard and mattress a shiny black gun, a pistol. She jumped, as if it were a snake. She lifted it up, holding it away from her body, and left the room, closing the door quietly.

Aurelia laid the gun on her dresser and ran a bath. She slipped into the tub, moving her body down to let water brush against her breasts. She held soap in her hands, running it over her arms and legs, letting the milky film form on her shoulders. She rubbed her armpits, then her shoulders, the length of her arms, her breasts. She soaped her feet last, wanting to massage them, felt the instep and the tissue surrounding the anklebone. Then she lay back, submerging herself up to her neck.

Was it Bobby's gun, or might it belong to one of the other boys? She imagined Bobby might be keeping it for someone. That was probably it. She tried to remember Bobby as a two-year-old, holding a toy. Do all parents, when they imagine something monstrous their child might have done, think of that child as a baby, or as a one-year-old, a two-year-old struggling to stand, to run, to reach for doorknobs, to pull the tablecloth off onto the floor?

She lifted herself out of the tub and dried her body carefully, as if she were a baby herself. From the bathroom window the last edges of the sun went behind the mountains, and she closed her eyes. She thought of what lay beyond the mountains. She dried her hair and legs with her eyes still closed and thought finally of contacting Robert.

She had loved Robert for eighteen years. But in the end she didn't know what love meant. Love came in so many forms. We love for weakness or strength, she thought, for security or wildness, for money, or beauty, or sometimes for sadness. Whatever reason, the brain turned giddy with self-worth, and self-worth became indelibly linked to the one who was loved.

Then when that person does something outrageous, do we still love him? Do we move away, kill off the loved one, because we can't find ourselves anymore in the definition love provided?

Aurelia had done just this. Robert's actions were finally something Aurelia was not able to absorb. Even back then, when she was still a practicing lawyer, she could not easily allow an infraction of the law or unethical behavior to invade her private world. She prided herself on hard-heartedness. Robert would go to jail for ten years. She would not wait for him. She planned to never see Robert again. She was that moral.

A divorce agreement was drawn and signed, and she moved back to Tennessee, where she had grown up. Aurelia Bailey's career as a judge had earned her a reputation for fairness in her decision making; and the verdicts declared in her courts accorded very well with the principle of justice. For the past six years she had made promises to the community, saying that "the violence creeping into other communities would not urge its way into South Pittsburg, Tennessee." She developed an after-school program and raised money for a youth center, still to be built. She was tough on crime.

Bobby liked to tease his mother about being a "crackdown" judge. He seemed proud of her, but that was last year. Lately he had grown secretive, sullen.

For years Aurelia had refused to answer Robert's letters, but after a time she relented, writing, sending him pictures of Bobby, giving him news of Little League championships, the Bandits. Still, she never allowed their arrangement to change. She felt confident in her decision to raise her son alone. She felt obliged to keep Robert's past from Bobby, and couldn't think of any good that would come from Bobby knowing. But now she felt the urge to ask for Robert's help. Robert had built a new life in Kentucky, and his disgrace (which Aurelia once thought would never leave her mind) was receding.

As she opened her eyes she saw the reflection of her face in the mirror. Her wild auburn hair curled in all directions. The pins she used to tame it in the courtroom had come out, and her hair framed her face like a wreath.

She heard tires on the gravel driveway. She slipped a nightgown over her head, tying her robe around her, and quickly pinned flat some loose strands of hair. She waited for Bobby in the chair where, when he was young, she had rocked him.

Twenty-five

As Bobby drove up to his house, he could see that the light in his mother's bedroom was on. He would go in and say he wasn't feeling well. He didn't want to talk. Dog was waiting in the front hallway, his strong tail whacking the umbrella stand. "Hush, boy," whispered Bobby.

When his foot hit the stair, his mother called out. "Bobby, is that you? Come up here, please." Her voice sounded coarse, strange. When he got to the top of the stairs he could see her in a chair, wrapped in her old brown robe and setting down a book.

"I went to see Crow," he said.

"I figured as much. I waited on you." She kept her eyes focused hard on him, and he could feel the weight of her glare.

"He's all right. I mean, we talked a little while, but he was tired."

"Uh-huh." She stood up, her back to him. She held her book down by her side. "Did you speak to Helen and Carl?"

"No, just Crow."

Bobby felt the tension in the air but didn't know what it was about. When he turned to leave the room, his mother's voice stopped him.

"Bobby?" She took a breath and let it out. She sat back down again. "Why do you have a gun in your room?"

He was sure he had misunderstood her question. "What?" He turned to face her.

"You had a pistol in your room." She took the pistol, which she had laid beside the chair, and lifted it into sight. She put it on her lap. "And I want to know why."

"It's no big deal. It's just something I bought over in Red Bank."

"When?"

"A few months ago."

"You've had a gun in this house for months?"

"Yeah."

"Why?"

"I just wanted to have it. I don't do anything with it. I mean, I take it out sometimes. I shoot at bottles and stuff."

"You can't keep it, Bobby."

"But I bought it with my own money."

"You shouldn't have spent your money on it. You shouldn't have brought something like that into this house, Bobby. Not to mention the danger of it. I can't believe you." She took a deep breath. "What's gotten into you lately?"

"I didn't think that . . . I just bought it."

"You didn't think at all. That's the trouble. I don't want a gun in this house, nor do I want it in your possession. You could be arrested for not having a license, you know."

"Nobody's gonna see it."

"*I* saw it," she said. Then she asked a question that came from the ceiling. "When exactly did you purchase it?"

She seemed suspicious of him now, and he would need to watch what he said. He would need to be friendlier to ease her mind. He tried to let out a weak laugh.

"Sometime in February or March. I don't know the day."

He watched as his mother's expression changed.

"You know," Bobby said, "if I had a dad, he'd understand. If I had a father, he'd let me keep it, I bet."

"Well, there is no father here," his mother said quickly. "So you'll have to live with my lack of understanding about guns.

This mother, who is a judge and sees killings both deliberate and accidental thanks to guns, you'll have to listen to her advice." She took the gun and wrapped it in newspaper. "Where are the bullets?"

"In my room."

"Get them," she said. "I'm turning this in tomorrow."

"Fine." Bobby returned with four bullets and let them fall on the table beside the bed.

Both of them, mother and son, felt warned by the other, and when Bobby turned, his mother said, "Bobby, I worry about you."

"Well, don't." He fingered his ear. "I'm going to bed."

As Bobby got to his bedroom door, he heard his mother go downstairs to lock up and turn off the lights. Dog made two full circles on his dog bed before settling down.

Bobby wondered for a moment: If he lost her approval, would she throw him out? Would she insist that *he* leave, or would *he* have to pretend to be dead? He knew what she was capable of. Still, he would need to tell her about the letter. He longed to see his father. He would tell her tomorrow.

He dreaded going to sleep, dreaded dreaming. His dreams often jolted him awake, made him sit straight up in bed, sweating. Every night he dreamed of gigantic roots going to the center of the earth, gnarly roots that moved around like worms. No trees appeared above the ground in his dream, and the worms hardened before his eyes. He dreamed of Crow in the courtroom, and Sophie's mother, who looked wrung out now, a gray ash on her skin.

Sometimes he saw Rita Chabot in town and wondered if he should speak to her. Once he saw Sophie, coming out of the doctors' building. She didn't see him. He tried to remember kissing her. Why had she let him kiss her?

The next morning it was raining hard, a downpour. He woke with a briny steam on his skin and surged out of bed, going quickly to cup water under the faucet and drink from his hands. The room itself felt cold.

He opened the window. Mud built up in pools beside the brick walk, and he imagined the mud rising, flooding his room. The one word that kept going over and over through Bobby's head was: *Don't. Don't.*

Twenty-six

WHEN THE JURY acquitted Crow, Carl thought the decision was reasonable; Helen didn't care about reasonableness, she gave a rush of breath. And Crow, at the moment the judge dismissed him, didn't understand what had happened, or even if he was really free to go.

Late that same afternoon, Bobby sat with Johnny beneath the tree in Crow's front yard. Helen and Ava sat on the porch. When Louise Burden's car drove up, she waved, her large arm moving up and down out the window.

"Antony and the others are coming in a little bit," she called. Bobby nodded.

Helen embraced Louise just as Carl Davenport's car arrived with Crow riding in the front seat. Bobby stood up to greet him. Crow got out, but he didn't look at anyone. He walked straight to the house and spoke politely to Mrs. Burden.

"Bobby's here," said Helen. She thought Crow hadn't seen him. Bobby followed Crow upstairs. They didn't speak until he closed the door.

"It's over," Crow said. He made a sound, a groan.

Bobby didn't know what to say. "You got off, man," he said, trying to cheer his friend—though he couldn't tell if they were still friends.

Crow had not turned. He kept his back toward Bobby, standing like a tall block of wood.

"This was messed up," Bobby finally said. "Everybody knew you didn't do it. Most of us were just stoned." He looked at his shoes with absorption.

"That's what I kept thinking," said Crow.

"What do you mean?" Bobby pulled back, formal.

"I mean everybody, you know, everybody was out of it." He turned around. "But not me. I wasn't. Neither was Sophie. We'd had some beer, but not much. And look what happened to her. Fuck, Bobby. I just hope they go back and catch the guys who did this. Those goddamn bastards let me go to trial. They must've been real disappointed at the verdict."

"Maybe not," said Bobby. "Maybe they were glad you got off."

"Yeah. Right." Crow's room felt to him like a place in someone else's house. "If the police keep looking, then they're gonna find something, or else maybe Sophie will remember. I haven't even seen her. She won't talk to me. I keep wondering if she thinks I did it."

"She doesn't think that."

Crow sat on his bed. He felt like a balloon empty of anything but air. He breathed out.

Bobby grew uncomfortable in his skin. "Listen, everybody's going to the river tomorrow. You wanna come?"

"What for?"

"We're planning for the Battle of the Bands, which songs and stuff. You can put this behind you now. We can focus on something else. We have a lot of work to do to be ready." He was trying to make his voice sound upbeat.

"Maybe. But, Bobby . . ." Crow's chest became concave. "I don't know if I can still be part of the band. I don't know if I can do anything until they find out who did it."

"But you'll come to the river." The statement seemed to be a question.

Crow could hear the other boys coming up the stairs, his mother leading them. He stood up as Tom opened the door. The boys entered and lined up side by side like posts.

"Listen," Crow said quickly. "I don't wanna be with anybody right now. All I wanna do is sleep."

"That's cool," said Tom. "Bobby tell you about tomorrow?"

"Yeah."

"We thought you'd want to do something," Antony said.

"He does, he does," Tom said quietly.

"C'mon," Lester said. "We'll see you tomorrow, Crow."

They all looked relieved.

"Hell, I'm just tired," Crow told them. "I'm glad it's over, and I'm tired."

"Let's go." Bobby urged everyone out the door. Tom looked slightly irritated, and Casey, who had not said anything, turned to leave.

Helen Davenport stood at the door as the boys drove away. Crow could see her watching them leave. He closed the door to his room and imagined that she watched them until they were out of sight.

The next day Crow went to the river, though he arrived late. He didn't want to go, but his mother urged him to get out, do something, try to get back to normal. The boys were already waiting when Crow reached the river.

Bobby spoke first. "If we're ever gonna get out of this place and make a name for ourselves—"

"Get famous," Casey said.

"—then we've got to decide some things. We've got to decide which songs we want to do, and how we're gonna arrange them."

Crow had brought a spiral notebook filled with songs written several months ago. He put it on the ground. "I might not be part of this," he said. He looked around at their faces, as though he had never seen any of them before. He wanted to be far away; and he also wanted everything to be the way it used to be.

"We can't do it without you," Tom urged. "Not without you and Antony."

"Give him some time," Lester said.

Casey flipped the notebook open to one of the new songs and began to suggest where drums could come in.

"Where's Antony?" Casey asked.

"He couldn't come. He's working at the diner."

They agreed to begin practice on Saturday and Sunday afternoon in Casey's garage, and to make their rehearsals more regular. Crow thought about going home, getting away from them.

"Anybody wanna swim?" Lester said.

"Hell, no," said Crow, "that water's spring-fed." Yet his face clearly showed pleasure in the idea of doing something they used to do.

"C'mon, man." Casey pulled his T-shirt over his head.

"Listen, Crow," Tom said. "What happened, I mean you getting arrested and all. That really sucked."

"But now we can all get back to normal," said Casey. "Hang out again. Kick ass in the band competition."

"What happened didn't just happen to Crow." Lester grew angry. "It's not just Crow it happened to, you know." He was yelling.

"Je-sus, Lester!" Tom shouted. "Don't be so self-righteous."

"I mean, what happened that night?" Lester looked as if he might hit someone. "What the hell happened?" His tone sounded accusing.

"You tell us," snapped Casey. "You were there that night. You think we know any more than you do?"

"Everybody shut up," said Tom. "This is not the kind of shit Crow needs to hear today."

Crow shook his head, silent. "She won't even talk to me." He looked stunned admitting this. She had heard what he said in court. Had she heard everything? He had had to say it all. Did she hate him for what he said?

Everyone grew quiet, then Bobby asked, "Lester, you've talked to her. What does she say to you?"

"She doesn't say anything. That's the problem. She can't remember."

"Maybe she shouldn't remember," Casey said.

"I want her to remember whatever she has to to be all right," said Lester.

"Je-sus, Lester! Why don't you act like a reasonable person instead of somebody who fucks his hand." Tom looked disgusted and began to take off his shirt. Everybody thought he was going to fight Lester, but instead he slipped off his pants and jumped from a high rock into the river.

Casey grumbled loudly, calling them all pricks, then took off his own clothes and jumped from the rock. He landed flat on his belly and rose out of the water, laughing and complaining. For one moment their lives felt innocent again.

Bobby and Lester began to remove their shirts and jeans, then Crow followed, last. They went into the river, not leaping from the rock but going in running, their particular alienation visible to the world. Sun broke out from a passing cloud and threw sparkles onto the water.

They dove and rose up like dolphins, ducking, pushing each other underwater, pretending mischief. They didn't want to think about the price it took to be men, wanting instead to be the blaze, the rage, the danger they *thought* were men. So they willed themselves back in time to when everything was just a game, their affection for each other real, not easily dismissed.

III

Evidence of Things Not Seen

Twenty-seven

THE TRIAL WAS over, but nothing seemed over for Sophie. She still had sleepless nights and was afraid to close her eyes for fear that something terrible might happen in her dreams, or in her life. Teachers had allowed her to finish up the year's work by taking exams at home. She had passed, or they had passed her on the basis of her previous work. Finally her mother had suggested that Sophie see a therapist on a daily basis, instead of just twice a week; and in only one week of daily visits, Rita saw a change in Sophie's sleeping habits.

Today Rita walked into Sophie's room to find her sleeping on the floor in a bed of blankets, a sheet folded neatly under her arms—a pillow for her head. In this manner she had slept all night for several nights in a row.

"So what did he say?" Rita asked when Sophie returned from one of her sessions with the psychologist.

"You're not supposed to ask me that," Sophie said.

"I mean about sleeping on the floor."

"He said it was fine and that when I wanted to get back into the bed I could, but to use the same blanket and use the sheet for a pillow. He said it was fine."

Rita opened the refrigerator door, took out some Cheez Whiz, and got Ritz crackers from a tin box she kept on the counter. "Sit down. Let's eat gobs of cheese on these crackers like we used to do."

"I don't want gobs of cheese," said Sophie. Her hair fell forward.

Rita opened the box and used a spoon to glob the cheese onto crackers.

"Mom!" Sophie smiled. "That's gross."

Rita opened her mouth wide and put the whole cracker in, her cheeks puffing out like a fat lady's.

"Give me one." Sophie spooned a huge hunk of cheese onto her cracker, then ate it in small bites. Her eyes looked rested, finally. "You know what I've been thinking about?"

"What?" Rita spooned another dollop of cheese onto a cracker.

"When we flew down here to look for a house?"

"Yeah."

"You fell asleep and I looked out the window in the plane. We were *above* the moon. It was a half-moon, and it was just coming up. And I was looking down at it. Looking *down* to see the moon. It was weird."

"I don't think I've ever done that." Rita reached for another cracker. "Did you paint that? I think I saw one of your drawings that looked like that."

"Yeah, I tried." Sophie changed the subject. "Did anybody call?"

On Friday nights Nikki and Stephanie often came to the house. They brought movies and sometimes spent the night. Or sometimes Lester Dunphy came by. Lester was the only boy Sophie wanted to see; though at times she seemed to be waiting for Crow to call or come over. Rita didn't know what to think.

"Nobody called," she said. "Sophie, tell me, what does Nikki say to you? Do you talk to her about what happened?"

"Yes." Sophie made a little hissing noise with the word *yes*. "She said she knew somebody this happened to, not as bad as mine, but she knew a girl."

"And how is that girl now?" Rita asked hopefully.

"She's okay, I guess. She moved away. Nikki thinks maybe she was pregnant."

"Oh, honey. Did they find who did it?"

"Yeah, but nothing happened."

"You mean the man never went to jail?" Rita had trouble keeping her voice at a level pitch.

Sophie began to cry. When she cried, blotches appeared on her face like red marks, and though this had been true since she was a little girl, when it happened now Rita could not bear to see it.

"Listen, honey," she said. "If you remember who did this I promise you that whoever it was will be brought to justice. They have to be."

Sophie shook her head, her hands in her lap.

Rita thought for a moment. She was trying to be careful, trying to discern how much Nikki might be affecting Sophie's actions. "What does Lester say?"

"He tries to help me remember."

"Well, he's your real friend, Soph. Did you tell this to Dr. Brooks?"

"Not yet," said Sophie, indignation in her voice.

"Maybe you should. See what he says."

"He doesn't say what I should or shouldn't do, Mom. He just helps me decide."

"Okay." Rita closed the tin of crackers and put the cheese away. "Okay. That's good."

"Lester's coming over," said Sophie. "He's bringing a movie."

"You want me to fix some dinner for the two of you?"

"I may never eat again." Sophie smiled. "But yeah, that'd be good. Fix some burgers."

Something new had happened. Not only had Sophie smiled, but she also gave a small laugh-sound. The moment between them felt like a Before moment, before anything bad had happened, and Rita knew healing had begun. She was briefly hopeful, and determined to make the moment fit realistically into the day.

Twenty-eight

HOW MANY TIMES had Crow tried to speak to Sophie? He had lifted the phone twenty, thirty times; he had followed her in town. But whenever Sophie saw him she looked mortified. He wrote notes to her, but they went unanswered.

Then, on the Saturday before school let out, Crow saw Sophie come out of the drugstore, walking toward him. He stopped. When he saw her, her hand moved up to her face. She touched her cheek, neck, and hair. Crow approached, trying to think of what to say. At night he spent hours planning what he might say to her, but now all words went out of his head.

She held his gaze and even greeted him, though it was only a nod. So Crow asked, "Did you get my last note?" Crow had written a note a few weeks ago, and left it in Sophie's mailbox, asking to talk to her. He had a birthday present he wanted to give her. Her birthday had been the last day of May. She was fifteen.

"Yes," she said. Her voice sounded flat. "I got it."

He fell into walking beside her. "Where're you going?"

"Home."

"Can I drive you?"

She didn't give assent, but she didn't object either, so they got into his car and rode in silence until they reached Sophie's house. Crow followed her across the yard to her porch. Sophie motioned for him to sit on the steps.

"For a while, I thought you might have done it," Sophie said. "I thought you might have hurt me."

"No. No."

"I know you didn't, but that's what I thought at first."

"And now?" *Maybe she has remembered,* Crow thought. "Have you been talking to the police? Have you told them?" *Maybe she knows who did it.* "I mean, do you know?"

His barrage of questions made her flinch.

"I'm sorry. I shouldn't have asked. I just wanted—"

"I can't remember," she said. "Anyway . . ."

"Anyway what?"

"I might go away. I might go back to Montana."

"You're leaving?"

"I haven't told anyone yet, except Dr. Brooks. He's my therapist. And he thought it was a good idea. You know, to go for a few weeks." Sophie looked at him.

"Oh," he said. "I thought you meant for good."

"No."

Crow looked out across the yard. "Do you hate me for what I said in court?"

"I know you had to say that."

"But do you hate me?"

"I don't think so."

"I wanted to call you," Crow said. Sophie remained silent. "I didn't know if I had any right to talk to you. I couldn't get up the nerve for a while."

They sat stiffly for a moment.

"Are you still drawing? You know, painting?"

"No," she said, but it was a lie. She had been sketching for the past three days, watching something lurk at the edge of the paper. Then, when she tried to paint, she lost track of the edge of the canvas. She painted beyond that edge, spreading paint onto the wall or just moving the brush into the air, letting paint drip onto the rug.

"No, I'm not painting anything." She fingered her necklace, a gold chain fine as lace.

Crow made a sound in his throat, primitive and coarse. "When are you leaving?" he asked.

"As soon as I can."

"Sometimes," said Crow, "sometimes you imagine yourself in a situation, you know? And you think about how you might act, and in your mind you always act the right way? But when it comes, and you don't act the way you thought, when you turn out to be somebody worse than you imagined—there's no way to think about it. No way to make it right."

They waited, a terrible hiatus before Sophie spoke. "You said you had a present for me."

Crow stood up. "It's in my car. Want me to get it?"

"Okay." Sophie's interest was perfunctory, but curious. "Yeah."

Crow went to the car. Sophie called, "Crow?"

"Yeah?"

"Why did you get me a present?"

"For your birthday," said Crow. His shoulders sagged with something secret even to his own mind.

"I know that." She challenged Crow to be more than he was. "But I just wondered why, exactly."

Crow went across the street and leaned into the backseat of his car. He came back with a box wrapped in green tissue paper and a white satin ribbon; but when he got to the porch, Sophie wasn't there. The front door was closed, so he put the present on the porch steps and left. Their time together had ended, he thought, and nothing would be good between them again.

Twenty-nine

THE FOLLOWING MORNING Sophie asked her mother if she could go back to Montana for a few weeks. Her voice, when she asked, sounded shaky. "I want to go away, just go away. I called Grace, and she said it would be fine. Her mother said so too."

"Oh, Sophie. You can't leave now. You can't just run away."

"I don't think I *am* running away."

"Then why do you want to go?"

"I want to be somewhere where people don't look at me like I'm a freak. Grace won't do that."

"Have you told Grace?"

"I told her that I'd been hurt. I didn't say anything else. I think she guessed. She got real quiet."

"Even if you go," said Rita, "you have to come back." She sank back in her chair. "You finally have to face whoever did this. And what about your sessions with Dr. Brooks?"

"I already told him. He said I could call him anytime I wanted to. He said he would talk to me twice a week by phone. Or more."

"Well." Rita sighed. "I guess I could go with you. Charlie wouldn't mind if I missed a week or so at the store."

Sophie shook her head. "I want to go by myself."

Rita shifted. "Not for the whole summer."

Sophie cleared her throat. "How long?" She had her hands in the pocket of her sweater and could feel the card that Dr. Brooks had given her, listing both his office and his home numbers. "If I stay more than three weeks, then you can come for a visit." She leaned toward her mother. "I really want to do this," she said.

Before choosing a therapist for Sophie, Rita had discussed with friends the advantage of seeing a man instead of a woman. She had made the right choice. Dr. Brooks had the patience that Sophie needed, and his willingness to be available had given Sophie a kind of confidence. Sophie had told Dr. Brooks that sometimes he seemed to say the things her father might have said. Sophie needed to believe again in the trustworthiness of men.

"When you leave town," Dr. Brooks told Sophie, "you might begin to remember things."

His words had made her sit bolt upright in her chair. Sophie had looked at him as if he were telling her something that had never occurred to her. The thought of what had happened could not enter her mind completely; but neither could the horror of that night leave her head.

"And you can call me. Anytime at all."

Dr. Brooks also talked once a week with Rita. He did not want the rage of the mother to affect the daughter's progress.

"Every time I pass a boy in town," Rita told Dr. Brooks, "whether it's Tom Canady, or Bobby Bailey, or Lester Dunphy, I think: *Was it him? Was it him?*" Rita kept her hands held tightly together, pushing against her knees as she spoke. "And Lester, he comes over to the house all the time. Sophie's glad to see him. He's been a friend to her, but I look at him and, Dr. Brooks, I want to scream. I think, *What if he did this? What if I'm letting the boy who did this into the house?*"

"Don't, Rita. Lester was in the Fairchild house at the time it happened. He was with five or six people. Let him be a friend to her."

"But I look at him, or I see Bobby Bailey walk across the street to catch the bus, and I think, *Did he do it?* Judge Bailey has called me several times, but I can't talk to her. I seem to hate everybody."

"Even Sophie?"

Rita could not answer.

"Rita," he said. "You must guard yourself against bitterness."

Rita could see what Sophie liked about this man. No matter what you said, he made you feel that everything was going to be all right.

That night Rita went to Sophie's room. "You still want to visit with Grace?"

"Are you letting me go?"

"Well, I've been thinking, maybe it's a good idea."

"Really? You mean it?"

"I'll call her mother tonight. It might be just the right thing for you."

"Oh, Mama." Before Rita closed the door Sophie said, "How long?"

"What?"

"How long can I stay?"

"As long as you want," Rita said, but before she closed the door completely, she added, "but not the whole summer."

She could hear Sophie's sigh in the room's air.

In the airport Rita told Sophie that she was glad that Grace probably knew. "Now you won't have to explain. Maybe that's good."

"Mom, everything I do in therapy is trying to find ways to talk about it." Sophie smiled. The act of leaving South Pittsburg was making her strong again. "Did you tell Grace's mother?"

"I didn't think I should. That will be up to you." Rita handed Sophie the tickets. "You can stay longer if you need to."

"I want to stay forever."

Rita shook her head.

"I know, I know," said Sophie. "When does the plane leave?"

"In forty-five minutes. You want something to eat?"

"Sure."

Rita put her arm around her daughter. "You are being very brave, you know."

Sophie's lip quivered and she began to shake uncontrollably. Rita took her into a restroom and held her until she stopped shaking.

"It's going to be all right," she said. She rocked Sophie and casually wiped away some drool that had appeared in the corner of her mouth. The medicine Sophie took made her drool sometimes. "We'll work through this. And we'll find who did it, and we'll send them to jail." Rita's voice sounded hard, determined.

"But people say that . . ." Sophie stopped and began to cry.

"What do people say, darling?"

Sophie shook her head. Several women came into the restroom, walking by, staring. Rita led Sophie back out to a place by the window where they could be alone. The loudspeaker announced the boarding of her plane.

Sophie continued. "I'm afraid if I accuse somebody, that the accusation will backfire. Lawyers could make it look like it was my fault, the guys could get off and—"

"And you think that could happen to you?"

"If I accuse somebody, they'll say that I wasn't wearing clothes, they'll say it was my fault. And I'd had some beer, so that too." Her words came out in huge sobs.

"Oh, honey. Nobody could blame you for this."

"But Nikki said that when her cousin went through this, the boys got off. They said her cousin was drunk, and that she led them on. They weren't found guilty, and the girl looked like a slut. That's what Nikki said."

Rita leaned back slowly. "Nikki's wrong." She tried to keep her voice calm. "Listen to me," she said. "Nothing like that is going to happen to you, Sophie. It didn't happen at Crow's trial, did it?"

"I didn't testify," said Sophie. "But if I did remember, and had to get up on the stand . . ."

Rita kept her hand on Sophie's shoulder, thinking. "That happens when a girl has a reputation for leading boys on, or has even slept with the boy accused—not in a case like this, not in this case." Rita knew Sophie's fear was legitimate. "I can ask Judge Bailey about this. She's called me several times and I haven't returned her calls, but I can call and ask her about this."

"You could?"

"Yes."

Sophie sat up and wiped her face with the hem of her blouse. "Okay."

"Sophie?"

"What?"

"Do you remember something about that night, and you're not saying the names because of what Nikki said?"

"I remember some of it," she said. "But not a face. I remember things like somebody's hair, and a smell, and a watch ticking. I remember a watch next to my ear." She began to cry again.

"Oh, honey." Rita reached again to comfort her.

Sophie stood up, a fast motion. "Let's go," she said. "I want to get on the plane. I want to get there."

Thirty

ONE AFTERNOON IN late March, Tom saw Johnny walk across the school parking lot with Melanie Bowen. Melanie was taller than Johnny, willowy, with hair past her shoulders. She leaned her head toward him, listening. Tom stood against the wall and watched them go past. Melanie laughed at something Johnny said. Johnny sounded confident, older. He put his arm around her waist, and she wore it like a blessing.

The next morning, Tom got to school early and swung around the north side of the building to the middle school entrance. When he saw Johnny approaching, he jogged over to meet him. "Meet me at the old house later. I have something to tell you."

"Today?" Johnny looked irritated by the request.

"Yeah."

"I can't stay long," said Johnny.

Tom nodded.

For the past few weeks they had been meeting at an old abandoned house. They sat on a pallet, ate food from McDonald's or Burger King, and sometimes smoked pot. They spent hours touching each other, exploring what they felt.

Now Johnny showed up at the old house a little late, and the two boys sat a few moments before speaking.

"So what's up?" Johnny asked.

"How's Crow doing? How do you think he's doing?"

"He's okay." Johnny sat down on the floor. "Is that what you wanted to talk about?"

"Not really."

"Then what?"

"It's just that I finally know something about myself," Tom said. It was not the first time he had confided in Johnny. Outside this old house Tom was simply who he was, but in this place he felt connected to the world. "I mean, I finally know what I am, and I'm glad. I think I'm glad I'm like this."

"Like what?"

"You know what. We're homo, man. We're gay. I suspected it before, but now I'm sure." His face shone with excitement. "I'm not even ashamed anymore."

Johnny got up.

"Hey, you okay?"

"Naw. I'm okay. I'm just not as sure as you are."

"Hey, I know. C'mon. I wouldn't have been sure either. Not at your age. I know what you mean."

"No you don't." Johnny had gone along with everything at first, curious about sex, any kind of sex. He liked the feeling of a shared privacy with Tom. It was as though they both kept a secret life, and for a while Johnny thought his father's suspicions about him might be right. But as time went on, he felt that his secret life was not a gay one, just private. Still, he had learned something about sex, about risk.

Now Tom was pushing him to admit something he didn't need to admit. "You are. You know you are. Hell, you couldn't do this if you weren't."

"Lots of guys try this," said Johnny.

"You been talking about us to other people?" Tom turned and trained his eyes on Johnny.

"No way. But I know other guys who've tried it. They've told me."

"I know what you're doing," said Tom. He was angry. "You

want this to be something that you just tried out, but you don't want to say it's who you are."

"It *isn't* who I am." Johnny stood up. "I'm not homo. I thought I might be, but I don't think so now."

Tom grew rigid. "You can't just turn it on and off like that. You can't just decide you're not this way."

"I'm not deciding. I'm just not. I know it now."

"You been talking to Crow? You said anything to anybody about this?"

"No."

"So are you into somebody else?"

Johnny hesitated. "Not exactly."

"You know what I think?" Tom said, trying to sound understanding. "I think you don't know how to handle it and you're trying to be like everybody else. But I'll tell you something, you'll have to deal with it sometime. I tried going out with girls too."

"I didn't say I was doing that."

"Yeah, but that's what you're doing. I've seen you with Melanie." Tom leaned close and spoke low. "Maybe you just want somebody to see you with a girl. Is that it? Hell, I've been there."

"I like her," said Johnny. "I like being around her. Listen, I don't want to do this anymore. I'm not like you."

"The hell you're not."

Johnny picked up his book bag, leaving.

"That's okay. You'll be back."

"I won't come back," said Johnny. "I won't." His voice sounded adult, severe.

Tom picked up the pallet and his own book bag and walked toward the car. "Let's go."

"I won't come back," Johnny said again.

"I heard you," Tom said. "I said let's go."

All the way home Johnny wondered what would happen if he told someone—Crow, or the police, or Coach Post—about what Tom had done to him. If he made it look as if Tom had molested him, then sympathy might fall his way. He didn't know if he could do that.

That night Helen Davenport noticed a change in Johnny's mood. He had been moping around all evening, snapping at anyone who spoke to him.

"Johnny? What's wrong with you? Are you sick?"

"Yeah, I think so."

She felt his forehead with her cheek. "No fever," she said. "But maybe you should stay home tomorrow."

"Maybe I will."

"Oh, I forgot," she said. "Tom Canady called." She laughed. "I thought he was calling for Crow, but he asked to speak to you. Was it about a lesson?"

"He said something today about one. I don't know." Johnny forced a cough, two coughs. "I don't want to talk to anybody though. I'm going up to my room."

He walked upstairs, his gait ramshackle, like a man crippled, or shot.

Thirty-one

WITHOUT JOHNNY, THE things in Tom's room became arbitrary: huge posters on the wall, old army boots belonging to Peter, a baseball from the championship game when he was eleven. They became things he could have or not have. He didn't care now. He began to feel numb, and longed for just an inkling of emotion. Before, with Johnny, everything he owned carried weight. The things in his room told him who he was. He had felt his whole life opening ahead of him, but now a great train had stopped and let him off in a place he hadn't seen before.

Johnny. Now there was nothing left to dream about. Tom's bones had been unstrung and strung back again. Johnny had dissolved the embarrassment of loneliness, and music that had been their dream still swam in Tom's head. Their intimacy had ended weeks ago, but his mind still rang every moment with what he had lost.

The sheriff had questioned Tom repeatedly about that April night—about who or what he had seen. Today they brought him to the station, questioned him in a small room.

Tom answered as best he could, though a few times, when they caught him in a lie, he imagined a blade of judgment falling suddenly, and when it did, things in the corners of his mind blazed upward. When he left the police station the sky above the horizon glowed like a candle.

On the way home, not five miles outside of town, Tom hit a dog crossing the road. It had come out of nowhere. At first he thought the dog was dead, but then he saw its legs move slightly, eyes looking up. Its small body shivered.

Tom's first impulse was to lift the animal and take it to the vet, but the idea seemed like more trouble than he wanted right now. He turned the dog over with the toe of his shoe and heard it whimper. It was a light-colored terrier, wiry and scruffy-looking. Its eyes looked glazed, shiny, but its back legs still trembled.

If he could get the dog to the car, maybe he could save it. He leaned to lift the body up carefully, but the dog snapped and growled, tore Tom's shirt. So he thought to leave it, let it die naturally, but he couldn't do it—the dog was in such pain. Tom looked around for a big stick and saw a limb about the size of a baseball bat. He picked it up to feel its heft. It felt right in his hands. He held the limb firmly, and as he saw the dog move to stand, he hit quickly, hard; and to his great surprise the dog let out a high, jerky sound, then it crawled a couple of feet forward. Tom hit the dog once more. Blood came out in spurts onto the bat, spattering Tom's shirt and face.

"My God. Die! Why don't you fucking die!"

The dog's feet jerked, but reflexively this time. The head split open from ear to mouth. Gray matter came out of its ears and eyes. Tom kept hitting, thinking it was probably dead but wanting to make sure. He had to be sure. He was grateful that no cars had passed while he performed these machinations.

That night his mother asked Tom how he got blood on his shirt.

"I cut my hand on an arrow," Tom said. "It was just a little cut, but it kept on bleeding."

She looked at his hand. "When?"

"Can't even see it now," he said. "I mean, I can't figure out how so much blood came from such a little cut. Hell, I can't even find it now."

"It is a lot of blood," she said. "I won't tell your father."

Tom looked at her quickly, without blinking, but she'd already turned away and was gathering piles of dirty clothes to wash. "You want anything else washed?" she asked.

The air seemed full of friction. Tom slipped off one shoe, then the other. He pulled off his socks and put them into the pile of clothes. "I'm not hiding anything," he said.

"I didn't say you were." She took his socks and smelled them, from habit. "If you'd been hiding it, I wouldn't have seen the blood on your shirt, would I?" She looked at him to see if he was amazed.

"I found a dog in a ditch coming home," he said. "I tried to help it and got blood on me." He liked the feel of confession.

"The preacher's dog? The preacher can't find his dog. Where is he?"

"He's gone. He was suffering so much that I put him out of his misery."

"You killed him?"

"He'd been hit. There wasn't anything anybody could do. He was suffering."

"We don't have to say this to anyone," his mother said. She looked more worried than she'd looked earlier.

"There are worse things," Tom said.

His mother didn't know what he meant. Before she left the room with her basket of clothes, she turned and asked, "Why didn't you just take the dog to the vet, Tom?"

"I'm telling you," said Tom. "This dog was gone. I tried to pick him up. He wouldn't let me."

When his mother closed the door, Tom couldn't stop thinking of the dog and how his own arms felt holding the branch, how they felt coming down on the dog. He couldn't get out of his mind the dog trying to get up, his paw just before he fell, slipping in the dust, his nose lifting a fraction before he was dead.

That night was the first night Tom went to bed with a sense of hope, a plan. He told his parents good night, and his mother noted what a good mood he was in. He got into bed and closed his eyes—it seemed a good thing, to be out of misery. He had given the dog what the dog most desired.

There are worse things than death, he thought. When he opened his eyes, the skylight above his bed was dark. The night held only a tinge of light.

Tom felt a dim anguish emerging, and imagined that life might be less preferable than death. His plan to leave with Johnny for San Francisco was not a plan now. It was less than a dream. All of his friendships were dissolving, and he was not the person he thought he was.

Later, when he opened his eyes again, the sun was full up. As he glanced at the clock he heard the faint sound of machinery in the distance—a lawn mower, a Weed Eater, or someone trying to start a car.

Thirty-two

A FEW DAYS after Sophie left for Montana, Rita went to Aurelia Bailey's house, marching up to the door as if she had bad news rather than urgent questions.

"I hoped you might come by," said the judge. "I've called you so many times, Rita. You know I've called you."

"I didn't return anybody's calls, Aurelia," Rita said.

"Come in." Rita looked as if she had been hit by a truck.

"I want to ask you about my next step," said Rita. "I'm going crazy at how slow the police work is going. I mean, since the acquittal."

"You need patience for this, Rita. The whole process is slow."

"How can I speed things up?"

"Let me say that things are probably moving along faster than you know. The police don't want to make the mistake of telling you something, getting your hopes up, then be wrong. They are questioning many boys, and E. G. Hollis is working with the detectives. So is Charlie Post. I think everyone knows more than they're saying, and in time you will know too. Tell me, how is Sophie?"

"She has good and bad days. She's gone back to Montana for a while. She wanted to stay with a friend of hers. I think it's the best thing. Just to get away, get a new perspective. Might help her to remember something."

"Yes."

Rita took a long, unblinking look at Judge Bailey. "Where is Bobby? Is he around?"

"He's spending time with his father," said Aurelia. "I don't know if you know, if you heard—"

"I do know, yes, that Bobby's father lives in Kentucky and—"

"Yes, okay. He went to visit. I'm going to get him next week."

"Oh."

"What were you about to say? I mean, before you asked about Bobby?"

"Just that I think I might go mad with this thing. You know, knowing how I couldn't keep her safe."

Aurelia dropped her head in what looked like submission. "I'm so sorry, Rita. I am truly sorry for all of us." When she raised her head, she was crying. "I feel so responsible for this horrible thing. I keep wondering what I could have done differently—you know, to make the community safer." She shifted and looked at Rita. "Is Sophie remembering anything at all? You know, does she talk to you about it?"

"Not really."

"I wonder what remembering will do to her."

"Dr. Brooks says she won't remember until she can handle it. What I want to ask you is this: If Sophie remembers, if she gets on the witness stand and names the ones who did this, will it backfire on her? Is there a chance that they will get off, or that Sophie herself will be blamed in some horrible and lasting way? Sophie seems to think it will. I'm not sure how to advise her."

Aurelia motioned Rita into the living room. They sat down. "It does happen that way sometimes," she said. "God knows why. And that's exactly why more victims don't come forward. You know, when several men attack a girl, people tend to remember the girl." Aurelia would not look at Rita. "The girl becomes tainted and people don't forget. I can understand how hesitant Sophie would be to bring this out, Rita." Aurelia couldn't believe she was saying this.

"Are you saying that Sophie should *not say* who these men are?" Rita stood up, visibly shocked by what she believed was Aurelia's suggestion. "Aurelia, I can't encourage her to remain quiet. If she remembers, I can't. I have to say"—she turned to face the judge—"I have to say that every time I see a boy in town, walking around, I wonder if that boy hurt Sophie. I wonder if he was the one. I've wondered that about Lester, and Antony. Tom. And even Bobby."

Aurelia brought herself back from some dark corner of protection. "Well," she said. "I don't know." She stood up herself now, assumed the authoritative tone of a judge. "I think the only thing to do is to prosecute whoever did this to Sophie. I hope it isn't the boys you named, and I don't think it is, but even so, we have to prosecute. But Rita, this town is so full of rancor right now that *anybody* she named might be found guilty. So try to be sure, will you?"

"So what do I tell Sophie?"

"Tell her that she can count on the justice system and *not* to withhold the truth. Tell her that." Aurelia walked to the door, planning to leave before realizing that she was in her own house. "Tell her, no matter who it is, to say the names."

The two women did not say more, and they did not look at each other when Rita left. The night sounds of cicadas and tree frogs created a sigh from the yard and woods. The breathing sound made them both calm.

From the porch steps Rita thanked Aurelia, but she didn't know if Aurelia heard.

Rita walked three houses down, and into her house. Tonight she would call Sophie and tell her what Judge Bailey had said; then, over the next weeks, Rita would find some way to put their life back on track.

She had done that before.

Thirty-three

AVA HAD COME back to South Pittsburg a week before Crow's acquittal. And during those weeks after the trial Helen came upon the idea that she might not love her husband anymore, or else that she might not want to love him. She and Ava had begun to argue about even the smallest things, their larger argument going unsaid.

"I have thought of marrying again, Helen," Ava spoke defensively. "Last year I almost got engaged."

"What changed your mind?" Helen asked.

"I'm not sure I want to marry anybody. I like to come here, but I always know it'll end and then I can go back to my own apartment. It's my apartment, and I don't have to do anything for anybody if I don't want to. Marriage would be different."

"Maybe that's the trouble," Helen said. They were packing Ava's clothes, taking them out of drawers and putting them into her suitcase. "Maybe you like to keep everything in a box, then when something real creeps in, you don't like it."

Ava felt embarrassed by the strong visibility of her shortcomings. Helen had said the very thing Ava feared was true.

Helen said, "Carl thinks you're stunted."

"Stunted?"

"He said he thought you were caught up in some adolescent idea about what love is. He said being with you finally wouldn't be very satisfactory to a man, unless you grew up a little."

"He said that?" Ava's shoulders became round, and she felt blood rushing from her head.

Helen amended herself. "He didn't say it exactly like that, but Ava, sometimes if you're stuck, you need something blunt to jog you out of it."

Ava looked thoughtfully at her sister. "So did he say it or not?"

"He said you were stunted and that life with you wouldn't be very satisfactory. He did say that." The lines in Helen's face grew hard. Ava wondered if her sister finally hated her.

Because Ava had been in Europe when Helen married Carl, she didn't meet her brother-in-law until after the wedding. Carl had dreaded meeting Ava, because she had been described to him by the family as "a difficult person." Ava's first visit, though, was a success. Ava and Helen had stayed up until 2 A.M. talking, and at one point they laughed so hard and so loud that Carl came downstairs thinking that one of them was crying. He found the two women leaning over each other's shoulders, tears of laughter streaming down their cheeks. They tried to explain what they were laughing about, but he couldn't make out what they said, and his confusion made them laugh more. He smiled, waved his hand as though brushing away a fly, and went back to bed.

Helen had always felt responsible for her sister. And though the visits became more trying as years rolled by, they sometimes laughed in their old childhood way. And though those times came less and less, still on certain nights Carl was awakened by loud laughter rolling up the stairs.

In past summers, or holidays, whenever Ava left the house after supper, claiming to look up friends, Carl called to say he would be home late.

Several years ago Helen had asked her sister where she went.

"If you go to a movie, I could go with you. You don't have to go alone." Her words had a razor-edge sharpness.

"I visit with people." Embarrassment settled onto Ava's face, but her arms moved in a voluptuous gesture. Ava saw the world as a vast secret that was hers to unfold. She was capable of discipline, but her discipline usually centered on not allowing herself to love completely.

"I didn't know you knew so many people around here." Helen lifted a rag and began to rub clean the counters and kitchen table.

"I've been coming back for years, Helen," Ava said. The veins on her temple were blue, and Helen thought if she touched them, she could feel them throb. "I've made friends here."

"Seems funny that nobody ever comes by, or calls. Don't you think?"

"I don't want them bothering you." Ava looked unnerved.

Helen had never before come close to confronting her, but now her blunt, no-nonsense tone dominated the room. Helen wiped the counter, rubbing the same spot over and over. "*Bo-ther-ing* me?" she said. A clashing sound, like metal, ran between them.

Outside the stars became visible. South Pittsburg still had starlight, since the town kept its backcountry characteristics and streetlights were few. Trucks on the bypass could be heard, more like far-off thunder or rushing water than like traffic.

In bed that night Helen pretended the traffic wasn't there. A dog barked in the neighborhood and a loose window in the house slammed shut.

"What was that?" Carl said.

"Nothing," said Helen. "Go back to sleep." The wind had picked up and the air smelled like rain. By 4 A.M. everyone was asleep, but Helen quivered under the weight of her suspicions. She felt waves of anger wash over her.

She had married Carl and had the child that was not his, but one that he had claimed without complaint. But his claim came with discomfiting knowledge that eventually bored its way into their bed and made their marriage pale.

She regarded him in sleep. She looked for motive in his face, looked for guile, something malicious, but she didn't find either. She got up and went to the closet, lifted one of Carl's sports jackets, trying to imagine where she would go if she left him. The idea lay in her mind like an egg, broken, its yolk running through her body, making yellow the dreams that came with leaving.

She eased back into bed and listened to Carl's uneven breathing, the snoring, and saw the small twitching that came a minute or two before his whole body grew quiet. She tried to imagine different possibilities for her life. Then Carl woke suddenly and said, "What's the matter?" She thought maybe she had spoken her thoughts out loud.

"Nothing." She felt apologetic. "I must've jerked in my sleep. You know how I do."

"Yeah," he muttered. He lay at an angle, one leg thrown over her legs. "You getting up?" he asked. She moved to sit on the side of the bed. "It's early, isn't it?"

"I'm hungry for eggs," she said.

He didn't answer, already lulled back to sleep. She walked to the bathroom and threw cold water on her face, looking into the mirror to see it drip off. She did this three more times, as though the ritual were interesting, amazing. She stood straight, turned sideways, sucked in her stomach and observed how her nightgown fell from her breasts and brushed over her bottom. She thought she looked pretty good at almost forty, and tried to imagine someone else loving her. If she left Carl, would she be alone for the rest of her life? Would that be such a bad thing?

"Get me a glass of water, will you, honey?" Carl called from bed.

She turned the faucet on and ran water into the glass he kept on the sink. She brought it to him.

"I thought you were asleep," she said.

"I was. You getting up?"

"I'm hungry for eggs."

"Oh yeah." He drank the water and sat up. "Might as well get up too," he said.

He smelled stale. As she kissed the top of his head, he touched her breast.

"Sleep a while longer," she told him.

And it was that touch, that gentle hand touching her breast as it had done a thousand times before, that convinced her. The naturalness of the moment when he asked for water and she brought it and watched him drink, the light kiss on the head, a few repetitions of words, his touch—this progression of things made her know she would not leave, would probably never leave him.

Carl had asked Helen many times in their marriage: "What do you think it'll be like when the boys are gone, when we're all by ourselves?"

"It'll be fine," she always answered.

"Really?"

"We can do lots of things," she told him.

"Like what?"

"We can travel."

Carl grumbled.

"Don't get mad," she said.

"I'm not mad."

In truth Helen didn't know what their life might be like when they were by themselves in the house. Maybe they could find their way back to themselves again, if they could just get past Ava.

Ava.

She closed the bedroom door and went downstairs. The kitchen had dishes in the sink from various nighttime snacks. She made coffee, then washed the dishes, finishing them just as the coffee stopped burbling. She sat at the kitchen table and looked out into the backyard. The cat wanted in, so she opened the door. She would let it eat the dry food already there. She wanted to sit awhile in the field of dim light of that particular morning. Sitting there, she decided she didn't want eggs after all. She didn't want anything, though her brain still kept the yolk of her thoughts about leaving.

Thirty-four

SOPHIE HAD BEEN away for a week, and though Crow often drove by her house after practicing with the Bandits, today he drove home along the road beside the river. The river sparkled with afternoon light, and he pulled the car over, wanting to hear the sound of water. A few dead fish lay on the bank, and he got out to throw them back into the river. They smelled rotten and made the air stink. Maybe something in the water would eat them. The fishy odor stayed on his hands.

He heard a quick rustle in the bushes, and without turning he could see, not six feet away, a buck. For a long moment neither of them moved. Then the buck took a few steps before jumping quickly into the woods, antlers angling through the trees. Another sound came, and another deer ran by, and another. Crow thought of the moment as a miracle, a sign of something good. A minute later he moved carefully back to the car, hoping to see them again, but they were gone. All the way home he thought of how he felt when he stood close to the buck.

Crow drove up to the house but did not call out when he walked in. He heard a quarrel going full force between his mother and Ava.

"Well, how perfect is your own marriage, Helen?" Ava asked. "Look at how you and Carl started out—you got pregnant and he had to marry you."

Crow had heard rumors about his birth. He knew he had been

born only a few months after his parents were married. He stood, not moving.

"No," his mother protested. "That's not what happened. Everybody just thinks it happened that way."

"What do you mean?" He heard Ava walk across the bedroom and sit on the bed.

"I was pregnant, but not by Carl. Carl offered to marry me."

"He agreed to take on another man's child?" Ava's voice grew stiff. "I don't believe you."

These sisters had put hurt on each other over the years. They knew exactly how to hurt each other, so that their hearts now had grown separate and hard, like two small kernels.

Crow closed the door to the kitchen. The sun came in and made a pattern of windowpanes on the floor.

"The man was already married," said Helen. "He was my professor, and I thought I loved him. He was smart, and he thought I was smart." Helen laughed derisively at her younger self. "But I never really wanted him. I always wanted Carl."

"Did Carl *know* it was someone else's child?" Ava spoke as if Helen might be lying. She could not believe Carl had never told her this.

Crow heard his mother sigh. "He knew everything. He had the idea to get married. He thinks of Crow as his own. Always has."

"And Crow? Does he know?"

A shifting occurred, a rustle of clothes. "We never told him. We meant to, but we haven't done it yet. It'll be a hard thing to say."

Ava looked around nervously. "Is Crow here? I mean, in the house?"

"No. He went out."

"But his car's here." She pointed to Crow's car parked in the driveway.

"Hey, I'm home!" Crow called out as though he had just come in. Both women sighed with relief. Ava touched Helen's shoulder with the tips of her fingers. Her hands shone pale against Helen's dark blouse. A tangle of words emerged, both of them speaking to Crow at once.

"Ava's leaving tomorrow," his mother called. "I hope you'll be here for dinner tonight."

Crow waved them off and went upstairs to his room, striding his new hurt with long legs. He carried this new weight like luggage he could not put down. He closed the door of his room, the presence of deer still in his head.

That night Crow lay in his bed, shocked by the way life could turn so fast. What went through his mind was how Bobby's lost father was found; how his own father, his real one, had been lost. One person gets something; another has something taken away, like coins traded in a private war. He tried to imagine who he really was. The offering of the deer, the fish; then the argument between his mother and aunt; and finally the words, overheard and charged, that changed his belief in what was real.

The air in his room grew thick and all these thoughts came in. Crow didn't know who anybody was anymore. He felt as though he was seeing a photograph of himself standing with the family, and in the photo his eyes looked startled, as though the person taking the picture had not warned him.

His hands still smelled like fish. He had scrubbed them, but the odor lingered. He put them under the covers, as far from his face as he could get them.

Thirty-five

AVA, HER STRAIGHT hair and dimpled cheeks, her eyes blazing, had oriented Carl's life for years—something she herself had often told him. But her absence disoriented his marriage. She seldom left his thoughts. Whenever he saw a girl, or a woman, in town or in a neighboring town—someone's wife, a secretary, a prostitute—he thought of Ava. He saw the woman, and an image of Ava would haunt him for days.

When Ava offered her body, with nothing held back, Carl felt lucky. He convinced himself he could have this happiness without damaging his marriage.

The first time Ava went with Carl to a shabby motel a few hours outside town, the sky was moonless. She wore a plain black dress.

"Is she okay?" Carl's first question was about Helen.

"Yes. I told her I was going to a movie. She encouraged me to go." Ava looked confident, determined.

"Don't you feel bad about this? I mean, your sister?"

"I can't think about that. If I think about it, I'll leave right now." Ava didn't ask how he felt. "You want me to leave?"

"No."

By the set of her mouth, he knew she meant what she said. If he had stopped at that moment, then these years would not have happened, or maybe they would have happened with someone else.

But Ava.

She walked as though she had invented walking. Men watched

her move across the street or enter a restaurant. Nothing about her movements was rehearsed. Her body carried the music of moving or speaking, like an instrument. And she looked at Carl as though some secret might be revealed in a second—or not. Carl waited to see what she would do next.

"You haven't done this kind of thing," she said, entering the dingy room. "Have you?" She looked as if she were fire, and would set them on fire. He watched her undress, noting a birthmark, small as a dime, on the inside of her thigh. She opened her mouth onto his neck and shoulder, and Carl felt the moment of long imprisonment vanishing in a rush. They lay together naked for a while before turning toward each other, before being pulled completely into the blue Tennessee evening.

Ava believed that someday Carl might marry her. Carl said from the beginning that he would never leave Helen. Still, he needed Ava. She gave him the spontaneity he lacked. Helen, over the years, had turned practical, businesslike. The business of raising children had preoccupied her. Ava lived in the realm of senses, and when he thought of her he wanted to turn off the lights, to sit in half-light or firelight, to be aware of shadows and smells. When he was with her, he felt he was entering a safe cave, and over the years he had found it a place too difficult to give up.

"Nothing is finished," Ava told him. "Not love, not grief, not being alone. We pretend it's finished, but we're just fooling ourselves."

After Crow's trial, Carl decided he would end it with Ava. He would prepare himself to be without her. Helen's sleep had been fretful all spring. He felt her restlessness at night and his own panic during the day. He hoarded the details of a slow day, the way Ava had taught him. He wanted the small moments to carry him, but he kept alive his regret and found no peace. Ava had made him into someone new, though she was also the source of his regret.

Every June the river flooded, like clockwork. The current moved heavy with debris, breaking up piles of leaves and sticks left by earlier high water. Carl knew the habits and inclinations of this town. He had lived here all his life and he knew the currents in both water and people.

The town, constructed on a bend of the Tennessee River, was home to people from a wide range of occupations: farmers, store owners, the regular mix of teachers, doctors, and lawyers, scientists who studied river currents and erosion, disorderly wanderers who landed in town out of necessity, hoping to find work or kindness. A new group of commuters—people who worked in Chattanooga—built sprawling farmhouses where they lived like landed gentry. With the new people came a few fancy shops, along with one pricey restaurant that arranged food on the plate in artistic fashion, sprinkling its offerings with exotic sauces and herbs.

Carl tried to remember summer days full of details so small that no one even spoke of them. Could he go back to the time before sidewalks, when pebbles pushed through the soles of his shoes? He had walked to school along railroad tracks, past street lamps stoned dark by boys, past familiar stores and woods that bordered the town. He walked to the small hobbled schoolhouse with a dirt yard, fenced at the perimeters, and a tire swing that hung from the limb of a huge oak. All of that was gone now, whitewashed by concrete.

The trial had brought them all into a new place, and Carl felt that he could not be visible again until the windows were open and he could hear the high creak of trees in the wind and the rush of morning through the screen door, see the blurry light of evening.

He wondered if Ava's absence might unravel his marriage more than her presence did. He wondered if he was about to orient his life or disorient it.

At the end of June Carl told Ava that it was over. He told her straight out.

"I'm glad you're leaving tomorrow," he said. "And if you come at Thanksgiving, or Christmas, either way"—he squinted in concentration—"it's over. I mean, now." His voice sounded dry. He had thought about giving her something, an expensive bracelet or a CD player.

They met at a place outside town. Usually they would stay in the room a few hours, resting on the soft sheets, shower together, drink wine, eat in bed.

But this time, when Ava got out of the car, Carl could see that she already knew what he would say. To his surprise, she didn't argue.

"Okay," she said. "Okay. I know."

She hadn't cried. She hadn't been angry. And after those few words she told him she would leave the next day. She kissed his mouth, her small wrists, dainty like the wrists of a girl, rested against his cheek.

The whole thing ended just like that, with a whimper.

They went back to the house, arriving at separate times. A skyline on the west side gave view to the sun going down below the curve of the earth and tree line. Mongrel dogs wandered the streets—new mutts each year, expecting to be fed.

Thirty-six

AURELIA BAILEY TOOK the old highway going from Lexington, Kentucky, to South Pittsburg, Tennessee. It was the long road home, but she grew tired of the interstate and took this back road to slow things down, see some real country, maybe stop at a diner, something with local flavor. Aurelia felt absolutely sentimental about local flavor. The road followed the river for many miles.

She had gone to Kentucky to get Bobby. Until a few months ago, the idea of such a trip would have been inconceivable; now she wondered if it might turn into a regular occurrence. She hoped Bobby would talk about his time there, but she prepared herself for the closed-lipped attitude he had been exhibiting for months.

Bobby came out to the car, saying goodbye to his father and the new wife. He put his suitcase into the trunk, got into the passenger seat, then leaned his head against the window. He moved immediately into a quiet defiance. He did not think about how the experience felt to his mother. He had watched his father walk to the car and embrace her—a gesture unfamiliar to him since he was four years old. The new wife stood in the doorway.

"Well, what do you know," Robert Bailey said—a phrase, an expression of greeting that he had used all his life. Even Bobby remembered it.

Aurelia felt startled of soul. Robert did not look the same at all. Prison had turned his hair gray, given his skin a rough-edged, lineny texture. He still had small, perfect teeth, large brown eyes.

An aura of caution surrounded him. To hold him felt illicit. They talked for a few minutes, and as she got back into the car she imagined herself consoled, uncrowded.

"So," she started, ignoring that Bobby's eyes were closed. "How was it?"

Bobby sat up, waiting until the house was out of sight. "It was okay," he said, then he turned toward the door to settle into a hazy tent of sleep. His legs, too long for the front seat, pushed against the dashboard. Aurelia hoped that when Bobby woke he might answer a few questions about Robert's life in Kentucky. She felt she deserved to know.

Rain came down in rivulets across the windshield, softening the pink dust along the shoulders of the road. A steady rain had followed her most of the way there, and now when she crossed the river Aurelia noticed the water had risen a few inches since yesterday. Swollen mountain streams roiled with whitecaps, flooding the ground, leaving an edge of foam on the lip of the bank.

"Where are we?" Bobby asked when he woke. "Are we lost?"

"I just thought I'd take this old way," Aurelia explained. "I get so tired of the interstate and the same old look of everything. So I got off. I like riding alongside the river."

"Can I drive?" asked Bobby.

"I guess so."

"Cool."

They pulled onto the shoulder, opened the car doors, and switched sides—like people in flight. Bobby took the wheel, turned the key.

"Listen to that motor," he said. He loved to drive on long trips, on strange roads.

"What's the matter with it?" Aurelia cocked her head to listen.

"Nothing's the matter. Just listen."

"Oh."

As he drove, the tires hit pavement seams and ticked down a rhythm that kept them both quiet for a while before Aurelia asked,

"You want to tell me about how it was to be with your dad for the past two weeks? You know I have to ask, Bobby."

"It was fine," he said.

"Maybe a little more than that?" She laughed at his resistance.

"No. It was good." Then he broke into life. "At first when I got there, I was mad at you, thinking about how I had a dad who'd been around all these years and I never knew where he was."

"He talk to you about that? About going to prison?"

"Yeah. He said he was glad I never saw him there. He said he kept up with me through you. Still, though, you should've told me about him. I thought he was dead all that time."

"He made me promise not to tell you he was in jail, Bobby," Aurelia told him. "I tried to honor what little pride he had left." She decided to test his mood. "Did he tell you why he was incarcerated?"

"Embezzlement," said Bobby, trying to minimize, keep the crime at bay. "He said it was embezzlement."

In fact, Robert Bailey had spent ten years in prison for creatively stealing money from his law firm. He and Aurelia had met in law school and fallen in love so fast Aurelia could hardly believe it. They married and moved to Washington, D.C., both lawyers, but in different law firms.

At first Robert waged small battles with nameless faces, often winning. He was quickly promoted, until the battles became larger, involving more money. He imagined himself wealthy and successful. He imagined he should receive more money than the firm was giving him and eventually was discovered performing illegal activities. He was arrested and convicted, and though some of his partners also participated in the scheme, they let him take the blame. (Aurelia suspected they offered him money to be the scapegoat. And that he had started his new life with this money.)

One night during that glassy band of days, Aurelia dreamed that Robert was an eagle flying in an arc of wind, wings barely turning as he rode the current, a graceful slide. But when she woke inside her own room, in her oversized bed, she saw the cage of air around him. He lay beside her, the edges of dream around them both, a blue air choking her. She would not be pulled down with him. She went to Bobby's room, dressed him, and told Robert that they were leaving. She had seen her husband only one time since that day.

"He said we just left one night," said Bobby. "Just left. He said he didn't really blame you though."

"I didn't know what to do, Bobby. I felt ashamed. I was afraid the trouble he got into might affect whether or not I got a judgeship somewhere. In fact, I think it did keep me out of some places, but the people in Tennessee already knew me. I had to earn a living in order to support you, you know."

Bobby had not thought of this.

"I also paid off some of what Robert owed."

"You did?"

"Yes. I did."

"Did you ever visit him in prison?"

"Once. Once I did. It was his thirtieth birthday. I took the train to Maryland. Left you with the Davenports. Remember when you spent the weekend at their house? You were about seven."

Bobby remembered.

"I rented a car and took him a chocolate cake with candles. Of course, the guards pretty much destroyed the cake looking to see if anything was hidden inside. I tried to smooth it before I took it to him. I don't think he cared that it was messed up. He was glad to see me. He ate that whole cake, almost, during the hour I was there."

"That's the only time?"

"Yes. I'm ashamed now of just leaving him like that. Plenty of shame to go around, I guess." She waited. "I loved your dad, Bobby. I really loved him." As she said this she turned on the radio, trying to find music Bobby would like.

Bobby had never heard his mother say those words, but as he

thought about it, he remembered photographs she kept around the house. He thought the photos were more for him than for her. His father did not have old photographs in his home. He had a new family.

During Bobby's visit his father acted affectionate in an offhand way. He had a wife and two children now, so that even when they did things together as a group, Bobby felt like an outsider. Bobby's ideal version of his father and the actual experience didn't coordinate. He didn't know what to think about the discrepancy.

"This doesn't seem like the road home," Bobby said as he turned up the volume on the radio. He began to pound a percussive beat on the steering wheel and dashboard.

"Well, it is."

They drove leisurely through the small towns and at noon stopped in Bell Buckle, Tennessee, for lunch at a place called Hot Thomas's Bar-be-que. "His first name's really Hot," said Aurelia. "He's about six-four. He's always behind the counter, or used to be."

"Who'd name a kid Hot?"

"He probably acquired the name as a teenager," Aurelia said. She could tell that Bobby was impressed by the name, even envious.

"Cool," he said, nodding.

Bobby drove again after lunch, and Aurelia noticed how he was less surly while driving, more willing to talk. The rain was over and streaks of late light poured like water through the trees.

"I wondered," said Aurelia, "if you might decide to live with your father." She was unable to hide a catch in her voice as she spoke. "I mean, if you might want to move to Kentucky."

Bobby looked at his mother.

"If you do want to, I won't stop you, but," she added, "you can't leave soon. Everybody who knew Sophie will have to be questioned."

"They've already talked to me."

"Yeah, but they will again. I'm sure." She tried to gauge his mood.

"Well," said Bobby, "I don't want to live with him anyway. I want to live somewhere, but not there. If we win the Battle of the Bands, some doors are going to open."

"Bobby," she said, then decided that this was not the moment to warn him about the possibility of losing.

Bobby sensed her warning. "We'll be up against some good bands, I know that. But I think we're going to win. We've got to."

Aurelia couldn't quite fathom the fragment of anxiety in his voice. She let them ride in silence. They passed through a small town, a stretch of low houses and stores, then a couple of horses in a pasture.

"Did you call Crow? I mean, did you talk to him while you were away?" Her tone was accusatory.

"I called him once." Bobby did not say that Crow wasn't home when he called. "About the band and stuff."

"Does he think you're going to win?" Aurelia studied the folds of her skirt.

"Yeah, I guess."

Her mention of Crow had broken something, a trust, and the air between them felt strained now. Bobby grew quiet for a long while before he suggested that his mother drive.

Everywhere Aurelia's uncertainty as to what happened that night, and the fear of Bobby's participation, was abundant. After all, she was trained to see lies, had been schooled in the expert excuses and denials of the guilty. But she also knew her penchant for believing the worst of people, and she had tried hard all of Bobby's life not to bring her suspicious nature into the home. She knew how a lack of trust could so easily bring to life exactly what is suspected. She knew she could make true what she feared. She tried not to wonder if she had done this to Robert.

She tilted her head, a feeling of dreamlike confusion falling over her. "It's not im*poss*ible to imagine that someone we know might be guilty," she said, no ounce of threat in her voice. "Rita says that Sophie still can't remember anything. When she does re- member, though, *if* she does—she might say something that'll break apart everything."

"I don't know," said Bobby, in answer to nothing.

Thirty-seven

IT WAS THE first of July when Tom returned from a four-hour practice at Casey's house and found his parents watching for him in the yard. His father stood like a broad-chested statue. From the look of them he thought he was in trouble. Maybe they knew about Johnny. Or maybe all his secrets were known. As he got out of the car, he tried to think of how he might defend himself.

"Where were you?" his father asked, but his voice sounded almost jolly. "Your mother called around but couldn't find you anywhere."

"I went to—"

"Get ready," he said. "We're leaving as soon as you pack."

"Where are we going?"

"Peter's docked in Norfolk, Virginia," his mother said. She walked behind them into the house. "He'll be there for several days, and we're going to see him."

"Our stuff's already in the car," said Mr. Canady.

"But we're playing in Sweetwater this weekend. They booked us months ago."

"They'll have to play without you," his father said. "They can get along without you for one night, I guess."

"You want to see Peter, don't you?" his mother said.

"Well, sure, but—"

"Get packed. I want to get on the road. We don't want to hit the late-afternoon traffic."

As he packed he realized that he didn't mind leaving town. With the dismissal of charges against Crow, the police had grown even more suspicious about Crow's friends. Mr. Hollis and Coach Post had asked Tom questions every time they saw him, and last night Hollis saw Tom coming out of the drugstore and called him to his car.

"Sophie went away for a few weeks. Did you know that?" Hollis said. "Maybe, while she's away, we can get people to talk about what they know. So, if you hear anything, anything at all, I want you to call me."

"No sir," said Tom. "There've been rumors about some boys from Chattanooga. That's all I heard."

"What about boys from around here?" Hollis asked. "The sheriff thinks this is local."

"I haven't heard that," Tom lied.

"Well, I have. They seem to think it's more possible that Sophie knew the ones who attacked her." He paused for a moment.

"I don't think that's right." Tom's voice grew whiny. "I know that's what they're saying though." The deputies had questioned Tom several times, even at the trial they put him on the stand.

"I'm told that Bobby liked Sophie, that he pursued her for a while," said Hollis.

"Yeah, Bobby was hot for her, but he's hot for a lot of girls." Tom hoped that Mr. Hollis couldn't tell how clammy his face was, how the blood had left his head.

"You all right?" Hollis asked him.

"Sure. I was sick last night, but I'm okay now."

"You better go on home," said Hollis. As Tom turned to leave, Hollis added, "The sheriff might question you some more." His words felt like a warning. "If you know anything, Tom, you should tell them. If you withhold information, you can get into trouble. Very deep trouble."

Now Tom pretended to doze most of the way to Virginia. He

had wanted to drive, but his father wouldn't allow it. After checking into a motel, they made plans to meet Peter for dinner, and Tom said he needed to call Bobby and tell the others that he couldn't play the gig in Sweetwater that weekend. His parents left to get a drink at the bar.

Bobby wasn't at home, so Tom dialed Johnny's number. Johnny answered.

"Hey. I just wanted to call, see how you are. We're in Virginia now, to see Peter. He wants to take us out on his ship, I think. Anyway, I was gonna come see you tomorrow, but I can't now."

"I don't want you to call me anymore," Johnny said. "I already told you. I don't want to see you either."

"You afraid Crow will find out?"

"That's not it. I told you already."

"But we can still hang out, right?" Tom was pleading.

"No," said Johnny. "Listen. Stop calling, okay?"

"Okay. I'll stop calling."

"Stop everything. Okay? I mean, if you don't, I'm going to say something."

"What do you mean?"

"Just what I said."

"Right, like you're going tell about us."

"That's not what I mean," said Johnny.

"Je-sus, don't get weird on me."

"I'll make it sound like something else, like it was your fault."

"What the fuck are you saying, Johnny?"

"Nothing. I gotta go." He hung up.

At dinner Peter told his family how he was learning to land a jet on a carrier in the ocean, and Mr. Canady looked transfixed by his son's words. The next day Peter would give his family a tour of the ship. He might take Tom up in a plane. Tom tried to act pleased, but all he could think about was what Mr. Hollis had said and Johnny's threat. He was glad now to be away, and hoped that in his absence the tension might die down.

"How is Crow, Tom?" Peter asked. "I know he was acquitted, but did they find the guys who did it?"

"Not yet." Tom reached for the basket of rolls. He took two.

"They will." Jack Canady sounded sure. "Charlie says he thinks they have some suspects and that they are close to an arrest."

"Crow's all right," Tom told Peter, "or at least he's getting better. We've been playing again—a few gigs."

"Still trying out for that Knoxville competition?"

"Yeah."

"You'll attract some girls there." Peter nudged Tom, nearly spilling his water. "Being in a band is almost as good as wearing a navy uniform."

"It's all been so sad," said Mary. She ate small bites. "So sad."

"They'll find them," said Jack. "It was a brutal thing. Not at all like South Pittsburg. Of course, you never know. Maybe that girl brought it on herself."

"I hope they catch the bastards," said Peter.

Tom nodded and kept nodding. For a long moment he was unable to swallow his food.

Thirty-eight

GRACE AND SOPHIE were not alone until the evening. Grace's mother and father took them first to a restaurant and then back to the house.

"I'm glad you're here," said Grace.

"Me too." Sophie pulled Grace into the room and closed the door.

"What's the matter?" Grace did not say it, but she thought Sophie looked terrible. Sophie was thin, her skin looked like plastic, rubbery, her expression one of forced reasonableness. "Are you all right, Sophie?"

"That's not the right question." Sophie lay down on the bed, her legs curling into a fetal position.

Grace locked the door. "What do you mean? What do you want me to ask?"

"Do you know what happened to me?"

Grace nodded and approached the edge of the bed, quilt folded neatly, a white rug with large soft loops. "I think I do."

Sophie parted her lips but didn't speak, then plunged ahead. "I'm hardly ever sick, and in fact when I was five, or six maybe, I decided not to be sick, ever, and I haven't been—not really—just a headache sometimes. But now, since this happened, I feel sick all the time, nauseated, you know? I feel like I have the flu all the time. I threw up every day for two weeks."

"You did?" Grace didn't know what to say. "I don't know how you did it."

"How I did what?" Sophie sat up.

"You know, how you stood the thing that happened to you."

"I didn't have any choice," said Sophie. "And you can say it." She took a deep breath. "You can say the word *rape* in front of me."

But Grace couldn't say it.

"Do you think that I'm different now, because of what happened?"

"Aren't you?"

"Well, but I mean, do you see me in a different way"—she nodded once—"because of it?"

"You're my friend, Sophie. I still see you as my friend, but . . ."

"But what?"

"I don't know if we can talk about things anymore, you know, like about boys."

"You told me about Garvin and you. You can still talk about him. I want you to."

Both girls changed into their pajamas, tiny tops that barely covered their midriffs, and long, baggy, soft cotton pants.

"They had a trial," said Sophie, "but the wrong person was on trial. I didn't say anything, I just let it happen, because I wasn't sure. I wasn't sure what happened, Grace."

"Are you still not sure?"

"Remember when I told you about Crow and how we were going out?"

"Yes."

"We had talked about doing everything that night, but he had to stop because he forgot his condom. It happened while he was gone."

"Oh." Grace waited. "But he didn't do it?"

"No, but I wasn't sure for a while. I couldn't remember anything. Even now. My doctor said I might remember more if I left town." Sophie lay back, sprawled on the bed, looking away from Grace. She didn't want to see Grace's face.

"Crow wrote me notes, but I didn't answer. He gave me a present on my birthday. Some oil paints and a set of Isabey brushes, and he made a tape of songs we liked. I know he feels bad about leaving me there."

"Why didn't you tell them he didn't do it?"

"I couldn't remember. And he ran away. So I wondered about it. I didn't know what to think. My mother said we had to make some kind of accusation, or else it wouldn't look right for me. And the D.A. was all fired up to nail somebody fast—"

"Sophie." A wave of dread flew over Grace's face.

"Everything's gone," said Sophie. She felt pushed down into a small box, smashed into a form that might never unbend. "I don't even feel like I'm human anymore. My mom . . ." She sat up, hating the life that had turned into this impossible rattling. A few strands of hair fell along her cheek.

"What about your mom?"

"She treats me different. I don't want to be different to her. *She's* the one who's different. I don't even like her."

"What's she like? When I talked to her on the phone, she seemed okay."

"You don't know. She's calling the sheriff's office every minute, she cusses them, and she's so mad all the time. She wants me to be mad like that. She's mad at me for not being mad."

"But you are, aren't you?"

"Yeah, but Dr. Brooks says I'm not acting like a victim. He says that's a good thing. He thinks that's good."

"But you are a victim."

"Not for the rest of my life, Grace." Sophie backed away as though something around her were radioactive. "I don't want to feel like this the rest of my life."

Grace flinched. "So you came back here."

Sophie's small pale mouth lifted into a smile. "I wanted to see you. And to be someplace different, someplace I used to be. To see if I can remember."

The cat scratched outside the bedroom door, and Grace opened it to let him in. "Hey, Bruno. C'mere, Bruno." The cat was huge and yellow, weighing nearly thirty pounds—affectionate and rumbling. Grace rubbed his head, but Bruno went straight toward Sophie. "He remembers you. Look at that."

Sophie scratched his neck and head. "I'm glad *some*body remembers," she said. The cat licked Sophie's arms. Sophie looked around the room. "Are those new curtains?" White eyelet-lace curtains swung in a wave at the window. The breeze brushed Sophie's face and arms, and in that one moment she tried to think of herself as worthwhile.

Grace's mother went to work the next day, and the girls walked to the swimming pool down the road. They packed up some sandwiches, cookies, and chips to take with them. They would stay all day. Bruno followed them down the sidewalk.

"Go home, Bruno. Go back home now." He continued to follow, then turned in another direction, not caring.

The pool was full of teenagers who seemed to all know each other, but many of them greeted Sophie with welcome and surprise. She felt good and settled herself happily into a chair. She was glad that no one here knew what had happened. Grace sat beside her.

"Go swim, if you want," said Sophie.

"Aren't you coming?"

"I will. Not yet."

"I'll wait for you." Grace didn't want to leave her friend, not even for a minute.

Sophie waved her off and said, "Just be normal with me, okay?"

"Okay."

"Then go swim. I swear, I'm tougher than I look."

Grace's carefulness with her—it was not something Sophie had expected to be a problem. Grace removed her shoes and ran to the diving board. "Watch this!" she yelled. "I can finally do a jackknife. You're next."

Sophie saw Grace's body fold in and out again, elastic before hitting the bright water. "Do it again," she yelled.

"You think I can't do it again?"

Sophie's request wasn't a doubt or a dare but rather the wish to see her friend in a state of suspension over the water, a shiny moment of mindless ease, and she felt the ease of it being given to her.

Grace came toward Sophie, smiling.

"That was perfect," Sophie said.

"Now you do it."

Sophie's first few tries were disastrous and funny. The laughter of her friends did not feel like jeering. It was comforting, familiar as old radio music. So she kept trying, almost making it, hearing applause as she pulled herself out of the water. "Almost there!" one boy yelled. "Keep your head tucked."

So she did, and the jackknife was formed above the board, above the blue water, a holding pattern, like some magic moment before she slipped carefully and silently into the wash of clapping and cheering.

"Talk about perfect!" Grace said, handing her a towel. "It took me a week to learn that."

"Well, I tried it a week's worth of times," said Sophie. She fell onto her chair, sagging comfortably like a small child. "Oh," she said. "I could stay here forever."

The girls, half naked, their bare legs and bare midriffs shining with water, settled into the privacy of talk.

"What do I look like, Grace?" Sophie asked.

"You mean right now?" Grace laughed, not realizing the solemnity of the moment, not wanting to acknowledge it. "Your hair is sticking up in back."

"But what do I look like to you now? I mean, I don't know anymore. I wash and dry my hair and put on makeup, but I can't really see my face anymore, or my body. A few days ago I caught a glimpse of myself in a window, and what I saw surprised me—my reflection surprised me. I've gotten thin, but still, what do I look like?" Her voice fully commanded Grace to give her an answer.

Grace had listened intently, nodding like a student who didn't quite understand. "You look great," she said. "Sophie, you always look beautiful. I thought you knew that. You're thin but not too thin. You look good, but you look scared too. Your whole body moves like it's scared, like you're about to jump away at any minute."

"Yeah."

"And that's what seems different about you—that's what makes me treat you in a different way. It's not because of what those men did—it's more like what you're doing now. How you seem to be afraid somebody's going to say something wrong to you."

"I'm not afraid of that."

"But you act like you are."

A ragged edge of pain moved right through Sophie's chest and down her spine and up into her head. She felt dizzy.

Grace shifted to get up. "Let's get dressed and walk to town," she suggested. "Okay?"

"Sure."

Sophie felt dazed by the realization that Grace (and probably everybody at home, even her mother) saw her differently; and that even back in Montana, where she thought people would not see the white, shapeless bones that had become her body, nothing could be hidden.

That night Sophie felt restless in the closed trap of her body.

She fretted herself to sleep, trying to figure out how she could go back to being herself again. And just before she went into dream she felt her body above the blue water, her head tucked as if in prayer, and her bones light again, suspended, then cutting through the water like a blade.

IV

Now We Are Awake

Thirty-nine

ON THE FOURTH of July Sophie and Grace went to see fireworks and dancing held on a small platform in the middle of a field. The whole night seemed constructed for a chance to explode into something new. For a time Sophie had been feeling ruined and grotesque, but tonight the flare of fireflies, the sparkling sound of fiddles, the honeysuckle and clematis casting a spell, the lustrous sounds of laughter—her own and Grace's—turned the dissonance of the past months into a bad dream.

Tonight Grace's mother had told Sophie she looked beautiful in her pink sundress. *Beautiful.* A word people had been hesitant, or negligent, to say to her anymore. But Grace's mother told her, "Oh, honey, you look so pretty. Beautiful really. You're turning into a lovely young woman." These words had made Sophie feel exquisite, and she asked to borrow Grace's sweater with plangent pinks and purples, sharp greens and iridescent blues, that rocketed into wild spokes, and she felt light-headed and tearful watching the fireworks bloom open into falling stars.

Everything around her seemed mortal and alive. She felt drunk. She felt she was going to be all right now. She leaned toward Grace and said it. "I'm going to be all right. I know I'm going to be all right."

But at that moment three more fireworks went into the air and Grace misunderstood. She laughed and said, "Me too. But my mother won't let us stay out all night." She smiled at Sophie, and Sophie turned to see another rocket expand into a puff of tiny stars that hung suspended before disappearing.

Eventually, people began to leave, the fireworks done, children crying for more. The girls walked back to Grace's house and sat on the porch steps still watching the sky for explosions.

"It's actually happening out there," said Grace. "Fireworks we can't see, spectacular ones." She pointed, pretending. "See? See that one?"

"Yeah," said Sophie. "And there." Then at the same moment they saw a shooting star and laughed uncontrollably. The laughter felt like something Sophie used to do when she was still Sophie, her back still straight, without the censure of every morning sunrise and every eye.

The next few days lumbered on without Sophie losing the context of hope that had come on the night of fireworks. The days turned into weeks, and Rita called to urge Sophie home. "It's been three weeks," she said. But Sophie stayed. She ate meals and swam at the community pool with her old friends and Grace. No one looked at her with morbid curiosity. No one knew how different she was, and so for a while Sophie slipped back into her body and lived as before, but Before would not come back completely.

"What does your doctor say?" Grace asked. "Does he say what you should do?"

"He says it takes time. He says that I need to let myself remember before I can forget." Sophie thought for a moment. Her expression showed that she had thought of something.

"What? What're you thinking?"

"Well, Dr. Brooks suggested once that I write something down about what I remembered, something about each man. Then to draw, or paint, and maybe something will come back then. He thinks it would help me to remember."

"You want to do it now?" Grace asked. "Let the memories come in?" She spoke as though this might be simple.

"Maybe I will," said Sophie, without any movement to do so.

Sophie did allow small parts to come back, but mostly she kept in abeyance any memory that moved into consciousness. She felt tired much of the time. She could not let anyone touch her. Whenever Grace's mother tried to kiss her good night, she turned away.

Sophie had started smoking about a month ago, and when she was alone, she lit cigarettes, keeping the butts in a coffee can under the bed. She was sure her mother had been able to smell the smokiness in the house, but Rita hadn't said anything about it. Sophie kept her habit a secret from Grace, but she suspected Grace had seen. She wished she could hide it from herself.

She wanted to redefine her life, though not the way her mother seemed to hope for. Each day she rose with a singularity of purpose: to find some small brightness in the day, just one moment, so that she could begin to reenter the world.

The water glistened as it dripped from the bathroom faucet. She could see it from where she sat on Grace's bed. She liked watching it drip and hoped Grace's mother would not get it fixed. Each time a new drop formed she thought of possibilities—all of the life swarming around in one drop. Her biology teacher had let them look through a microscope, and Sophie felt amazed at all that was going on in that small world. But that was before. Everything now was divided into Before and After. Whenever she thought of Before, she remembered the girl she had liked being. She remembered how powerful she felt Before, and could not get her mind around what went wrong.

She thought of something observing her as she had observed the life in the drop of water. She hoped that Whoever was watching could see a better life down the road.

*   *   *

On days when Sophie wanted to paint, Mrs. Jackson set up a place in the basement. Sophie stayed there for several hours, and when she came up Grace would be waiting for her, ready to take her swimming or to the movies.

"What's happening?" Grace asked one day. "I mean, are you remembering anything?"

Sophie nodded.

"So what'll you do? Can I see what you've painted?"

"Tomorrow maybe. I'm not finished."

"But have you remembered?"

"You know the worst thing about going back home?" Sophie said, not answering Grace. "People feeling sorry for me, you know?"

Grace nodded, but she didn't know.

"And I just don't know if another trial is going to help me feel better. I mean, how can that help?"

"It'll keep them from doing it again."

"If I'm right, if I'm remembering right—"

"Then you do remember!"

"Listen, I'm just tired of being 'the girl who was raped.' That's all. I'm afraid that if I say who it was that people, even my mom, will see me that way all over again."

"But you can't make yourself *unraped,* can you?"

Later that night after Grace was asleep Sophie went outside and sat on the ground. The word *unraped* kept going through her mind. And she thought she knew now how getting unraped happened: by going back through the memory of it all. She had done that earlier today, and she remembered lying on the ground, the shirt around her head slipping off, seeing the shadows of boys—three boys moving through the woods—their height, the turn of their hair, the way they walked, small gestures she had seen before. And she knew who they were.

The field beside Grace's house held a phenomenon of fireflies hovering close to the ground. Sometimes cars passing by stopped to watch the field light up, sparkling with movement.

Tonight Sophie had the field all to herself. She felt rich. The moon rose low, like a piece of fruit, over the hills. The orange-gold light sifted down around Sophie, dropping its yellow gown, a soft silky mantle covering her. She didn't know what was happening, but felt dared to do something bold.

"What?" she said out loud. The moon was taking off its clothes, making a deal with her: you can be as polished as a petal of light—your body, without clothes.

So she slipped off her shoes and socks, pants and shirt, slowly removing her bra, her panties, then she stood—open-bodied, her heart like a fountain. She conspired to be a literal moon. She moaned and heard herself moan. She didn't know how long she stood there waiting to become blossom, or leaf, shuddering, breaking into her body again.

It was the hour of moths, and the moon came close to her face—a simple touch of wings, and she was done. She reached to put her clothes on, but she knew that the evening had changed, and that the night had become for her, in those few moments, a revelation. She was coming back to the world.

The next day Grace's mother made soup in a huge pot and the girls helped cut chunks of meat, carrots, celery, three kinds of beans, and potatoes to go in it. The house smelled of a flavor you could almost taste, even without putting your lips to a spoon. This morning they had eggs and bacon or waffles and the family sat around the table eating and talking the way Sophie used to do with her mother and father.

Grace's parents teased and kissed each other, bickering in small ways. Sophie wished she could go back to that time with her own mother and father. She wanted everything to be the way it was when her father was alive.

"Your mother called," Mrs. Jackson told Sophie. "She'd like to come this weekend. She misses you. She says six weeks is too long to be away."

"She doesn't have to," said Sophie. "I'm going home. I want to stay through the weekend, then go home."

Mrs. Jackson leaned toward Sophie with a large spoon for her to taste the soup. "Try this. But *foof* it first." Sophie blew on the hot broth and tasted. She nodded approval.

That night Sophie spoke to her mother on the phone. "I'll stay through this weekend," she said, "then come home on Monday."

"Oh, darling," Rita said.

"I'll call with the flight time," said Sophie. "Mrs. Jackson will help me change it." She sounded happy. What she really planned to do was come home early, on Sunday, to surprise her mother. "So don't do anything till I call."

"Well, good." Rita could hear something different in Sophie's voice. "Oh, honey, you sound so good. I can't wait."

That night Grace's parents had a fight. The girls could hear them arguing, and the next morning they found Mr. Jackson asleep on the sofa in the den.

"What happened?" Grace asked.

"Nothing we can't work out," he told her. "You girls been up long?" But his face looked pinched and unhappy, and Sophie wondered if this was an After time for Grace's father and mother. She wondered if they would look back on the time of Sophie's visit as Before.

Forty

SUNDAY MORNING WAS gray and misty. At eleven-thirty Rita sat at the kitchen table in her robe and underwear. She had bathed and washed her hair. At noon Charlie would arrive and they would climb the stairs for a long lunch. Rita had made roast beef sandwiches and bought potato salad from Charlie's favorite deli. The night before, she'd made brownies, sprinkled with powdered sugar, and stacked them on a blue plate. Charlie liked to eat a bite of dessert before every meal. Even at breakfast he might have a few bites of doughnut or coffee cake before eating cereal or eggs.

Sometimes they made love before lunch, sometimes after. Rita didn't care which. She put the sandwiches in the bedroom and looked forward to his knock at the back door.

"Rita?" She felt pleased to see the image of him through the screen, and opened the door, hugging him slowly. When she went to hand him a mug of coffee, he was smiling.

"You think coffee's what I want?" He reached beneath her robe to feel the soft curve of her body, and pulled her toward him. "Coffee's not what I want."

"Don't make me spill this," she said, placing the mug on the counter and untying the sash of her robe. The weeks without Sophie had spurred their romance. They spent many days and nights together and were beginning to talk about how to explain their relationship to Sophie when she returned home.

"I only have until two o'clock," he said, grinning.

"Sophie's coming home tomorrow," she told him.

He kissed her mouth hard, and they stumbled upstairs to the bed.

Rita had surprised herself with Charlie. She hadn't really been able to be with anyone since Ben, but the first time Charlie kissed her in the back of the store, she felt herself opening.

She had been searching in the storeroom for a particular type of hammer for a customer. "The ball-peen hammers, Charlie," she said. "Where are they?"

Charlie was unpacking a box that had just come in. As she waited for his response (he seemed to be thinking about the answer), he swerved and kissed her without warning, his arm wound tightly around her waist, his body pressed against her. The kiss was soft but took her breath away. Then he handed her the hammer she needed.

When Rita went back to the customer, the woman said, "Well, that must be it." Then she looked at Rita and asked, "Are you all right, honey? You look kinda pee-kid."

Rita smiled weakly. She left early that day. When the door closed behind her, she heard the small bell announcing arrivals and departures and felt a shift toward something good.

In the bedroom Charlie folded Rita into his arms, wrapping the blanket around them. He buried his face in her neck as though she were a smell he couldn't inhale enough of. He held her close. "Sweetie," he said.

Rita didn't know how many years it had been since she had heard that particular endearment come her way. Ben had called her honey, darling, and various pet names, but only her grandfather had called her sweetie. And since he'd been dead now for more than twenty years, the familiarity of it had gone. She'd heard other couples use the term, but now it was hers again, along with this man who loved her so easily.

"What's this town saying about us?" she asked.

"They're wondering if we're going to settle down," he said. "That's the rumor."

"Should we settle down?" She spoke to the ceiling.

"Maybe. Ben's been dead for almost three years, Rita." Charlie lay back. Rita didn't say anything and he wondered if she was mad. "Anyway," he said. "I wasn't asking you to marry me."

"I know that." She laughed.

He smiled wickedly. "Not yet."

In the spring Sophie had questioned her mother about Charlie. "You like him a lot, or what?"

"Charlie's a good friend," Rita had said. "I do like him. Don't you?"

"I just keep thinking about Daddy," Sophie answered. "I don't want you to forget about him." She watched her mother's face intently. Rita went to the sink and washed off a pear, took a bite. She chewed slowly, as if she were remembering something but not saying it. Sophie walked over and took a bite of her mother's pear.

Rita was startled. "You can have it," she said and reached to wash another one, but Sophie threw the pear out the back door and went to her room.

That night Rita made all of her daughter's favorite foods for dinner: macaroni and cheese, baked pork chops, tossed mesclun salad, and Sara Lee crescent rolls. All through dinner they spoke about school and Rita's work at the store. Neither mentioned Charlie's name.

An afternoon rain came down hard, and thunder and lightning made the privacy of the bedroom seem like a tent. By the time they made love, ate lunch, and made love again, the wind had abated, and they both fell asleep.

Charlie sat up quickly. "What time is it?" he said. "How long did we sleep?"

"Not long," she said, stretching.

He took a sip of the water Rita kept beside the bed, and she watched the liquid move down his throat. His chest and arms glowed with a light sweat. He smelled vinegary and clean. He put down the glass, wiped his mouth with the back of his hand, and saw her watching him. He rolled over onto her.

They heard someone come in. The front door slammed, and they heard someone running upstairs.

"My God," said Rita. "Someone's in the house!"

Charlie looked at his watch. "Two-thirty," he said.

Footsteps came down the hall toward their door, and as the door opened, Rita heard, "Mom? Where are you? Mom?" Sophie was excited to be home and her voice rippled as she opened the bedroom door.

Rita pulled the covers over Charlie, reaching for her robe. No one could speak. They could see a taxi pull away from the house.

After a long moment Sophie ran downstairs; she ran outside and down the street. Rita hurriedly dressed and chased her, going to the edge of the yard, calling. Charlie was dressed by the time Rita returned to the bedroom.

"She's gone."

"God, I'm sorry," he said. "Did you know she was coming home today?"

"She probably wanted to surprise me. Oh, God, Charlie, what have we done?"

"You want me to find her?"

"No. No." She could hardly look at him. "Just go."

Charlie slipped on his shoes without tying them. "Let me know if there's anything I can do, anything I can say to her. Je-sus, I can't believe this happened." He gave Rita a swift kiss on the ear and left the house.

By the time Sophie came home, Rita was bending to clean up some spilled coffee grounds. "Come here," she said and opened her arms.

"You lied to me."

"No, I didn't."

"You didn't tell me. I feel so stupid."

"Oh, honey." Rita held her daughter tight against her breast. The power was scattering between them. "You shouldn't feel like the stupid one. I'm the one who's stupid." She pulled back and looked at Sophie, the heartrending tenderness of her daughter's face and hands.

"I wanted to surprise you," Sophie said.

"You did."

Sophie nodded. They smiled at each other.

"I'm so glad to see you." Rita hugged her daughter and would not let go. "Surprise or not. I am so glad you're home."

As they held each other, Rita thought how far they had come from drives along Montana roads seeing fields of horses, cows, and happy lambs.

At the store Rita could not keep her mind on work, so Charlie told her to go home early. On the way home she bought a pizza and the car smelled deliciously like tomato sauce and sausage. As she pulled into the driveway, she saw Sophie sitting in the backyard. She took the pizza out on a tray with some iced tea and paper towels.

Sophie's expression seemed unusual as she lifted a slice of pizza and a paper towel from the tray her mother set before her.

Rita sat on the ground. "What's wrong?" she asked.

"Well, I just have something to say."

Rita waited to see what might come.

"Remember when Dr. Brooks said that I might start to remember?"

"Sophie. Oh, honey."

Then Sophie said *out loud* the names of the boys. Rita had to keep herself from cursing, though under her breath she railed. She burned.

"When did you know this?" Rita asked cautiously. Dr. Brooks had advised Rita to stay calm if Sophie told her anything.

"A few days ago. I was waiting to be sure in my head."

Rita barely moved, trying to be careful. She watched Sophie take another piece of pizza, pick off the sausage, leaving the mushrooms. "I remembered one day at Grace's while I was painting on a canvas they had in their basement. And I saw their faces."

Rita handed her daughter a glass of tea and saw her drink almost all of it. She poured more. She didn't know if she should encourage Sophie to continue. "Honey," she said.

Sophie pulled away. She was trying to tell more.

Rita put her hands on her ears, even though she wanted to hear. She thought she might vomit, and gagged slightly. "Have you talked to Dr. Brooks?"

"Yes." Sophie sobbed. "I told him. He told me to come home."

"May I hold you for a little bit?"

Sophie leaned against her mother's shoulder, and Rita rocked her back and forth. A sound came out from Rita, like an oboe, coming from her mouth and arms and legs. They swayed like this for a long time.

"You want to go inside now?" Rita lifted Sophie's head, wiping tears away with her thumbs. They brought the rest of the pizza and iced tea into the house and Rita locked the back door. Sophie sat motionless at the kitchen table, gathering her arms around her as if to protect her chest and heart.

"You want a cigarette?" Rita asked her. An impossible question, since Sophie knew her mother didn't allow anyone to smoke in the house. But Rita took out a pack of cigarettes from the kitchen cupboard, and lit one for Sophie, handing it to her. "Better take it," said Rita. "It'll be the last and only time I'll ever offer you one." A hint of laughter hung around her mouth and eyes, but the laughter couldn't quite let go.

Sophie took the cigarette between her fingers and drew in

smoke as if she'd been doing this for a long time. She held the smoke in her lungs, then blew it out.

As Rita watched her daughter, she thought her small body might burst into flame. She thought the smoke curling through her vessels could hardly be the healing Sophie needed; but for now, the offering had been right.

Forty-one

BOBBY KNEW THAT Sophie had come back home, but he did not expect her to call his house. When he answered the phone, even though he recognized the voice, he could not believe it was Sophie. She told him to come over to her house, that she wanted to speak to him about something. Her voice did not sound angry or tentative. Bobby tried to answer her in the same way, but his hands shook and he felt sure his voice sounded trembly. He said he would come over right away. He didn't want to have to spend hours wondering what Sophie wanted to say to him.

When he came in the back door, Sophie stood in the kitchen and told him without hesitation, even before Bobby had closed the screen door, that she remembered who had raped her that night. She remembered, and she planned to tell the police.

"But before I do that," she said, "you and Tom and Casey have to turn yourselves in. I want you to admit what you've done. It will be easier this way—just a confession."

"Why's that easier?" Bobby asked. He did not deny anything.

"Easier on me. I don't want a trial, or to have to testify or be questioned. I've thought about this." She paused. "So you've got to say what you did, Bobby."

Bobby took a deep breath.

"Anyway, it'll be better for you if you turn yourself in." She didn't want him to refuse. She didn't think she could go through another trial.

"God, Sophie. I don't know what made us do it. We'd been drinking. We were all fucked-up."

"So you'll turn yourself in?"

He hesitated. "Yeah." He sounded relieved.

"I'm going to the sheriff tomorrow," she told him. "So you better do it before then—if you're going to."

"What about Tom and Casey?"

"You tell them, if you want. I'm not talking to them."

"I'll go tomorrow," Bobby said. "We'll all go in."

"I'll wait till noon," she told him. "But no later than that."

On that night in April the boys had seen Crow and Sophie leave the party. "C'mon," Bobby had pulled Tom and Casey toward the door and outside. "Where're we going?" said Casey, already drunk. They followed the couple into the woods, quietly watching, inching closer for a better view. And when Crow took off, leaving Sophie exposed, a dark excitement broke loose, urging them forward.

Bobby saw Sophie try to push her arms through the sleeves of a shirt. When she heard them running through the woods toward her, she tried to cover herself; but Casey jerked the shirt away and wrapped her head like a ball. No one said a word.

Sophie struggled and cried out, "Wait! Don't! Please!" She kept saying, "Let me go!" But the scream was muffled inside the cotton of the shirt. Casey and Tom held her down.

"Don't. Don't hurt me."

Casey had stuffed Sophie's mouth with the shirtsleeve and held her arms down while Bobby got on top of her. Her skin white, white. As Bobby entered her he felt strange, otherworldly—as if he were having a fantasy that showed him doing this. The fantasy lingered even after he got up.

"C'mon, c'mon," Casey whispered. He motioned to Tom, but when he moved to stand up, Sophie grew strong and struggled out of Casey's hold. Casey hit her, wrapping the shirt tighter around her head. "Go on," he mouthed to Tom.

"Don't smother her," Bobby whispered.

Tom moved on top of Sophie, her body so slight beneath him. She whimpered, mumbling unrecognizable words. Bobby saw Tom pretend to do what he had done, even pretending to like it. Sophie grew limp.

As Casey climbed onto her, Bobby and Tom held her down. When he was through, he pitched the shirt so that it landed on Sophie's legs. She looked asleep, though her arms and legs resided at odd angles.

The whole thing took less than twenty minutes.

Then the boys ran into the woods, toward the river. The act had sobered them. The entire episode, even as they ran away, seemed like something from a life that was not their own.

"They'll match footprints to our shoes, you know," Tom said.

So each boy removed his shoes and threw them into the river. One by one tennis shoes flew in various directions, to sink quickly or float hopelessly away.

"We got to go home," said Bobby. They ran to the church parking lot, where Tom's car was parked. "We can't say anything about this. Not even to each other. Nothing." He knew more about the law than the other boys.

"Yeah," said Casey. "Oh, man."

"Why'd you have to hit her?" Bobby asked.

Tom pulled the car up to Bobby's house. His mother's bedroom light was off. *She must be asleep,* Bobby thought.

"Just get out. Go on, get out."

"Listen, we messed up," said Bobby.

"Get out, man." The consequences loomed large in Tom's head. He gunned the engine. "I've gotta get Casey home. Just go on."

Dog barked once as Bobby walked into the house. His mother had not locked the door. She used to always be awake when he came in, but lately she had been asleep. The next day she would ask what time he got in. Bobby usually lied. He seemed to be changing from the inside out.

A few years ago he would not have thought himself capable of doing what he had done tonight. He wondered if he even cared if he got caught. If he got caught, maybe his father would come to South Pittsburg. Everybody could see that he had a dad. He imagined having a father who would take care of difficult matters for him.

Bobby stood, without his shoes, looking down at his bed. He thought: *Have I murdered someone and not remembered it?* He thought that his face might have become invisible, his eyes black holes. He had heard an owl then—during the time with Sophie— and he heard one now outside his room. He felt a slight flutter of his hair in the night breeze coming through the window. He could not move. He could not climb into bed, he could not step back- ward, could not even move his head to look up, or turn off the lamp his mother had left on on the nightstand.

A car passed and he turned quickly to look, then turned off the lamp and pulled off his clothes. He put them under a pile of laun- dry next to the door and got into bed. Another car went by, throw- ing light onto the walls and ceiling, and the light felt heavy, like a horse running fast into his room; the threat of being crushed came to his mind. Then the light unhinged sideways down the room, and it was gone. It was gone.

When Bobby awoke, his first thought was how he would confess to the sheriff. He spoke the words aloud in bed, and his voice had a new thickness. He barely recognized it as his own. He felt a rhythm in sitting up in bed, going into the bathroom, washing his face. His actions felt ritualistic and final. He kept being amazed at his face in the mirror—how it looked the same. He still could not imagine consequences, couldn't let the idea of guilt enter his head. He stood in the shower a long time and tried to picture his mother's face when he told her.

At breakfast he ate little and his mother mentioned something in the news. She asked him a question, but Bobby didn't answer, his tongue too thick. The truth had begun to knit itself into a form of shadows in the corner, visible now.

"I spoke to Sophie Chabot yesterday," he said, not offering more. His expression suddenly like someone older, older even than his mother.

Aurelia got the look of someone who had just seen a terrible car crash, close up. "Oh," she said.

As he left the house a wind blew dust from the driveway, a swirling dust that had in it the vagaries of a different weather, colder. But it would be months before cold weather came.

Forty-two

ANTONY TRIED TO sneak upstairs. His watch gleamed 12:30, and he knew exactly which steps creaked and which didn't. But Louise Burden could hear an ant come in the door. She heard everything. He hadn't thought he'd made any sounds when her voice came from the bedroom. "That you, Antony?" Louise's voice didn't have a scintilla of sleep in it.

"It's me." Antony began to walk up the stairs at a normal pace.

"Awfully late tonight," she said. "Hard to believe you been practicing with the band all this time." She was getting up, putting on her robe and slippers. She would check to see if he'd been drinking.

Antony knew better than to lie to this old woman. "We jammed until about eleven, then we went to get burgers at the diner."

"You been drinking?"

"No, ma'am. Just Pepsi."

She was satisfied now. She could see him on the stairs from her room. "Y'all about ready for the band competition?"

"We better be."

"Go on to bed now."

When he closed the door to his room, he breathed relief. He had gone to practice, that was true; but no one had shown up. He had gone to the diner—that was also true. What he didn't tell was that he had seen Bobby and Casey outside the diner, arguing. He had overheard Bobby say that he was going to turn himself in to the police the next day.

"You can't do that," said Casey. "You're gonna screw all of us."

"You've got to come with me. I've already talked to Tom. It's over, Case."

They saw Antony, and Antony held up both hands.

"Antony," said Casey. "You can't say anything about this."

"I don't want to even hear it," Antony said, his hands still in the air.

"Okay, go."

So Antony went home. He hoped no one had seen him talking to Bobby or Casey—even the smallest thing might indict him. The next day he would claim to be sick. He awoke the next morning with complaints of nausea, flulike symptoms, begging not to go to work at the diner.

If Louise believed him, he would be safe. "You don't seem to have any fever," Louise told him, her large, fat hand on his head. "I don't want you missing work for nothing."

"I'm not," Antony protested. "I felt nauseated all night."

"Maybe it's food poisoning. That hamburger you had last night."

"I'm achy all over."

Louise watched her grandson try hard to bring on flulike symptoms, and she began to trust his fear of going out today. Something was going on. "Well," she said. "It *sounds* like the flu. You'll probably have a fever by noon." She kept looking at him, his eyes closed. His face was not even flushed, but his expression kept a hard plea. "I'll call the diner and tell them." She left the room, keeping the door open.

She told George, "He's got something, a fever, he's nauseated. The flu, I think. I'm letting him stay home."

"Didn't he stay out late last night?" George asked.

"Yeah, but that's not it. He's really sick."

·   ·   ·

Antony stayed in bed all day, alone in the house. Louise called him every few hours to ask how he was. He told her each time that he'd been sleeping.

Bobby called just before noon. "Okay, man. Listen, we're going in."

"I don't know anything about it." Antony hung up. He went to the refrigerator, finding a hodgepodge of soft celery stalks, two apples, milk, and some moldy cheese. He looked expectantly into the microwave window to see if Louise had left a bowl of soup for him. She had. He heated it and ate without turning on the lights. He liked the dark coolness of the house during the daytime.

The afternoon had begun to accelerate, bringing a heavy, gold haze over the houses and woods. The clock on the stove showed the time in digital red numbers: 3:45. When Antony turned on the TV, he heard the jagged news: three boys had turned themselves in for the assault and rape of Sophie Chabot.

But something else too—a teenager from South Pittsburg, Tennessee, had been reported missing. More news at six.

Forty-three

AROUND TEN O'CLOCK in the morning Bobby came to the house looking for Crow. Everything about him—his gait, his face, his shoulders—everything seemed urgent. Helen called to him from the garden.

"Bobby, where've you been?" She didn't mean it as a judgment, but as a statement about missing him. "I haven't seen you in weeks! Crow's upstairs."

For years Bobby had walked in without knocking, like family; this time he paused at the front steps before going in. He climbed the stairs slowly. Crow's bedroom door was open. Bobby saw that he was gluing a wing back onto one of the planes they had put together when they were ten. Crow kept them on a shelf above his bed.

"What's up?" Bobby said, trying to lose some of the urgency he felt.

"I knocked off a couple of planes throwing around my basketball." Crow studied the place where glue had to be applied. Bobby didn't come further into the room, and he didn't sit down.

"What's the matter?" Crow asked.

Bobby turned away. "Listen," he said. "I've got to tell you something."

"So tell me." The glue didn't hold and the wing fell off again. "Damn."

Bobby sat on the bed. "You won't believe this." His voice shook.

Crow shifted in his chair and looked at his friend. "What if I do?" he said.

"I did something pretty bad."

"What?" Crow set the plane on the bed. "With that gun? Shit! I thought your mother took it away."

"Not with the gun. I don't have that anymore." He turned his face away from Crow.

"So what is it?" Crow was beginning to realize what Bobby might say.

"Bad."

"What'd you do, Bobby?" He lifted the broken plane with both hands and laid it carefully on the shelf. "Hell, you gonna make me guess?" He kept his back to Bobby.

"I did it. The thing they accused *you* of doing."

Crow did not move, his hands in midair. "Say it, Bobby."

Bobby shouted now. "Sophie! Me and Casey and Tom! We were drunk out of our minds, Crow. We'd been drinking." Everything came out—excuses, confession, everything. "She was there in the woods. You weren't anywhere around."

Crow's voice was a whisper. "What are you saying?" Though he knew, somewhere inside he had known. He walked toward Bobby, close. A mountain was building itself inside him.

"Listen," said Bobby. "I know how this sounds. We weren't thinking. Like, it just happened." He threw his arms up. "We went to the river after. We threw our shoes in the river."

Crow stood. How strange to dislike so intensely the same person who, only moments before, had been a friend. The air in the room felt heavy.

"Listen . . ."

"Get out." Crow lunged, hitting Bobby's chest, pushing him hard.

Bobby fell. "Listen, Crow."

"Get out!" said Crow. "You bastard!"

"I wanted to tell you. I wanted to—" Bobby got back up.

"What do you expect me to do?"

"Say something. Just say something."

"You *ass*hole. You did that to Sophie? Who *are* you? And you let me get blamed without saying *any*thing?" Crow swept his arm across the shelf of airplanes, and they all crashed down. "You didn't say *anything*? Shit, man. I don't even know who you are."

"I'm turning myself in today," Bobby said. "We all are."

"Get out. Fuck you. Get OUT." Crow opened the door and pushed Bobby out.

"I'm going to the police," Bobby said. "I'm doing the right thing now."

Crow heard Bobby lean against the door and whisper, "Did you hear me?"

Crow didn't answer. He was leaning against the door too. He heard Bobby stumble downstairs toward the front door and leave. He felt a shaggy hate toward his friend.

In the moment when he left Crow's room, Bobby looked like a man hanging on a branch over a cliff, one hand out for someone to take hold of. The truth had circled and finally landed, forming a tight band around them.

Forty-four

CARL CAME HOME at two. He was leaving to pick up Johnny at camp this afternoon. Johnny had been away for the last two weeks in July, and Carl looked forward to driving him home.

Helen heard Carl's car door slam, and she met him in the hallway as he came in. "Have you heard yet?"

"What happened?" Carl put down a large folder of papers and went to fix a drink.

"Bobby confessed to Sophie's rape. So did Casey Willig and Tom Canady. Charlie Post came by and told me," she said.

"What's Charlie saying?" Carl didn't believe it.

Helen shook her head. "It's not what Charlie says, it's what Sophie told. It's what Bobby Bailey told the police."

Carl drank long sips of his bourbon. "My God, Helen."

"They've all turned themselves in."

"Crow's friends." Carl shook his head. "And they let him be blamed. Go through a trial. I can't believe it."

"Charlie wondered if Crow knew anything about it." Helen spoke tentatively.

"What're you saying? Did Charlie make some accusation against Crow?"

"He didn't accuse. He just asked us if we had ever questioned Crow about his friends."

"Damn. Of course we did! And so did the police, the D.A., Butler . . . We had a whole trial. Crow was acquitted. Isn't that enough?" Carl looked enormously sad. He downed the last of his drink and got up for a refill.

"Stop yelling at me! That's exactly what I told Charlie."

Carl walked into the kitchen. He wanted to get away from her. "I hope Johnny will be easier to raise than Crow," he mumbled. "I don't expect to go through anything like this again."

Helen lifted herself out of the chair. "Because Johnny is *yours*?" She followed Carl to the kitchen. "How convenient for you to be able to choose when you claim someone and when you disclaim them!" She was yelling.

He kept his back to her, looking at the floor. "Helen, I wasn't saying that. You know I didn't mean that."

Helen was working up to something hard-edged. "Haven't you ever done anything wrong, Carl? If I know something about you, something that has been kept secret for a long time, if I find out about it, what do you think I do?"

"Helen?" He looked up now, surprised at her fervor. He hadn't expected the conversation to go in this direction.

Helen took her words further than she had meant to go. "You think I should disclaim you because you've done something reprehensible?" She had her hands on her face, weeping into them. Carl walked over to her.

"Helen." He didn't know what to say.

"I want you to speak to him, Carl. You need to talk to him."

"I don't believe Crow knew more than he told us," said Carl. "Damn that Charlie." He shook his head. "Okay," he said. "I'll talk to him." But Carl couldn't leave Helen, couldn't leave the room. "I know I've hurt you," he said.

"We all hurt each other." She buried her face in his shoulder. "We hurt each other all the time."

When Crow came downstairs, his mother said, "Do you know?"

The back lot of Crow's memory kept the shock of that night hanging precipitously in his mind. As the memory came forward again, his face grew haggard. A white haze fogged his mind. He nodded.

"What did you hear?" Carl asked.

"Bobby went with Tom and Casey to confess. Bobby told me before he told the sheriff."

"Is that why he was here?" Helen asked. "He told you then?"

"Yes." Crow's voice took on the timbre of a young child.

Carl felt like a relic asking these questions. His voice seemed to have an odd inflection. "So you didn't know anything until . . . ?"

"Until today." Crow grew angry at this third degree.

"I had to ask," said Carl. "I just had to ask you about it. That's all."

Helen had left the room, trying to take in the news of Bobby, but she could see them both through a space between the hinges of the door. She saw Crow's stringy muscles and Carl's jaunty underlip.

She saw Crow's hands worrying his forehead and hair, and she tried to push from her eyes the image of her son's unchildlike face.

When Crow looked at his father, he held a hard, straight glance. He wanted to bring out all their secrets. "Now, let me ask *you* something," he said.

"What's that?" Helen saw the dread creep into Carl's face.

But Crow's question went unasked, because at that moment someone knocked loudly at the door and Carl stood up. Helen answered the door and entered the room with two men. "They're asking where Johnny is," Helen said. "These men work at the camp. They say that Johnny is gone."

"He's been missing for almost five hours," one man said. "The camp director has been trying to reach you." He looked at Carl with eyes that could not find a place to land.

"Mr. Davenport." The other man stood very still. "Your son has been reported missing. Though there's been no evidence of foul play. Do you know where he is?"

"I was going to pick him up today. This was his last day at camp."

"He was going to pick him up," Helen said dumbly.

"Well, sir. We think that he ran off. He took some of his clothes with him, and some camping gear. Somebody could have taken him, but we think he more than likely ran away."

Helen screamed. "Carl? Carl?"

"Well, I don't believe that," Carl said. He touched Crow's shoulder. Everything that happened from now on, he felt, would be completely his fault.

Helen could not move. Outside the hills rose, and trees wilted in the heat. Everything looked as though it wanted to sit down.

"Did anybody at the camp say where he might be?" Crow asked.

Both men took a step toward them. "Can we sit down?" one asked, and led Carl, Helen, and Crow into the living room, as if they were guests in a new home.

Forty-five

AURELIA BAILEY STOOD in the kitchen pouring a cup of tea when she heard someone knock at the back door. Dog, napping under the table, lifted his head, ambled to the door. She thought of the dream she had had last night about a visitor who came to the house, one who kept knocking but, when she opened the door, was nowhere to be seen. Then she heard knocking again at another door, or at a window. She wasn't afraid in the dream, but when she awoke she thought the experience nightmarish. She imagined her mind playing tricks on her, and she ignored the knocking. She put some honey in her tea and decided to go in late to the office.

She heard the knock again, louder this time, more urgent. She went to open the door and saw a young deputy standing before her. His manner was serious, but his hands twitched nervously. She didn't like the lack of confidence that seemed to go with his youthful appearance. He looked like someone who was performing a task for the first time.

"Mrs. Bailey?" he said. Not *Judge* Bailey, but *Mrs.*

"Yes?" She knew what he would say, and thought of the persistent knocking in last night's dream.

"Your son's turned himself in."

Aurelia's knees grew weak, and the young officer caught her as she began to buckle. She stiffened as he took her arm.

"He's at the station now?" she asked, her judgelike voice trying to take hold. It was here.

"Yes, ma'am," the officer said. "I'll drive you." His name tag read ALEX JAMISON. He looked not much older than Bobby.

"Just a minute," she said. Then, "No, you go ahead. I'll take my car."

Aurelia disappeared upstairs and yelled something to the officer in a tone that sounded dismissive; so Deputy Jamison closed the door, got into his car, and waited for her to come back down and drive her car around front, then pull out onto the road. He followed her to the police station.

Bobby sat in a chair with his hands in his lap. When he saw his mother enter the room he tried to read her face. She had hoped for a chance to speak to him before the D.A. came in, though Jeb Wall had already thought of that too and had started talking casually to all three boys. She whispered something to Jeb, and he nodded.

She looked at her son, trying to ask him with her eyes what he had said, but Bobby's expression was sheeplike and foreign.

She'd seen them first through the one-way glass: Bobby at the table, an investigator sitting across from him, and Jeb standing, very tall it seemed, behind Bobby. She saw their heads and bodies, their faces in bas-relief. When she entered the room, she felt a change in their mood.

The police investigator looked up slowly and acknowledged Judge Bailey's presence. His skin stretched tight, like a balloon, and he squinted in concentration as he began to ask another question. Wall stopped him. The afternoon dwindled into evening, and the idea of her son going to jail seemed more a part of last night's dream than today's reality.

"May I speak to him a moment?" she asked. "Could I take him outside and speak to him?"

Jeb Wall nodded.

Bobby walked out of the station and sat with her on the courthouse steps, his head bent forward.

Aurelia could not tell from his face if he felt remorse, guilt, or fear. She'd never before seen this particular expression and wondered if it was false, or if every expression up until that moment had been false—this one being true. His skin, a sick blue shade, and his breathing, slow, made him seem oddly unfamiliar.

"Are you going to talk about this now or later?" she asked, not without anger.

"I don't know."

"Then let's say *now*."

Bobby looked as though he might pass out.

"You will go to jail. You know that already, I guess."

He did not know she meant now, today.

She paused. "You've been lying to me about everything." It was not a question.

"You lied to me too. You lied to me my whole life." Bobby began to sob, his head down. His shoulders shook with despair. Aurelia leaned to hold him. She already believed that what Bobby had done arose out of the secret she had built around his father. She was alarmed to realize that this secret had caused more harm than Robert's own particular disgrace, or his actual absence.

"Can we go home?" Bobby asked.

"No," she said. She could not believe how much he didn't understand. "I have to take you back in there. I'll get a lawyer and try to get you out on bail, but it may not be possible."

She held him until the sobbing lessened, then they went back into the station. She promised again that she would try to help him.

When Aurelia entered her house, the wind blew and rattled the windows, reminding her of the knocking, and the absolute end of life as she had known it before last night's dream.

Forty-six

"Seems like nothing good happens anymore," Louise told George.

"Why you say that?"

"Because it's true. One thing after another—those boys' confessions yesterday, and now this thing with Johnny disappearing. I'm going over to see Helen. I dread seeing her face. What am I going to say, George?"

"Just be a friend to her, I guess."

"Yeah."

"Oh, God. All I could think about was if this was my Antony—if Antony turned up missing, I don't know what I'd do. What am I gonna say to her, George?"

"Won't matter what you say. Hell, you can't really say anything. Just go on over there now. Talk to her a little."

Louise drove up to the Davenport house and got out. Helen sat by herself in the living room, dressed like she was going to church. Her face was blank, no expression at all; then as she choked back a greeting, she leaned her face down into her lap.

"I don't want to upset you," Louise said.

"No, come in. I count on you to be the one to come by when I need somebody."

"Where's Carl? And Crow?"

"Carl went into town. He's coming back in a little while." She

looked up, her face and eyes pooling into a mask. "Crow's upstairs." The pain moved beneath her skin, hovering, steel-edged.

Louise sat beside her on the couch.

"When the men from the camp came by and told us Johnny was
missing, Louise, I couldn't stop screaming. I couldn't stop. I
thought they had told me he was dead. I thought that's what they
were not saying, you know? I'd be screaming now if my doctor
hadn't dosed me up on pills."

Louise nodded. "I know," she said. "You keep thinking you
could lose him. I know about that." She reached for Helen, then
pulled back, not wanting to touch such raw heat.

"Carl looks smashed down," Helen said.

"What can I do?" Louise asked. The muscles in the back of her
neck began to ache. "Oh, Helen."

Helen pressed her mouth tight, trying to keep her lips from
trembling. "When I was young, kids didn't have such a dangerous
world. Nobody would've raped somebody's girlfriend. That was
what *criminals* did, not regular boys. And I never knew anybody
who ran away. I think somebody's taken him." She had not even let
herself think this thought, and now she said it out loud.

"You just wait," Louise said. "Thing's are going to be fine." She
squeezed Helen's arm. "You've got to hold on now."

Helen struggled to do just that, to hold on. "Sometimes I wonder if we try to protect our kids from too much, then when they
enter the real world, they're not ready."

Louise didn't know where this was going, but she could see
how Helen's talk was unraveling a fierce knot inside her. "You
can't really protect 'em," she said. "That's the thing."

Helen leaned forward. "What do we do?"

She heard the back door slam and jumped. "Carl, that you?"
She looked up quickly, her eyes wild.

Carl walked into the living room. "Any news?"

Helen shook her head.

Crow came downstairs and stood behind his father. They looked as separate as stones.

"You want to go with us to the camp, Louise?" asked Carl.

"No. I got to get back home."

"Okay. Crow and I will wait outside," Carl told Helen. "You come on when you're ready."

Helen nodded. Her hair was unwashed, though brushed, and she wore no makeup. Her long fingernails had been chewed down to nubs, and dried blood clotted in the corners. Louise felt she could see a tiny pin shining in the center of Helen, piercing her just below the heart. She could *see* it: a sliver piercing the edges of ventricle, cutting away at tissue and vein. A hot white pin embedded in sinew and muscle.

It could take years for that to go away, thought Louise. *Years.*

Helen stood up and turned out the light. Through the kitchen window they could see the bright weather of the day. Both women thought that if they looked hard enough, they might see the face of the God they both trusted, some contour of a face that was recognizable against the endless canvas of blue sky. They both wanted to see it.

As Louise drove away, she thought about the suffering of white people, how it had never seemed the same as, or even comparable to, the suffering of blacks. She had always felt that way, and even felt superior because of the difference; but sitting with Helen she knew that she, Louise Burden, had not had Helen's troubles. She saw how no one but Helen could hold her particular load.

Then Louise wondered, for the first time, if she had taught Antony how to bear his own sadness, or had taught him to blame. Had she allowed him to resent others for what he didn't have? George liked to blame. He liked to resent and hold a grudge. It frightened her to think of what she had taught, or not taught, Antony. And in the secret part of her heart she hoped that Antony knew nothing, nothing whatsoever, about the problems of these white boys.

George and Antony waited for her on the porch. Antony kicked at his shoe. Both looked so handsome in their bright white shirts. "You look nice," Louise told them, and George got in the front seat.

"We're taking you out for dinner," he said. And they drove in silence to the nearest restaurant.

V

The Slow Moon

Forty-seven

THE JAIL HELD heat like steam in a barrel. The boys had been in their cells for almost a week, just five miles away from Pittsburg, but it felt like a different universe, or a bad dream. The jail cells in Jasper County were small and clean, and each one had a high window.

When they were first taken to their cells, each boy was allowed to talk to his family. Jack and Mary Canady entered a large room and sat at a table. One guard walked Tom into the visitors' room and stood beside the door. He pretended not to listen, but noticed how Jack kept complaining about small matters. The complaints came steady, relentless, and rarely had to do with Tom. He seemed chained to these complaints.

When he complained about the lack of air-conditioning, Tom said, "They have it. It's just broken."

"Well, it's unbearable in here." The complaints lessened after a while, then started up again. Neither parent wanted to talk about the rape, instead they told Tom about Johnny's sudden disappearance.

"What do you mean?" said Tom. "He ran away?" Tom did not admit to having called Johnny at camp before turning himself in. He had pretended to be Mr. Davenport so they would be sure to call Johnny to the phone. Johnny had been sent for right in the middle of a swimming competition.

"Dad, what's wrong?" Johnny's voice sounded young and worried.

"Relax kid, it's me. Tom." He took a deep breath and spilled out his story, telling Johnny what he, Bobby, and Casey had done, and explaining their plan to turn themselves in.

"Why would you do that to Sophie? And my brother." Johnny's teeth were chattering.

Tom could just picture him, wrapped in a wet towel and dripping on the floor. "You think you can judge me?" He felt his voice grow harsh against the back of his throat, raggedy. "Like none of this is your fault? Think about what you did to me. One day you can't wait to kiss me and squeeze my cock, and the next you won't even take my phone calls. Actions have consequences, Johnny. And the way I was feeling, in that black, crappy hole, half drunk, I just went along with my friends."

Johnny swallowed. "So you're saying that this was somehow my fault?"

Tom sighed. "I don't know what I'm saying. I guess I just wanted you to hear about this from me, before your brother had a chance to trash me or you saw it on the news. You're the only person I really care about, Johnny. I wish you cared about me the same way. If you had . . . I wouldn't be in this mess."

Now Tom worried that Johnny might hurt himself, or that his own problems could be compounded by what Johnny might tell.

"They haven't found him," said Mary. "People are thinking somebody took him."

"Nobody took him," said Tom. "Johnny's just real private. He likes to go off alone sometimes."

"Well, this seems different," his father said. "Nobody can find him. He didn't tell anybody he was going away. That's why they're worried."

Tom felt supremely conscious of his body, its weight and heft. As they talked, something flicked through his head, made him start, as if he tasted something sour.

His mother, stuck in her funnel of doubt, asked, "Are you all right, Tom?" A dry question. Tom nodded. He caught his father perusing his hair and shirt.

"You need some other clothes, son?" Jack Canady sat, still as a carving. He had settled into meek embarrassment. "They let you wear your own clothes in here?"

"I can wear my own stuff until I have to leave," said Tom. He didn't say "prison." Mary made a list of things to bring to Tom, glad to be talking about something she could do. She felt pleased that Jack had asked the question. Tom felt that his parents might be trying to pretend that he was leaving for school.

"We'll come back every day," his mother promised.

"Let me know if you hear anything about Johnny," Tom said.

The boys were in cells near each other. Bobby and Casey on one side, Tom on the opposite side. They would remain there for a couple of more weeks, maybe a month. The D.A. had decided that these boys should be sentenced as adults. Now everyone had to wait for the judge to consider this decision. Many people in town did not agree with the D.A. Letters and editorials were written. The judge could take his time deciding.

Every night for several weeks one of the mothers brought supper for them—an unusual request made by Judge Bailey and accepted by the sheriff. The boys preferred meals cooked by Mary Canady, but tonight Judge Bailey brought them chicken tetrazzini. Casey's mother could not be counted on to bring anything.

As Aurelia Bailey entered the visitors' room, thunder shook the building and lights flickered. A deluge of rain fell on the jailhouse roof. She sat with the boys while they ate. The room had a TV, and sometimes the guard let the boys stay an hour or two to watch TV before going back to their cells.

Bobby took a bite of the casserole. He liked the taste of noodles and chicken and cheese. He ate quickly.

"Bobby," said Aurelia, "when you're through I'd like to talk with you."

"Okay."

She gathered the plates and her casserole dish, then led Bobby to a different room. Bobby stayed for nearly thirty minutes, and when he returned he looked puzzled but inflated with importance.

The next flash of lightning made the lights flicker again, and the TV went off.

"That's it," said the officer, whose name was Seldon. "You're going back now." He seized and handcuffed each boy, and they followed him down the dingy hall to their cells. Pearly hard drops of hail hit the roof and the sides of the building. Officer Seldon closed the cells, and just as he was leaving, the lights went out completely. He had a flashlight and flipped it on.

"Don't you have some kind of emergency lighting in here?" Bobby asked.

"Yeah, but it must've got the transformer."

"At least leave us the flashlight," said Bobby.

"Can't do that," said the officer.

"Aw, man. Don't leave us like this. What could we do with a flashlight? Leave us something."

"I have a small penlight in my desk. Guess I could get that." The officer went to get the smaller light.

"What'd your mother say, Bobby?" Tom asked. He could tell that Bobby's mood had lifted.

"She said my dad's coming tomorrow," Bobby told them. "He's coming here."

"You're shittin' me," said Casey.

"She said he's coming around four o'clock." Bobby's voice had a tinge of restoration in it, an oddly happy inflection. (All those nights in bed, imagining a father somewhere in a boat, or camping in the woods, in an office high up in a building in Chicago or New York City. Or he imagined his father walking into his room, or coming home at dinnertime and sitting down with him forever.)

Officer Seldon returned with the penlight and handed it to Bobby.

"Here." Tom pitched a couple of books outside the bars of Bobby's cell. "Read something to us. I mean, read it out loud. You got the flashlight."

"Which book?"

"Anything," said Casey. "Something funny."

So Bobby read as they settled on their cots, getting beneath their slim blankets. And the dark air took the words, creating a story above them, a comic scenario that made them laugh out loud. When Bobby grew tired, he stopped reading. "Okay," he said. "That's all."

No one answered, but he heard them turn over on their cots. He flicked off the penlight, its thin ray going back into the small stick canister.

"You know what, guys?" Casey said. "The Battle of the Bands was yesterday. I wonder who won."

That night Bobby tried to pray. But as he lay there he began instead to laugh. He thought of passages he had just read, and the laughter that rose up in him was real, not nervous, and became contagious as he tried to explain what he was laughing about. Tom remembered something else, then Casey added to it, and their laughter wouldn't stop. It moved from cell to cell like a feather. And the joy that comes with laughter came in, like a stranger to them. Just before sleep, Bobby wondered if that was prayer. If, for the first time in his life he had prayed, really prayed, and that that was it.

The next morning a robin flew off the roof, its wings skittering in front of the cell window; another one ducked and fluttered toward the ground.

"I wish it would come in here," Tom said. He was looking out, trying to see it again.

"Tom's turning into the Birdman of Alcatraz." Casey laughed.

"Kiss my ass," said Tom.

"You ever held a bird?" Casey asked.

"Have you?"

"Once," said Casey. "It had a broken wing and I picked it up. I could feel its heart, you know? Like its heart would beat right out of its chest."

"Did it die?"

"I guess."

"You didn't take it somewhere?"

"No."

"Shit, Willig," said Bobby. "Why'd you even pick it up?"

"It wadn't my fault it got a broken wing," Casey said. "Don't blame me."

Tom thought of the reverend's dog on the side of the road.

"What're you thinking about?" asked Casey.

"Who?" asked Tom.

"Anybody."

"I'm thinking about how we got here," Bobby said.

"My head's fuzzy," Tom answered. "I can't think about anything at all."

"Willig?"

"I'm thinking about my brother and how he felt when he was in jail. Did I tell you he was in jail? He stayed for four years."

"I wish I'd done what I planned to do," Tom told them.

"Which was what?" Bobby thought he might say something funny.

Tom didn't answer. No one spoke.

"Je-sus, Tom."

"I was going to San Francisco. I was going to live there." He had not said what he was thinking, but the words sounded good. "I swear, I don't think I'd be in all this trouble if I had a different dad."

"Well, if we're blaming, then I'm the son of a bitch who has a dad I thought was dead, and a mother-judge. I wouldn't mind having a few things different too."

"I'm following after my brother," Casey said. "Right in his footsteps."

They stood around blaming whatever they could think to blame.

Tom leaned against the wall, looking out into the other cells. He wanted someone to speak, to talk to him and make him feel normal. He wanted them to find Johnny. Casey sat on his cot, his head in his hands, looking at the floor. He mouthed to himself as if talking in his sleep.

Bobby kept coughing, not as if anything were caught in his throat, but nervously. From time to time he stood on his cot and looked out the window. "I see Coach Post," Bobby said. "He just got out of his car. He might be coming to see us."

But Charlie headed toward the 7-Eleven. Bobby said nothing about his pause, his slow turn toward the jail before going into the store.

Casey sat on his cot, cursing, a sluggish sound to his voice. Each boy could hear the other moving in his cell. In a short while they grew still.

"Guess Coach isn't coming," said Tom. The day moved slowly toward noon, and they slept to pass the time.

Bobby lay on his cot. He wished he were outside doing something free. And with the wish came an image of wings over the river, a flicker of a hawk or bright robin.

Last year Mr. Hollis had told his classes an old story of slaves who were packed tightly into ships for many months, how the slaves had dreamed of flight back to their homes, their families, back to their sisters and fathers. Each man held his breath, hoping to fly, believing that if only he could swallow his tongue, then flight might be possible. By swallowing his tongue a slave could fly out of the dark hull of a ship, over the water and bright shore, over the hard moon and its edge of shadow, until he reached the hut where he had lived. And when he got there, he could breathe in the smell of home. He could bring his father's hand to his face.

Bobby experimented with his tongue, but instead of flying he coughed and choked, and the face that came to his mind was Sophie's—Sophie hovering small on the ground. He could see her— her shoulders and arms, the shape of her eyes and mouth. He could smell her hair. And then he saw her body lift up above the trees and she was gone. But Bobby was not gone. Bobby was still here inside the realm of mistake. He could not swallow his tongue, nor could he fly, but he did feel the crazy thrill of joy. He had seen Sophie leave that place of ground. And by midafternoon he didn't know if he had slept, but he knew the burst of flight, of Sophie's freedom, if not his own.

Forty-eight

JOHNNY HAD BEEN gone for thirty-six hours. A slow August light settled into the ground, burning at the edge of hills. People wondered now if the Davenport boy was even alive. They suspected something more than just a boy running away. They had found a T-shirt and a sock in the woods outside Chattanooga, and suspicion stirred through the town. Police in other states had been alerted.

Helen barely slept at all. That night she saw Johnny at the end of her bed—she awoke suddenly and saw him there. She knew she was not dreaming because Carl had gotten up and was in the bathroom. The bathroom light was on and water running. She called to see if Carl was all right. "I'm fine," he said. She could hear him pacing.

Then she saw, at the end of the bed, the form of Johnny, his face and shape, though not his clothes, not even his body—just his shape, his size, his head and features. And he motioned for her the way he motioned every time he wanted her to come, whenever he wanted to show her something. She gasped so loud that Carl turned off the water and called out, "Helen?" So concerned they were about each other. Then again, "Helen?"

Helen couldn't answer, for fear her voice would send Johnny away. His shape moved to the side of the bed, and she reached quickly to touch him, but he moved back.

"Oh, Johnny, honey, is it you? It is you, isn't it?" And then she heard a sound—but not a voice—come from the charge of light that he was.

When Carl came back to bed, Helen pretended to be asleep. She hoped the shape would come back. She felt greedy with hope. She lay with her eyes closed, and for moments she wanted to leave the world, to allow holy sleep to pronounce its own loneliness.

Helen felt her throat collapse, a small cry coming out. Carl reached his arms around her. He held her close.

The next morning, in the half-light of dawn, Carl could hear Helen's light footsteps, barefooted going through the house. He could hear her walking from room to room, passing Crow sleeping, then down to the carpeted hallway to their own bedroom.

Worry surrounded Helen like smoke, like clothes she could not take off; and she became aroused. Her groin and breasts ached with a fever, her belly and arms, her legs, trembled with want.

Carl saw Helen pull her gown over her head, her body gleaming white with shadows. He had forgotten how slim her hips and legs were, how full her breasts. She climbed into bed beside him and lay on her back before she said his name. He didn't answer immediately. He wasn't sure he could do what she wanted. How long had it been since they were close?

But as she began to touch him, knead him with her hands, he caught some of her hunger and turned toward her. He said her name, then said it again, kissing her. Her mouth became young, and remembering, his tongue took hold.

He entered her and they rocked, investigating the whiteness of legs and belly. "Carl, love me, Carl." Then she said, "Fuck me," as if she were mad at the world. Carl grew strong with desire. Helen had never come to him with such abandon, and he imagined Ava instead of Helen, though the nights with Ava were over. Those last nights with Ava had even become humdrum, expectable; and now this desire from Helen had brought him back to what he thought was an irretrievable domain. He had missed her.

How did this happen? Had the presence of children in the house over the years taken away their spirit of lust, and now had it come back? She rode him, rolling until they were half off the bed. Helen's head hung down like someone drowned. Still she wanted more, so they moved to the floor. A long final sigh and tiny tremblings convinced Carl of her satisfaction.

"Helen."

"Don't," she said. "Don't say anything. Anything." Helen's pleadings came out in a rhythm, rather than specific words.

They heard the sound of birds, many birds in a field behind the house. The noisy calls came in so suddenly that Carl got up to see what it was.

"What is it?" Helen asked.

"Blackbirds," Carl told her. "So many. Come here and look."

"I can't move," she said. "I don't think I can move." When Carl didn't return to the bed but kept standing at the window, Helen got up to see.

Hundreds of starlings were rising up, then landing in a nearby meadow. Helen stood beside Carl, their bodies shiny with sweat, their arms around each other. They watched the birds' trembly pecking, moving together, from one side of the field to the other.

"They're starlings," said Helen. "I've always been fascinated at the way they move in droves like that." They swerved up again. She and Carl remained at the window thinking about how their world had shrunk down to this ledge: the rise and fall of so many black wings against the morning air, and harsh calls cutting the air like a knife. They clutched each other as if they were about to fall.

The telephone rang and Helen hurried to answer. Carl heard her talking in the hall and could tell by the tone of her voice that it was news about Johnny.

"What?" Carl yelled, hearing her run toward the room.

She rushed to the closet to get dressed. "They found him."

Carl leapt up. "Where?"

"I don't want to believe anything until I see him," Helen said.

"Where did they find him? Tell me." Carl was pulling on his pants.

Helen laughed, almost laughed. "Wake Crow up," she said.

"Helen?"

"State troopers found him on the road to Chattanooga. They're dropping him off at the police station."

She put on jeans and a sweatshirt, and touched Carl's cheek as she left the room. "Crow!" she called loudly. "They found Johnny!"

Carl rushed to Crow's room. He was already in the bathroom and had not heard his mother. They all dressed without washing, without doing anything but going to the car and rushing to where Johnny was.

Forty-nine

JOHNNY HAD HUNG up the phone, shivering, horrified. Tom's news turned the world upside down. Could all of this be Johnny's fault? Even partly? Because he'd let himself go with Tom and spent those afternoons exploring in the abandoned house? Because he'd cut Tom off so completely? Would Tom tell everyone what they did? Johnny pictured his father hearing about it. It would probably kill him. And all the kids at school would look at him differently. Melanie would think he was gay. Would she be wrong?

Johnny felt like he'd swallowed a fireball, and the idea pushed him into motion. Instead of going back to swimming, he'd headed to his cabin, grabbed his backpack and some water, and started walking.

He needed to be alone, to think about who he was, or who he could be now. In the small river town of South Pittsburg, Tennessee, a shock spent itself wave upon wave, where even things in the corners or the backs of closets kept rising.

His memories of sex with Tom confused Johnny, and even though Tom had never forced Johnny further than he wanted to go, he had always urged for more, finally growing frustrated and angry. ("C'mon. Shit! Are you with me or not? What are you so scared of?")

Maybe Tom was right. Maybe Johnny *was* gay, but then why did he have such strong feelings for Melanie? He had kissed her over and over, not wanting to stop. He wanted to touch her legs and breasts—could barely keep himself from doing so. He felt a stronger pull toward Melanie than he had with Tom. Should he feel guilty? Should he tell Melanie about Tom? If he could get off somewhere, he might be able to figure things out. So he wandered from the camp and didn't come back.

The smell of leaves and old roses hung in the air. Crab apples, sour and dark on their axis in the deep earth, hung beside thick webs in the limbs. Johnny kept thinking about regret; but these thoughts seemed useless, like a sentimental weakness.

A breeze worked like a courier to bring him new thoughts: *I am not to blame. Tom did what he did. He did it, not me. And I know that I want Melanie more than Tom.* He began to feel a subtle unstringing in his bones. *But I treated Tom badly. I started something in him that turned destructive. I have to go back and face that—the part that was mine.*

Sympathy and outrage fought against each other. There would always be the appearance of shadows in the woods, of a sky luminous with gray pearl, and long dark streaks of road. *We carry our own mistakes,* he thought. *Sometimes when you stand on a precipice, it becomes impossible not to slip. Something went terribly wrong. But how, exactly? What did I not see or understand?*

Johnny slept all night on the floor of the woods, and the next morning he awoke with a clear plan. He would go to the jail to check on Tom. He would look him straight in the eye.

Feeling touched by a finger bone of hope, Johnny walked all morning until he found himself at the edge of a cemetery near Chattanooga. The cemetery gates were large and rusty. And as he passed them, a chord struck. *Was the chord in his head? Was it a bell in the town, a church bell? It seemed far off. Was it the sound of the gate closing?*

When he looked up he saw a white cruiser in the cemetery parking lot, and two flat-eyed men coming toward him, fast.

"Are you Johnny Davenport?"

"Yes, sir, I'm Johnny." He knew who he was, and it felt good to say it out loud.

"We've been looking for you. Where have you been?"

The next day Johnny asked his mother to go with him to the jail.

"I don't want to see those boys," Helen said. "Not yet."

"Just drive me," he pleaded. "Don't go in if you don't want to."

Helen was so glad to see Johnny she would've done anything he asked. "Well, but we won't stay long," she said.

The smell of urine in the jail filled even the visitors' room.

"Canady!" the officer called. "You got vis-ters." He led Tom into the visitation room, to a large wooden picnic table.

"Is it my mom?" Tom asked.

"No," said the officer. He opened the door, and Tom was startled to see Johnny and his mother.

"Hello, Mrs. Davenport," Tom said. He nodded slowly to Johnny and slid onto the bench facing them.

"I wanted to come by," Johnny said.

"He asked me to bring him," Helen spoke stiffly. She barely looked at Tom. She couldn't look at his face.

"I wanted to see how you were." Johnny kept nodding, could not stop nodding.

"I'm pretty good," Tom said, trying to sound normal. "I get hungry though."

Johnny took a sack from his mother. "We brought you these." He looked embarrassed. "It's just some comic books and candy."

"No, that's good." Tom took the sack and looked inside. "That's real good. Thanks." He had tears in his eyes. "You ran away?" he said to Johnny.

"I don't know why I did it. It was stupid."

"Not that stupid," said Tom, his mouth curling slightly toward a smile. "Not nearly as stupid as the stuff I've done."

"Yeah."

Helen felt the current between the two boys and wanted to shut it off. "Johnny, I told you we couldn't stay but a minute."

"Okay then." Tom rose to go back to his cell.

"I'm sorry about all this," Johnny said.

"Yeah," Tom said, and he looked as if he might touch Johnny. "I'm glad you're all right." Tom tucked the sack under his arm, but it broke open. Johnny leaned to pick up the items. When he handed them back, Tom's whole body appeared sad and raw, sick even.

"Listen." Tom wanted to prolong the moment but didn't know what to say. "Maybe you can come back again."

"I don't know," said Johnny. "Maybe."

They both nodded.

As Helen walked with Johnny back to the car, she asked, "What was that about?"

"Nothing."

Helen took the long way home, not wanting to stop driving but thinking about Johnny with Tom. What exactly had transpired between them? "Is there anything you want to tell me about Tom?" she asked. "Anything I should know? Why did you tell him you were sorry?"

"It was just something I wanted to do," said Johnny. "Go by the jail. I just feel sorry for him."

"He's getting what he deserves," Helen said. "Don't you think so? What he did to Sophie, and letting your brother be blamed for it? I'm having a hard time feeling sorry for him."

"Still," Johnny said.

As they drove, Helen saw clearly her own rancor hitting against Johnny's acceptance. Evening came down over them like a large cup.

The next morning Johnny awoke early, spending an hour watching the half-moon and bright starlight work against the sun. As the sun rose, the air filled his room with a bluish tint, the light transitioning night and day—the world was ether. For a moment he wondered: *Are we still human?*

Over the next few days the voices of his house returned to normal: his dad and Crow laughing downstairs, private voices rising like smoke, his mother's voice calling them to supper or saying good night through layers of brick and stone to a point above the roof, above the trees—landing like a light cover on the arms and legs of Johnny in bed, settling like a sweet touch on his head.

Fifty

AURELIA COULD REMEMBER when her family seemed normal. They lived in Washington, D.C., she was with one firm in Georgetown, Robert with another. They struggled with money, as many other young couples did, but Robert didn't complain when Aurelia worked part-time in order to be home with Bobby in the afternoons. She remembered how the house smelled of baby powder and food, and how she slowly became aware of Robert's dark moods creeping into their days.

But on Christmas Eve, when Bobby was five, Robert rose early with a kind of excitement that Aurelia was pleased to see. His face had a familiar light, though his eyes remained dull.

"You going in to work today?" she asked.

"Yes." He put his arms around her. "And I might have a surprise for us when I get home."

Aurelia felt hopeful in ways she hadn't allowed herself for months; and when he came home with a puppy, she was as surprised as Bobby.

"I thought you didn't want a dog in the house," Aurelia teased. "You were so opposed." She reached down to pet the puppy as it ran in circles around the kitchen. "What happened?"

"Look at this!" Bobby yelled. The puppy followed him and barked. "He likes me!"

"I believe he does," his father said.

"Can I take him outside?"

"In the backyard," said Aurelia. "Don't go near the street."

Bobby ran out the door, the puppy following. They could hear him calling, "C'mon, buddy! C'mon!"

"You know he'll want the dog to sleep with him tonight, don't you?"

"I'd planned on it," Robert said.

Aurelia looked at this version of her husband, who could change his mind so completely. It would be another week—a few days after the New Year—before she realized what had changed.

When the call came for Robert in the middle of a January night, Robert did not deny his guilt. He was arrested, tried, and convicted. After the conviction, Aurelia said she was leaving him. "I want nothing to do with this," she told Robert. "I can't do this."

Aurelia would not bring Bobby to see his father. She told Robert they were moving away. His only hope of keeping track of his son was to agree to her conditions. He had never seen her so determined. So Robert agreed to a divorce, but he grew furious when he realized that Aurelia wanted to claim that Robert was dead. He refused to sign the divorce papers if she insisted on such an extreme measure.

"I'll keep you informed about Bobby," Aurelia said. "I'll write you, send pictures. I promise to do that. You know this will be best for him."

"No, I don't know that."

"Well, I do." If Robert didn't agree, she threatened to take away his son completely. "You won't know anything," she said.

Finally he agreed but suggested a clause in the agreement, so that after ten years they could renegotiate. He would be out of jail in ten years. "I can't do this forever," he said.

Aurelia did not know what he meant.

He coughed several times. "Send the papers and I'll sign them."

When Bobby told his mother about the letter from his dad, Aurelia felt slightly glazed over and oddly appeased. She had been thinking about Robert for weeks and felt sorely in need of his help.

"I thought you'd be mad," Bobby had said, as he held the letter with both hands.

"I'm not mad." She wondered what he was feeling. "Does your father want to see you?" she asked.

Bobby brought out the letter, opening the pages that had been handled so many times they appeared to be cloth. "I'll read it to you," he said.

She sat in a straight-backed chair as Bobby read, seeing how every word singed him, like neurons firing. She could see the words breaking him open. She blamed herself. In that moment she began to blame herself for everything.

She had wanted to keep order, the kind of order she imagined would protect Bobby—like a fence. But it had been an electric fence. A fence that, when touched, shocked his limbs into a rigid, bony shape.

And now it was the beginning of October and Bobby waited in jail. Tomorrow he would be transferred to the Marion County facility. This was the paradox that was her life: the practice of justice that she valued so highly hit first against her husband, now her son. She had become like a straight line, hard beside them. She shuddered to think what might become of Bobby now. The judge had sentenced the boys as juveniles, but each boy had received fifteen years. In the far corner of a neighbor's yard, a dog barked, and though Dog was sleeping again under the table, for a moment Aurelia thought the bark was his.

She had not turned in Bobby's gun, as she had threatened. Instead, she had placed it on the top shelf of her closet. If she had turned it in to the police, she might have drawn questions or even consequences for Bobby; so she kept it and half hoped the gun might disappear, might dissolve into the wood grain of the closet shelf. She felt it there, a small bag of bullets beside it.

Now she took it down and loaded it carefully. She sat in the rocking chair and laid the gun across her lap, putting both hands on it as she would a baby. She tried to decode all she had done, and why. She tried to decode what she might do now.

She had the feeling for a moment that she could make everything the way it used to be—that if she did something, she didn't know what, she could bring herself into another time, and then whatever was heaving inside her might stop. Stop. She heard a small sigh escape her chest. Inside us is something that has no name, and that something is what we are.

She sat for hours holding the gun, waiting, trying to decide whether to stay or leave. Her mind changed a thousand times. But finally she could not find in herself the decision to end anything. The bus would come for the boys tomorrow morning. Ending enough. She judged herself, then reentered her life with all its mistakes, and the hope that she could turn the next day into a bright, if brindled, thing.

So Aurelia Bailey held the gun on her lap all night, rocking it like somebody's life.

Fifty-one

THE PRISON BUS came for the boys on Friday, the first day of the town's October Carnival. The guards had told the boys they would leave by late morning, and their families had been notified. The townspeople were glad to have the Carnival as a distraction. They wanted to get on with their lives, to get this calamity behind them.

The Carnival arrived each year in early October, and roustabouts set up tents and carnival rides, transforming Joe Locker's field. The smell of animals and sawdust pervaded the far pasture, which was bordered by river on two sides.

The Carnival always lasted two days. Last year a cold snap had brought frost. Pumpkins rose ripe in the fields, and when people looked out their windows and saw frost they pretended it was snow. This year, though, the weather beamed sharp with sunlight, free of the summer's humid oppression.

Horses gave rides around one section of the field; on the other side, carnival barkers in bright plaid coats and straw hats used their voices like megaphones, urging people to enter this tent or that. They called out seductive descriptions of each sideshow; a few shows were limited to those eighteen and older.

People came from as far away as Chattanooga or Dalton, Georgia. They ate casseroles made by church ladies, or visited tents selling fried chicken, fried turkey, fried okra, fried tomatoes, fried Mars bars and Twinkies—or, for the more adventurous spirit, fried pickles. They came to ride the rides, to see the freak shows, and to try their hands at landing a nickel in a bottle or popping a balloon with weighted darts.

Cars lined the whole length of road, and all day people walked toward the pasture. Many did not know that the prison bus would pick up the three boys today, though some people came to the Jasper County jail and waited to see the boys come out. No one knew what to say when they saw them.

E. G. Hollis and Charlie Post stood at the door of the bus, taking the arm of each boy before he boarded. They promised to visit, and the boys knew that those two men, at least, would keep their promise.

The Canadys and Judge Bailey formed a group beside the bus. Casey's mother and father stood separate from the others. Crow waited too, several feet behind them, coming no closer. He saw Bobby flinch before allowing Hollis to take hold of his shoulder. All night Crow had awakened himself, afraid of oversleeping. *Is it time? Is it time?*

Coach Post stepped back to stand with Crow, but Hollis stayed near the bus. "Stand back, please," the sheriff said. Hollis requested a last word with the boys. Bobby, Tom, and Casey listened, their heads leaning forward, as though they were studying something on the ground. A moment later they boarded the bus.

Sophie and Rita stood farther away. Sophie saw Bobby walk toward the bus, recognizing his gait more than his face, his step that leaned slightly, then righted itself. Rita kept saying how relieved she was that they were leaving, but Sophie, who had expected to feel happy, or at least relieved, felt nothing.

When Sophie was a young girl, every time she left her house she would turn to look back, seeing the house as a place where strangers lived. So she would climb a nearby hill, thinking the house might look familiar again from that vantage point. She had left it only moments before, left the room she loved, her mother's powder lingering in the air. From the hill she focused on one high room in the attic where she liked to hide, struck by the feeling that the house would remain mysterious and uncollected until she went back and entered it again—the house not being changed at all.

Today Sophie herself was different, transfigured in ways both good and bad. And if she went back to that high room, went back right now, she might look out the window and see how the flesh of things that had lately been so clothed in ice was learning how to breathe again. Her bones trembled. She hoped she might see Crow today but did not know if he wanted to see her.

The early sky above the horizon glowed. As Rita turned to leave, she put her arm around Sophie, guiding her to the car. Neither of them wanted to see the bus pull away. Neither wanted to see the boys' faces in the windows.

As they drove back home, Rita suggested that they go to the Carnival later. "We'll spend the whole afternoon. How does that sound?" For the first time in months her mother's smile had returned to normal; but Sophie, still hearing the bus pull out—the thin sound of brakes lifting and gears shifting—was startled by her mother's suggestion.

That afternoon, when Sophie and Rita went to the Carnival, they paused at the entrance, drinking in the colorful scene. A Ferris wheel, merry-go-round, Tilt-A-Whirl, and small roller coaster kept children and mothers standing in long lines waiting for a chance to ride. Music came from every ride, as well as from the Dixieland Band playing around the picnic tables. As Sophie entered the gates, going to all that music and the strange sights, she became suddenly giddy.

She had felt burdened, for some time, her mouth full of dust, her head full of rain. Now the sound of melodies, all different, and people milling around calling to each other brought her back to life, and she surprised her mother when she said, "I wonder if Crow will be here today."

"He might," Rita said. "He probably will."

* * *

Sophie saw him first beside the ice cream stand. She waved and he came over to her.

"I'm glad you're here," he said. "I was hoping you'd come."

"I was looking for you too."

Crow felt a dull, tinny jolt of hope. "Want some ice cream?" He spoke nonchalantly.

"Sure."

They walked around the Carnival grounds, from the ice cream stand to the house of mirrors to the World's Longest Alligator to the small and childish roller coaster.

"Have you seen the freaks?" Crow asked.

"No, but the man with the tattoos is funny. He really made me laugh."

Crow licked the ice cream dripping down his hand. "Or the animals. We could see those."

"Okay."

"And we've got to ride the Ferris wheel. If you want to, I mean."

As they walked they smelled the river, the rich leafy scent of fall, and Crow imagined the shoes thrown in as far as the boys could throw, sinking into the soft silky bottom. Those shoes, never found, moving now in slow motion, their laces floating upward, a tiny phosphorescence glimmering on the soles and edges of heels. Shoes, without feet, in a light puppet dance.

"I saw you this morning," Crow said. "You were watching the bus leave."

"Oh." Sophie nodded. "I knew you'd be there."

"I didn't expect you to come though," Crow said.

"I probably wasn't there for the same reason as you." Sophie flinched slightly, a small jerk. "I came with my mother."

Crow could not look at her. They passed by one of the barkers, who tried to get them to come in and see the dog with four legs but six feet.

"Well," Sophie stopped walking and turned toward Crow. "Are you going to visit Bobby in prison?"

"I don't know."

A barker called out: "See the Fat Lady married to the Tattooed Man! Only three dollars!"

"He came to my house," Crow said. "Did you know that he talked to me before he went to the police? God, I hated him. I've known Bobby, and Tom too, since we were six, seven years old. Not Casey though. I never knew him very good. Nobody did." Crow looked in the direction where the bus had left earlier. "Bobby's always had this thing . . ." But Crow didn't finish. "You know his dad's moving down here with his family, so they can visit him."

"I don't think I care."

"I don't know, Sophie." Crow spoke uneasily.

"They have a long time to think about what they did," Sophie said.

"I guess so."

Sophie stopped again, and Crow stopped with her, standing with his arms awkward at his sides. She waited a long moment. "Something's over," she said quietly. "But not my life, and not yours either. You know," she said, her voice changing, "Crow, I still dream about you."

"You do?"

"Yeah, I do."

"Sophie, things get so ragged up." Crow spoke quickly. He cared about her so much. He ached to touch her. "Nothing's like I thought it was, not really."

"Well, we're all pretty ragged up, all of us." Sophie and Crow looked at the people around them. They liked examining the frailty of others.

"Where are the monkeys?" Sophie asked. "Lester told me this Carnival has a monkey tent."

Crow pointed in the direction of a small tent where children and parents waited in line for the next show.

"Let's go." Sophie took Crow's hand. They ran and were the last ones to buy tickets, entering and squeezing into a bleacher seat just as the trainer began to speak. The sign over the tent read MACKEY'S MONKEYS. Whether this was the trainer's first or last name was anybody's guess.

Mackey stood almost six feet tall and had brown hair that fell over his forehead. His ears stuck out slightly, and he resembled, in modest ways, the monkeys that he trained. Mackey introduced the monkeys by name, and each one came forward and took a bow or curtsied, depending on its gender. Everyone clapped. After the introductions, Blondie, the smallest monkey, made a high screeching sound, like a strange laugh. The trainer touched her back in a gesture of comfort. Mackey spoke to the animals with gentleness, and they seemed to trust him.

While Mackey stroked Blondie, she jumped into his arms and kissed him. Everyone laughed and clapped. He explained to the audience how he had brought three of these monkeys, recently orphaned, back from Africa. "Their mother," he said, "was killed, and hunters brought these babies to the hut where I lived." Mackey explained that he went to Africa to find animals to train for a circus that once employed him. He had trained bears, and even tigers, for ten years. But when the monkeys were given to him, his whole business changed. He loved these creatures. He found two more and started this show. "They are my children," he said.

The audience clapped again.

The monkeys waited patiently while Mackey talked, and as he placed Blondie back onto her stool, he turned and raised his arms and the monkeys gave him their devoted attention. They performed amazing tricks involving acrobatics, teamwork, the timing of somersaults that would be difficult for any human.

"No wonder everyone wants to see this show," Sophie said, her face lit from within. Crow fell in love all over again, watching Sophie's pleasure.

Children laughed at the comic interplay between monkey and trainer, and a settled satisfaction filled the tent. Suddenly, one monkey jumped on top of Mackey's head and began to bite his face, scratch at his cheek. The audience saw this as playfulness, but then another monkey jumped on Mackey's shoulders, a dark thatch of hair making a high-pitched shriek. One more came close, spat, baring its teeth in a mock smile. The trainer tried to cover his head with his arms, tried to shield himself. The monkeys began to run around the tent.

A little boy in the front row, maybe about five years old, was approached by the largest monkey, Sam. Sam reached for the boy's bag of peanuts, but the boy pulled it back. Sam bit him, and the boy's father hit the animal, a cracking sound.

Mackey frantically motioned to his assistant for help. "Call animal security!" he said. "And get some food. Get them back to their cages."

The monkeys moved to the edges of the tent, harassing and hissing. They pushed further into the crowd, and a shuffling occurred, women pulling their children close.

"Let's get out of here!" a man yelled.

"Oh, God. Hurry!"

"Mama!"

Mothers rushed their children toward the exit, clogging the door of the tent with the static of bodies pushing against each other. The boy who had been bitten was crying. Someone with a first-aid kit rushed past Sophie and Crow.

Crow held on to Sophie, steering her out of the frantic center of the crowd bearing down on the tent's main exit.

"They're everywhere, Crow. Look." She pointed. A monkey hid in the rafters, just overhead, jerking the frame as if his intention was to collapse the tent. A hulking shape scuttled across the ground and jumped on the first-aid man. The man let out a roar, and the monkey, frightened, shifted direction. Now he was heading straight for Sophie.

Crow planted himself between Sophie's body and the frenzied monkey. The animal leapt on Crow, tearing his shirt. Crow braced his feet and hurled the monkey into the stools that had created order for the earlier act. The stools scattered and fell on top of each other; and the monkey, its eyes baleful, leapt out of reach.

"Stay with me. C'mon." Crow put his arm around Sophie's waist and guided her outside, into the twilight coolness. A siren sounded from the middle of the pasture as they hurried away from the mayhem, through the scattering crowd. A raft of policemen moved in quickly, spreading around the tent.

And then Sophie dug in her heels. "Wait," she said, transfixed by a pair of animal security officers heading into the tent with their guns drawn. "Are they really going to shoot them?"

"I don't know," said Crow, squeezing her hand.

They could hear Mackey inside the tent. "Wait, don't do that! I can get them back in their cages," he cried. "Let me try."

The biggest monkey, Sam, emerged from the tent, clutching a bottle of chocolate milk left by a child. He looked around, seeming to weigh his options, then ran a few yards before the sharp bang from a gun caused Sam's eyes to roll. The monkey collapsed on the ground. He looked like a wet mass of fur, his mouth slowly opening. He made a sound like a human cry.

"We should do something," Sophie urged.

"What can we do?" Crow looked at her.

"I don't know."

They stood long enough to watch the boy who had been bitten be taken away in the ambulance, then Blondie and the rest of the captured monkeys were driven away in a large wooden crate, their faces looking through the slats. Next Mackey was ushered out of the tent. They saw Sam carried away, and saw that he was alive, just unsteady, sedated.

"They'll be okay," Crow said, trying to reassure. "Look, it was only a tranquilizer gun."

Sophie nodded. "Thank you," said Sophie. "For what you did."

It was not until this moment when they stood in the secure circle of folks outside the tent that Crow recognized how his action in that limited portion of time had been right—not cowardly. He didn't remember making a decision.

Sophie touched his torn shirt. "Are you all right?"

"Not even a scratch," said Crow. "I'm okay." He led her away from the crowd. "You want some more ice cream?"

Sophie smiled. She, too, felt his need to go back in time, to before the monkeys—or even further back to when nothing had been broken or lost.

The police spent thirty minutes tracking down one last monkey who had been spotted scampering toward the river. Over the loud-speaker a man's deep voice said that rides were now reduced to half price. The voice apologized for the "mishap" and reassured those who had heard the commotion but did not see it that the injured had been taken to the hospital and the monkeys gathered into a safe place. The voice spoke in an even rhythm, like a metronome, comforting the crowd, urging people not to leave—promising prizes, free ice cream, cheap rides.

The Dixieland Band began to play again, and slowly the murmur of voices hummed through the tents, around the ice cream, and into the ride area, where the lights of the Ferris wheel glittered in the half-light. Sophie looked up. "I want to ride in that red seat with a painted moon on the back," she said.

Crow bought two tickets and told the man running the ride to bring down the red seat. Sophie climbed into the cradlelike chair like a princess, sitting carefully, expectantly, trembling from the episode with the monkeys. Crow closed the long bar in front of them. There were many things they could do nothing about. They both held their breath as the wheel went backward and up.

The wheel went around several times, and finally they relaxed, even laughed, throwing up their arms to feel like falling. Crow put his arm around Sophie, and she leaned into him. "Want to have supper together? We can get some hot dogs. They have the best hot dogs."

"Okay," said Sophie, "but what time is it? I don't have my watch, and I told my mom I'd meet her at the pavilion at six o'clock."

Crow didn't want to look at his watch. He didn't want to tell her what time it was. He didn't want Sophie to have to leave, so he leaned over the bar and yelled down to the crowd, "Does anybody know what time it is?" The question carried over the heads of the people below, over the pasture to where the horses gave a last ride for the day, over the field to the road with all its cars, then to the river where shoes floated aimlessly on the river bottom.

A few people looked up and said, "What? What is he saying?"

Crow laughed as the Ferris wheel swung down and back up again. At the top they stopped while the man below let on new riders. And Crow could smell Sophie's fragrance beside him, still like oranges. He could smell her, and he did not know what to do. They sat high above the town, and both suddenly pulsed with a sense of new and possible life. Crow kissed her, unexpectedly and seriously—the cradle rocking slightly—and when Sophie lifted her head she saw a purple streak in the sky, like a long highway going straight into the setting sun.

She raised her arms, profoundly, and the Ferris wheel moved again, taking them over the top, down, then back up out of the earth; and each time they went around they heard the barker calling out about the man the size of a child; they saw the sky changing fast, and the bright strip of river the monkey had tried to run to.

The Ferris wheel rumbled upward, the kiss still hot on their lips. The chorus of crickets had lessened in the last month, but Sophie and Crow could see and hear every warp and woof of what was below them. Every shadow, every crevice, revealed itself, and they watched as though they were looking at the world through a ridiculous glass. All these things created a fabulous order.

But what they saw—what they really saw—was the thin, bright string of light along the hills, a horizon not yet captured, not held down by circumstance. What they saw was the world opening its margin of breath into their green, tremulous lives.

Acknowledgments

I am enormously grateful to my editor, Judy Sternlight, who has worked tirelessly with me on this novel and whose comments and suggestions I greatly appreciate; to Dan Menaker, who has shepherded me through this process; to my agent, Susan Lescher, who has sold every book I've written; to Brian Smith, a criminal lawyer in Tennessee, who gave me valuable advice concerning criminal proceedings; to my friends Ginger Smith, Beth Graham, and Jill McCorkle, for their encouragement; to Kittsu Greenwood, who, through many readings, pushed me to finish this book; and to my husband, Michael Curtis, who gives me everything.

About the Author

ELIZABETH COX is the author of *Night Talk, The Ragged Way People Fall Out of Love, Familiar Ground,* and the story collection *Bargains in the Real World.* She is an instructor at the Bennington Writing Seminars and teaches at Wofford College in South Carolina, where she shares the John C. Cobb Endowed Chair in the Humanities with her husband, C. Michael Curtis. She lives in Spartanburg, South Carolina.

About the Type

This book was set in Times Roman, designed by Stanley Morison specifically for *The Times* of London. The typeface was introduced in the newspaper in 1932. Times Roman had its greatest success in the United States as a book and commercial typeface, rather than one used in newspapers.